The bridesmaids and groomsmen for hire at Sweetheart, California's Something Borrowed have the cure for celebrity wedding headaches. But even a job that's strictly business can lead to the real thing . . .

RULE #2: DON'T UPSTAGE THE BRIDE AND GROOM

Rylie Templeton had big dreams, until she quit culinary school to take care of her father and signed on with Something Borrowed. Suddenly years have gone by and she's still a bridesmaid-for-hire, with her idea to open a gourmet bakery on the back burner. Scoring a high-profile wedding could help turn her life around, if only she didn't have to share the spotlight with her coworker, the insufferable—and undeniably gorgeous—Dustin Kent.

Instructed to make it work, Rylie plunges into the wedding festivities with Dustin by her side. If only she could convince him to turn his spectacular charm on someone else! But the enigmatic, reformed playboy has his own ideas about romance, and they all include Rylie. As the nuptials get closer, Rylie realizes that Dustin's wooing is actually working, and that the two of them might make a good team in more ways than one . . .

Visit us at www.kensingtonbooks.com

Praise for Codi Gary's *Don't Call Me Sweetheart*

"*Don't Call Me Sweetheart* is packed with laugh-out loud moments balanced by emotion that rings true."
—*RT Book Reviews*, **4.5 Stars Top Pick**

"Gary's novel will delight romance lovers who appreciate a strong heroine going after what she wants."
—*Publishers Weekly*

"Flirty, fun, and fabulous!"
—**Bestselling author Candis Terry**

"Fun, lighthearted, and full of emotion. You can't help but smile while reading Codi Gary."
—**K.M. Jackson, author of *Insert Groom Here***

"Codi Gary is the queen of romance. She'll make you fall head over heels."
—**T.J. Kline, author of the Healing Harts series**

"*Don't Call Me Sweetheart* is a charming romance that will leave you saying 'I do, I do' to author Codi Gary."
—**Leah Marie Brown, author of the It Girls Series**

Books by Codi Gary

The Something Borrowed Series
Don't Call Me Sweetheart
Kiss Me, Sweetheart

The Rock Canyon, Idaho Series
The Trouble with Sexy
Things Good Girls Don't Do
Good Girls Don't Date Rock Stars
Bad Girls Don't Marry Marines
Return of the Bad Girl
Bad for Me
Good Girls Don't Kiss and Tell
Good at Being Bad

The Loco, Texas Series
Crazy for You
Make Me Crazy
I Want Crazy

The Men in Uniform Series
I Need a Hero
One Lucky Hero
Hero of Mine
Holding Out for a Hero

Standalones
How to Be a Heartbreaker
Bear Mountain Rescue
Hot Winter Nights
Sexy Summer Flings

All Kensington titles, imprints, and distributed lines are available at special quantity discounts for bulk purchases for sales promotion, premiums, fundraising, and educational or institutional use.

To the extent that the image or images on the cover of this book depict a person or persons, such person or persons are merely models, and are not intended to portray any character or characters featured in the book.

Special book excerpts or customized printings can also be created to fit specific needs. For details, write or phone the office of the Kensington Special Sales Manager:
Kensington Publishing Corp.
119 West 40th Street
New York, NY 10018
Attn. Special Sales Department. Phone: 1-800-221-2647.

Kensington and the K logo Reg. U.S. Pat. & TM Off.
LYRICAL PRESS Reg. U.S. Pat. & TM Off.
Lyrical Press and the L logo are trademarks of Kensington Publishing Corp.

First Electronic Edition: February 2018
eISBN-13: 978-1-5161-0231-0
eISBN-10: 1-5161-0231-2

First Print Edition: February 2018
ISBN-13: 978-1-5161-0232-7
ISBN-10: 1-5161-0232-0

Printed in the United States of America

Kiss Me, Sweetheart

Something Borrowed

Codi Gary

LYRICAL SHINE
Kensington Publishing Corp.
www.kensingtonbooks.com

To my mother- and father-in-law, Karen and Mark. Thank you for all that you do for our family and for being so supportive of my writing. I love you.

Chapter 1

Rylie Templeton sat at her desk, staring at the box of death by chocolate muffins she'd made that morning, and wondered if throwing one at Dustin Kent's head could be considered assault.

God, he was an arrogant son of a bitch. He leaned a broad shoulder against the doorjamb of her office, and watched her with one raised brow and a sardonic smirk across his full lips. He'd been working at Something Borrowed Wedding Solutions for two months, which boggled Rylie's mind. Not only did he come from one of the richest families in Sweetheart, California, but he was a self-made millionaire. There was no reason he should need to work, yet here he was every day, walking around as though he was God's gift.

And he'd managed to get under her skin in the worst way. Constantly mocking her with his fake compliments and flattery, as if she didn't know he was full of shit.

Even worse, just a few weeks ago, Marley Stevenson, Kelly Barrow, Dustin Kent, and Rylie had all gone in on restoring the old ghost town, Buzzard Gulch. They were all technically partners, although Rylie's involvement had been more Marley being generous. Rylie couldn't afford to buy a house, let alone a town, but Marley had made her a working partner. They were turning the ghost town into a wedding venue and they needed a baker. The whole set up was pretty sweet, if not for the man with sparkling blue eyes currently watching her.

"You look very pretty today, Rylie. I love you in black. It really brings out the green flecks in your eyes."

Rylie narrowed her very dark eyes at him. "My eyes are brown, asshat."

He pushed off and started walking toward her, a long stride that ate up the length of her tiny office in no time. His gray suit was dapper and his blue shirt and loosened silver and blue striped tie made his eyes seem more like midnight than robin's egg. His short black hair was tousled with gel that was messy yet stylish. He was the ultimate pretty boy, the kind of guy who used to make Rylie's life hell, and she steeled herself as he approached.

He placed his hands on the desk and leaned over until he was almost nose to nose with her.

"Not true. Right in the center—"

She caught the finger he'd started waving in front of her face, tempted to bite it.

Not in a sexy way, of course.

She released him abruptly and stood. Why the hell would she go there, even in her head? Dustin wasn't sexy, and she had a boyfriend anyway.

"I know you are used to getting what you want from women, but your flattery will not work on me."

He stared down at his cuticles casually, a move that reminded her of James Spader in *Pretty in Pink*. "Too bad. I was just coming to tell you that Kelly wants to see us in her office. Something about the Rolland/ Marconi wedding?"

Rylie's heart almost exploded from her chest. This was it. With her friend Marley gone, Rylie was the top bridesmaid at Something Borrowed. Although she loved Marley, she had been praying for this chance since she'd watched Tonya Rolland, the governor of California's daughter, walk down the hallway into Kelly's office last week. The governor was a favorite for the next presidential election. The Rollands were originally from Alabama, and had moved to California when Tonya was six. Since then, the governor had risen through the political ranks and had become beloved by the people, as was his altruistic daughter.

Blake Marconi, Tonya's fiancé, had played basketball for UCLA and gotten his degree in political science before being picked up by the NBA. The Los Angeles Lakers had snagged him, and the big Italian was a fan favorite not just for his jump shot, but his extensive charity work. It was how he'd met Tonya; they'd been seated together at an animal rights dinner, and hit it off. It was a storybook romance and Rylie wanted to be a part of it.

Then, the entirety of his words sank in. "Wait, why does she want *you* there?"

Before she could blink, Dustin snagged one of her muffins and bit into it, chewing slowly. She watched his full lips as he chewed, waiting for him to elaborate with a pounding heart and her mind racing with dread. The agony was killing her, until finally he swallowed.

"I have a feeling the two of us are going to make this wedding very special."

The two of us? THE TWO OF US?

After years of being patient, her big account was a shared one with Don Juan Le Douchebag?

"Are you kidding me?" Stepping around the desk, Rylie mumbled, "There has to be some kind of mistake."

Dustin followed behind her, talking in a low, suggestive tone. "Oh, no mistake, baby. Just destiny."

"Shut up." Rylie knocked on Kelly's office door, ignoring Dustin as he came up to stand beside her, bristling when his shoulder brushed hers. She had no idea why he irritated her so much, beyond the fact that he was an obvious womanizer and liked to manipulate women to get his way.

That was probably reason enough.

But she hated to admit, even to herself, that when Dustin had first started working there, she'd naively thought that all his charm and snark was just a cover for the good guy beneath.

Then she'd learned that he had slept with one of Marley's engaged clients, and realized she was an idiot when it came to men's characters. While she'd been charmed by him, he'd been helping someone else break a promise.

She could tolerate a lot of things, but a cheater wasn't one of them.

Which was probably why she'd stayed with her boyfriend, Asher, for so long. Their relationship was far from perfect, but Asher wasn't the cheating type.

"Come in," Kelly called.

Dustin beat her to the doorknob. As he twisted it open, she looked up in time to catch his grin.

"After you."

Rylie passed him with a sniff and sat in one of the chairs opposite Kelly, trying to read her boss's pleasant expression. Did she even realize what she was doing? Did she not trust Rylie to handle an A-list client?

"You wanted to see me?"

"And me," Dustin said, taking the seat next to her.

Rylie gritted her teeth even as she caught his amusement out of the corner of her eye. He was really enjoying this, and it made her want to take her four-inch red heels and find an uncomfortable place to put them.

A striking woman with long black hair and green eyes, Kelly was the kind of woman Rylie used to dream about looking like in high school. It had taken years, but Rylie didn't look at her boss with envy anymore. She liked the way she was.

Kelly smiled and leaned forward, oblivious to the tension between them. "I'm sure you have an idea why I've called you both in here."

"The Rolland/Marconi wedding," Dustin said.

"Yes. They want to keep a very tight lid on everything, including the location. Close friends and family only and no press. You two are to get everything ready, so when they arrive, all they have to do is get dressed and walk down the aisle."

Rylie wasn't the type to rock the boat, but she couldn't help being irritated. She'd worked hard to get this account; she didn't need a partner, especially some playboy millionaire who couldn't keep his penis to himself.

Taking a deep breath, she blurted, "Kelly, I know this is a huge account, but I can handle it on my own."

The office went dead silent, and Kelly sat back, her brow furrowed. "Dustin, would you please step out and close the door?"

"Sure."

Rylie's whole face felt like her skin was burning off. God, she hadn't meant for it to come out quite like that.

"Kelly, I'm so sorry—"

Her boss held up her hand and Rylie shut her mouth, waiting for Kelly to tell her she blew it. The click of the door behind her was her only sign that Dustin had left; she was too terrified to look away from Kelly, waiting for her to tell her she was fired.

Instead, Kelly's expression was kind and concerned. "I didn't assign Dustin to this account because I thought you couldn't handle it alone. I know you can take on all of this and it would be spectacular."

Rylie waited for the *but* that was sure to follow that glowing speech.

"But as both the bride and groom have no siblings, they have made their closest friends bridesmaids and groomsmen. Their friends are not as well off, and so Tonya and Blake are paying for everything, but still, they can't take a lot of time off work to plan. This is why they asked for professionals to handle the position of Best Man and Maid of Honor. Do you understand?"

And she did. Everyone at Something Borrowed had wondered why Kelly had hired a man after all these years of only employing women. Now it was clear she'd been anticipating a request like this.

It still didn't explain why she'd chosen Dustin Kent. Even if he hadn't sold an app he'd designed in college and made millions on his own, his parents owned one of the biggest vineyards in the area, and half the town of Sweetheart. The guy should be sleeping his way across the U.S. and Europe, not playing at being a professional groomsman.

"Yes. I'm sorry if I was rude," Rylie said.

Kelly shot her an amused look. "Please. That is the first time you've ever questioned a decision I've made in what, four years? I think you've earned one or two."

The tension Rylie hadn't known was there leaked out of her chest as she released a heavy breath. Kelly passed her a red folder, and held on to it until Rylie met her gaze. "I also want you to keep an eye on Dustin."

Rylie blinked at her a few times. "You mean spy on him?"

"No, not spy. I just want you to make sure that he's doing his fair share of the work. I know how he likes to get one over on the other women here, but thankfully, you seem to be immune to him."

Rylie wasn't sure immune was the right word. When Dustin had first been hired, of course, she'd noticed he was good looking, maybe even enjoyed his flirtation a little bit... Until she realized he was a dog who flirted with *every* woman he met.

And she would never cross that line.

"I have a boyfriend," Rylie said.

Kelly's lips thinned for a half a second until she forced a smile. Rylie wasn't surprised. She knew no one liked her boyfriend, Asher Reid. Some were just politer about letting their feelings be known.

"Yes, I know." Kelly said. "Will you send Dustin back in when you leave? I'd like to finish telling him what I expect and then I'll send him back to you."

Rylie took the folder and left the room, making her way down the hallway to Dustin's office. He was sitting behind his desk, glasses slipped over that perfect nose, making him look like Clark Kent. For a second, she watched him, thinking she was due for a *Smallville* marathon.

Rylie shook her head. Dustin was nothing like Tom Welling, except for being insanely good looking, but beauty was only skin deep. Vipers were gorgeous too until they bit you.

She knocked on the doorframe and he looked up at her from his laptop.

"Kelly wants to finish talking to you," she said.

Dustin shut the laptop and stood up, stretching his arms over his head. Which, of course, lifted his button-up shirt and suit jacket. She had to fight not to look down and see if any skin was exposed.

God, I'm a terrible person.

"So, you didn't manage to get me kicked off the account then?" he asked.

Rylie glared at him. "It wasn't about you. It was about me wanting to handle this on my own." *Plus, the commission alone would have changed everything for me.*

Dustin walked around the desk and chucked her under the chin. "Don't worry, sweetheart. I promise that you're going to love working with me."

Rylie ignored the little flutter in her stomach and scoffed. "Just don't screw this up for me."

She left his office, her cheeks burning as his deep chuckle followed her down the hall.

She sat down at her desk in time to hear her phone beep. She checked the text message and winced.

Did u get BBQ sauce at the store?

Crap, she'd forgotten. Her heart sped up just thinking about how such a small thing could set Asher off. Taking a deep, shaky breath she tapped out a response.

I'll pick some up on my way home.

There was no response five minutes later, and she knew things were going to be bad.

A knock on her open door made her jump and Dustin threw his hands up. "Whoa, it's just me. Was going to see if you wanted to scout a few sites that the bride and groom have picked out?"

Rylie looked at the clock and calculated how long it would take to check out some places. With any luck, Asher would be asleep when she got home.

"Sure, sounds good."

Chapter 2

Dustin Kent enjoyed attention from beautiful women, and had never apologized for it. If a woman was already involved with another man, it was her own damn problem, not his. He never promised anything but a good time; it wasn't his fault if they thought he was some kind of prince charming.

He turned onto the driveway of Heart and Soul Vineyard, trying to shake off the text message from the last girl he'd hooked up with. He didn't know her name, he just had her in his phone as *Talks A Lot.*

Please, we belong together. Call me.

Why she'd become so fixated on him was a mystery, but he didn't do clingy.

Dustin glanced over at Rylie, who was quietly looking out the window and ignoring him. He had no idea what he'd done to upset her, but she'd gone from laughing at his jokes just a few weeks ago and blushing so prettily at his compliments, to lashing out at him.

It was too bad, because he genuinely liked Rylie. She was a nice girl.

Which is probably why she sees through me.

Dustin didn't have any illusions about the kind of women who were attracted to him. Gold diggers and thrill seekers; they saw him as a challenge because he didn't do relationships. Why bother? He already knew he wasn't cut out for monogamy, so why waste anyone's time?

Dustin parked in front of the clubhouse and got out. He had every intention of opening the door for Rylie, but she didn't wait for him to round the car and get it for her. As she stepped out, Dustin took a minute to admire her. Rylie had a curvy figure designed to keep a man warm at night, and she knew how to accent it. She was one of those girls who dressed to the nines; today she was wearing a black swing dress with cherries on it, a little red shrug, and bright red pumps.

Plus, there was something about those brown eyes that could suck a man in if he wasn't careful.

"I think your parents' vineyard is a little bigger, but this is still beautiful," Rylie said.

Dustin shook off his crazy thoughts. Rylie had a boyfriend and from what he'd gathered, she wasn't the cheating kind. And he wasn't up for more than being a side piece.

"You've never been here?" he asked.

"No."

"I thought maybe your boyfriend would have brought you here for a little wine tasting."

Her expression turned guarded, and he wondered why. He'd heard mumblings around the office that no one seemed to like Asher, but he hardly remembered the guy. He'd been two years behind Dustin and besides the fact that he played football and was a bit of a meathead, there was nothing else that stood out in his mind.

"I'm not a big fan of wine," she said.

Toni Hart, the owner of the vineyard, burst out of the door with a wide smile, forestalling any further questions from him. "Hey there!"

Dustin had known Toni since he was a kid. Even though his parents owned a rival vineyard, his mom and Toni were best friends. "Good afternoon, Toni! This is my partner, Rylie."

Toni held out her hand to Rylie, her hand lined with age, and sporting coral pink nails. Her white blond hair was styled in a perfectly rounded bob, and her green eyes sparkled in a face that showed every one of her sixty-two years in the best way possible.

Rylie grasped it, a beaming smile lighting up her whole face. That welcoming expression made Dustin's heart skip.

He frowned at the thought. Maybe he was coming down with something.

Rylie didn't seem to notice his momentary panic. "It's a pleasure to meet you."

"Likewise," Toni said. "It's so nice to see Dustin with such a lovely young woman."

Dustin spluttered. "No, Toni, we're not together—"

"I have a boyfriend," Rylie said at the exact same time.

Toni's face turned crimson. "Oh, well, when you said you needed a tour, I just assumed…" Toni trailed off.

"We work for Something Borrowed, Toni," he said. "We're scouting the winery for a client."

Toni seemed to recover from her initial discomfort and smiled. "Oh, well that is wonderful too. And it is still nice to meet you."

"Yeah, you too," Rylie mumbled, her cheeks a cherry red hue.

Toni shot Dustin a confused look. "Wait, you work there too?"

"Yeah. It's fun, and you know how good I look in a tux," he said, winking at her.

"Oh, well, you definitely do." Toni was probably still wondering why he, a multi-millionaire, would work at a place for rental bridesmaids. Everyone had been asking him why, including his mother, but he'd just changed the subject. It was nobody's business but his.

Toni seemed to regain her composure, because her saleswoman smile was back in place. "Let me show you around. Dustin, you've been here before, but we've remodeled the main clubhouse and our lodge rooms since then."

Rylie was all business now, walking beside Toni as they headed across the grounds. "And how many guest rooms do you have?"

"About fifty, including several suites."

"Wow, that's great. Our clients want an intimate affair," Rylie said. "Do you allow outside caterers?"

"No, but we have a varied menu that should work well for their needs. I'd be happy to set up a tasting."

Dustin didn't want to get her hopes up if they decided to go with another venue. "Let's just see what you've done with the place first, Toni."

"Certainly."

Dustin followed behind Rylie and Toni as they walked along a stone path. The grass was green, proving that Heart and Soul wasn't concerned about the California drought. Then again, Northern California never had the climate troubles that their Southern counterpart did.

Dustin's pocket vibrated and he checked the screen. Shit, it was his agent.

He hit the reject button. He'd call him later, when there was no one around to eavesdrop. It wasn't as though he could openly tell people he was writing a book.

Especially when the subject matter was about a groomsman for hire spilling all the dirt he could on the celebrity couples and their weddings.

He'd been trying to come up with a book idea for months, and frustrated by severe writer's block, had taken a drive out to his family winery. When he'd found his mother, she'd informed him that starlet Paula Riviera was celebrating her marriage to her wife, Julie Waynewright. There was only about fifty people in attendance, and absolutely no press. Dustin had spotted Marley Stevenson and her boss, Kelly, working as bridesmaid and wedding planner and it had struck him. People loved reading about celebrity dirt, and it was well known that weddings brought out the beast in almost everyone.

So, that Monday, he'd called his agent and pitched his idea. He'd gone wild for it, and Dustin had walked into Something Borrowed and offered his services to Kelly. He'd been surprised how receptive she was to the idea and before he knew it, he'd had his opening three chapters written and a proposal for his agent to shop.

And the Rolland/Marconi wedding was going to be his gold mine.

"Oh, this is lovely." Rylie's voice brought him out of his head and back to the present. There was a beautiful pond surrounded by flowers and several benches. A couple of swans swam across the clear water.

"Yes, the pond is a popular attraction," Toni said.

"How do you keep the water so clear with the birds?" Rylie asked.

"We filter and clean it daily."

Dustin's gaze shifted to Rylie's expression as she stopped and scanned the area, her forehead wrinkled in concentration. She worried her full lip, and the sight of those even, white teeth abusing the lush, pink flesh made his cock stir to attention. Shifting on his feet to relieve the pressure against the front of his suit pants, he stepped a little closer.

"What are you thinking?" he asked.

She jumped, as though she'd been lost in thought and forgotten he was there. He didn't like that; Dustin wanted her as aware of him as he was of her. It wasn't rational or even fair, but there it was. She got to him and he couldn't put his finger on why.

But she had no idea what was going on inside him. How could she?

Finally, Rylie answered him. "I was just wondering about the bird poop. If they are free to walk around the grounds, then they must make quite a mess. I would hate for our bride to step in something."

Dustin covered his mouth to hide his smile as Toni straightened up, obviously offended. "We have a groundskeeper who takes very good care of the property. There is no mess."

Rylie blushed. "I didn't mean any offense. I was just thinking that things may happen and we can't control everything."

Toni's lips were still pinched, and Dustin added, "Maybe the geese—"

"Swans," both women corrected.

Whatever. "Swans could be locked up during the wedding? Then the grounds would be clean and stay that way during the ceremony."

Toni seemed to be considering, and Dustin grinned as Rylie jumped on the suggestion. "They are beautiful, so maybe after the ceremony they could be released? Then they can be in the background of some of the pictures. Very romantic."

Toni nodded enthusiastically. "That is the reason we got them. We thought they would add a romantic element to the grounds."

"Oh, they do." Rylie glanced at Dustin, and he thought she looked appreciative.

Visibly appeased, Toni flashed them a sunny smile. "Let me show you the rest of the grounds, and then I'll take you through the buildings."

"Thank you."

Just as they started walking again, Rylie stumbled in front of him. Before she went down, he grabbed her, pulling her back against his chest. As she leaned into him, her butt pressed right into his crotch and it just made his erection worse.

"You okay?" he murmured.

She nodded, clearing her throat. "I hit some kind of dip in the walkway and my ankle turned."

"Does it hurt?" God, she smelled good, like the peonies and lilacs his mother had in her garden.

"No, it happens all the time. I'm okay."

That should have been his cue to release her, but it was the last thing he wanted to do.

What the hell is wrong with me?

Chapter 3

Rylie's heart continued to pound, even as Dustin's hands slipped away from her arms. She nervously tucked a stray hair behind her ear and stepped away from him unsteadily. Not because of her ankle, which throbbed and ached, but because of what she'd felt pressed against Dustin's front. He'd been excited to have her there and just the knowledge of that had been a rush.

Come on, he's a horn dog. Any ass will do. Besides, I have Asher.

It was probably a bad sign that she had to keep reminding herself about her live-in boyfriend.

"Should we continue?" Toni asked.

Rylie's face warmed, irrationally worried the older woman could read her thoughts. "Yes, sorry. I normally change my shoes when I scout locations, but I forgot today." Probably because she'd been so thrown about being paired with Dustin.

As they continued the tour, Rylie discreetly checked out the front of Dustin's trousers and could still see the evidence of his excitement pressing against the gray fabric. From the look and shape of it, it was no wonder so many women had no problem hopping into bed with him.

I am going to hell.

"You sure you're okay?" Dustin asked quietly.

Rylie's gaze shot up to meet his. His smile was wide, bright, and sexy as hell.

Oh, God, did he know that she was scoping out his package?

"Yeah, I'm good."

The rest of the tour, Rylie avoided looking Dustin's way as much as possible. When they finally got back to the car an hour later, she stared out the window as he backed up and headed down the driveway to Highway 16.

"I don't think it will fit," he said.

Rylie whirled toward him. "What?"

He glanced away from the road to shoot her a quizzical look. "Heart and Soul. I don't think it will be a good fit for the wedding."

Oh, God, why couldn't she seem to drag her mind out of the gutter? "Oh. Yeah, yeah, I agree."

"What did you think I meant?"

His handsome face had split into a grin, and she thought her face would catch fire. "Nothing, I was just deep in thought."

"Mmm-hmm."

She glared at him. "What? What did you think I thought you meant?"

"Oh, I wouldn't dream of hazarding a guess, Miss Templeton."

He was messing with her. She knew there was no way he could know that her first thought had been downright naughty, but still, his tone suggested he suspected.

"Where are we headed next?" she said, changing the subject.

"I thought we'd head back to the office and get a change of shoes for you."

"They aren't there. I forgot to pack them today, since I didn't have any plans to walk all over a bunch of venues."

"That's okay, we'll just swing by your place and grab some."

Rylie's heart skidded as she glanced at the clock. Asher probably wouldn't be home, but she could just imagine the fight that would erupt if she showed up with Dustin and he was there.

"That's okay, I can make it in these."

Dustin glanced over at her doubtfully. "No, you can't. Those are not functional shoes. Those are meant to look pretty and give men impure thoughts."

Just the mention of impure thoughts made her want to crawl under the seat and die.

"God, do you have to do that?" she snapped.

"Do what?" He seemed genuinely surprised by her reaction.

"Do you always have to talk dirty?"

A rich chuckle escaped him and she hated that she clenched her thighs together as the low rumble swept over her.

"Believe me, when I talk dirty, you won't want me to stop."

Rylie punched him in the arm before she could stop herself, and he yelled, swerving.

"Ow, I was kidding!"

Her knuckles throbbed. She hadn't quite expected him to be that muscular. "No, that's sexual harassment!"

"And you just assaulted me!" he sputtered.

"You're lucky I didn't assault you with my heel."

That grin was back and she held up a finger. "Do. Not. Say. It."

"Yes, ma'am."

Sinking back into the passenger seat, she sighed. "I should change my clothes too. One wrong breeze and I'll give everyone a show."

"I wouldn't mind," he said.

She sighed. "I guess I can't blame you for that one. I walked right into it."

"Yeah, you did."

Rylie needed to get them on a safer topic, one less laced with innuendos.

"To get to my house, you take Main to—"

"I know where you live, Rylie."

"How?"

"I've seen your personnel file."

So much for privacy. "Right."

He made a slight turn onto Highway 88. "I was surprised you didn't stay in the place you shared with your dad."

Rylie's chest hurt, thinking about her dad. Her father had been a good man, the best. She strived to be like him every day—selfless, understanding, and brave.

Nothing like her mother, who had found out that she'd had ovarian cancer and instead of staying and fighting, she'd run off to "experience life."

Her dad had been heartbroken, but never spoke ill of her, even when Rylie did. She'd hated her mother for hurting him.

And me. She left me too.

They'd gotten a call from a hospital in Florida that she'd been admitted and they'd flown down to see her. She'd been so far gone; there was nothing the doctors could do for her.

She'd asked their forgiveness, and her dad had given it readily.

Rylie couldn't. After sixteen years of being an amazing wife and mother, she'd bailed. She'd gone off and screwed around and who knows what. That's what she'd wanted to do with the rest of her time instead of being with the people who loved her.

After her mom died, her dad had sold their house to pay for the deductibles from her mother's medical care and used the rest to pay for culinary school for Rylie. Once she'd finished, she'd wanted to go to Paris and study under one of the top pastry chefs, and eventually, open her own gourmet bakery. It had been her dream since she was eight and got her first Easy-Bake Oven, and her dad had tried to make it happen for her.

It hadn't though.

She'd been in her last semester when she'd had to drop out and come home. Her dad had experienced a mild heart attack and needed help recovering. She always thought she would go back, but after he didn't survive his second one, she had been left with more debt....

And Asher.

"Rylie? You all right?" Dustin asked.

"Yeah, sure. I'm just surprised you knew where we lived."

"We grew up together. I wasn't oblivious to you."

She almost snorted. Everyone had been oblivious to her. She'd been fifty pounds heavier, worn her glasses like a shield, and had serious acne. After leaving Sweetheart, she'd attended dance and aerobic classes while she was in school, dropped some weight, got contact lenses, and started a serious face cleansing regiment. And she'd learned to love her body in the process.

When she'd come home, she was completely different than the shy bookworm she'd been in school and people had finally started noticing her. Before that, she'd been invisible.

"Please. It wasn't like we traveled in the same circles."

"Neither did you and Asher."

Her jaw tightened. She didn't want to talk about Asher with Dustin, but he didn't take her silent hint.

"How long have you two been together?"

"Three years."

"Long time. You two talk about getting married?"

A sour taste rose in the back of her throat. Once upon a time, she'd thought she'd marry Asher. Their first year together had been great, for the most part. The more she thought back on it, she had probably been so surprised that the guy she'd had a major crush on in high school, who she'd thought was totally out of her league, had asked her out, and she'd ignored some obvious issues.

By the time they'd moved in together a year later, she'd been shocked the first time he'd lost his temper and shoved her into a wall. She'd stared at him in horror for several moments before she'd walked into the bedroom and started packing. He'd come in, begging her forgiveness, and trying to hold her. He'd cried and she'd told herself that it was a mistake.

And she'd warned him that it was the only chance he'd have.

Then her dad had died suddenly and she'd been lost. It had been the two of them against the world; with him gone, there was no one who loved her, except Asher. The money in her dad's bank account went toward funeral costs and the medical bills insurance wouldn't cover. When she hadn't been able to cover everything, Asher had paid the remaining bills, and told her she didn't have to pay him back. She'd gotten the job at Something Borrowed so she could save up and eventually finish culinary school.

But without her dad, she'd relied on Asher more, and although it had started small, he'd slowly started tearing her down. Telling her she had stupid taste in movies. That she should stop baking so much because she was just going to get fat again. Accusing her of working at Something Borrowed so she could meet other guys. He'd become controlling, condescending, and she'd just let it go on. Somewhere along the way, she'd stopped fighting back.

It was only now that she'd realized how far she'd let things go. And that she needed to find a way out.

"No, we don't talk about getting married."

He pulled in front of the house she shared with Asher, and when he got out with her, she shook her head. "You should wait here."

He raised an eyebrow at her. "I can't use your bathroom?"

"Of course, you can. Sorry." God, she was acting like an idiot. There was nothing wrong with having her coworker use the bathroom while she changed. She wasn't doing anything wrong.

They walked up the path to the porch, the clip of his fancy shoes on the cement making her heart jump with every tap.

She unlocked the front door and she waved him toward the hallway. "Bathroom is that way. I won't be a minute."

He disappeared and Rylie went past the laundry room to the master bedroom.

She pulled out a pair of slacks, an off-the-shoulder floral blouse, and her black Skechers from the closet. The slacks would be scorching in the 103 degree heat, but they would cover the shiny black sneakers. It was disgusting how hot Nor Cal was in late September.

She was just pulling her blouse on when she heard the unmistakable rumble of Asher's truck.

Oh, no.

* * * *

Dustin wandered around the living room of Rylie's place, surprised at how bare it seemed. One picture of Rylie with her father sat on a bookshelf filled with paperback books. Another of Marley, Rylie, and Kelly dressed to the nines and smiling was set on the second shelf down along with a few of those silly Funko Pop! figures.

The walls of the house held pictures of Asher catching a fish when he was a kid. A framed article about him playing football. One after another of the man's achievements were hung up. The leather chair and couch, big screen TV, and tacky neon *It's Beer O'Clock* sign screamed bachelor pad. Besides that one bookshelf, Dustin wouldn't even have guessed that Rylie lived here. There was no color, no flair that said, "Rylie." Meanwhile, her desk at work held a hot pink cat-shaped cup with funny pens in it and more of those Funko Pop! figures.

Something was definitely off. The way that Rylie had reacted to him suggesting they go to her house for shoes and wanting to use the bathroom... She'd seemed almost afraid.

The door slammed behind him, and he turned to find Asher standing by the entrance, scowling at him. He was wearing jeans and a T-shirt, black grease stains covering both. Dustin noticed that even though his arms and shoulders were still muscular, there was evidence of a beer gut.

"The fuck are you doing in my house?" he growled.

Before he could answer, Rylie came running out of the bedroom, breathing hard. "Hey, babe. Dustin just brought me by so I could change. We're going to scout a couple of properties for a wedding and I forgot to pack my sneakers this morning. I almost broke my ankle in the heels I was wearing."

Asher glowered at Rylie and Dustin bristled as he sneered. "You actually expect me to believe that?"

Dustin didn't like all that anger directed at Rylie, who was pale and shaking. He moved between them, bringing Asher's focus back on him. "Hey, man, it's true. I just came in to use your bathroom."

Asher stepped into him, and Dustin held his breath. The guy smelled like he'd bathed in a brewery and rolled in motor oil afterward. Was he day drinking when he was supposed to be working?

Classy.

"Was I talking to you, shithead?"

"Asher, stop it!" Rylie's voice trembled. "We weren't doing anything."

Asher turned his bloodshot gaze on Rylie and stepped around Dustin toward her. "You think I'm stupid, Rys? I know this guy. What happened? He tell you you're pretty and you just spread your legs—*oof.*"

Dustin hadn't even realized he'd grabbed Asher until the other man was pressed up against the wall, Dustin's arm across his throat. His whole body trembled with barely repressed rage as he said, "You don't talk to her like that."

Dustin hadn't put his hands on another person in years; he preferred to handle disagreements without using his fists, afraid he'd lose control. But for this douche canoe, he was about to make an exception.

Asher's eyes popped out of his head as Dustin held him there. He wanted to drag Asher outside and teach him a lesson about bullying, but Rylie was tugging on his arm frantically, bringing him back to himself.

"Dustin, don't! It's okay. Put him down and let's just go back to work."

He turned in disbelief to look at her over his shoulder. "The hell I will! He's out of line."

"*Please.*"

Her shiny eyes cracked something in him and he let the prick go. As Asher bent over, sucking in air, Dustin stood over him.

"I'll meet you at the car," she said.

Every fiber in his body wanted to plant his feet and stay, but he just nodded. There was no convincing her to walk out; how many times had he tried that with his mom when his dad got violent?

It still shocked the hell out of him that Rylie would put up with this asshole though.

It's none of my business. Just stay the hell out of it.

With a curt nod, he walked out the door.

Chapter 4

Rylie stared at the front door, wishing she could have just walked out with Dustin. To not have to deal with Asher right this second. But he'd made it impossible to ignore *this*. He'd threatened her coworker, insulted and embarrassed her.

This couldn't wait.

"I'm going to kill that asshole," Asher wheezed as he clutched his throat.

Rylie grit her teeth, wanting to tell him not to be an idiot, but it would only make him more belligerent. By the look and smell of him, he was drunk, and probably high. He'd gotten his medical marijuana card a few months ago to help with the back pain from his football injury and since then, it had become a daily habit.

"Have I ever given you any reason not to trust me?" she asked.

Asher stood up to his full height of six foot three, and his gaze slid over her. "You mean other than the fact that you're a professional bridesmaid, whose sole job is to flirt and look pretty?"

"That's not fair or true. I organize most of the event, I am there for the bride, and I do not flirt with anyone."

He didn't respond right away. When he went to the fridge, and pulled out a beer, she wanted to say something about him having enough, but she bit her cheek.

"Not going to tell me it's the middle of the day?"

"What would be the point? I *would* like to have an adult conversation though. You flew off the handle for no reason, and I want to know why. Why don't you trust me?"

He popped the top as he sneered at her. "Maybe I'd trust you more if we'd had sex recently."

Rylie swallowed. It was true that they hadn't in a while, probably over a month, but it was hard to get excited when all Asher did was grab at her. No romance, no sweet words. Just a hand on her breast or between her legs and his heavy breathing against her neck.

Not the best way to get her in the mood.

"Maybe I'd want to have sex with you more if you weren't acting like such a jerk."

He took a long drink before he nodded toward the door. "And what, you think that guy is going to treat you better? That he's after more than sex?"

Rylie's cheeks burned. "This has nothing to do with him and everything to do with us. We aren't happy, Ash. We haven't been for a long time, and I think maybe we need to take a break."

He blinked at her, like he couldn't believe what she was saying. "You're leaving me?"

Rylie took a strengthening breath, but it came out shaky. "Yes. I'll come for my stuff after work. I'd appreciate it if you weren't here."

Asher set his beer down and turned away from her, gripping the side of the kitchen counter. The sunlight coming through the window hit his tan profile, his chocolate brown hair and strong jaw contoured in shadows and light. He was still handsome, but around his mouth were lines of bitterness. She'd known he'd been disappointed after he'd lost his football scholarship and come home, his back screwed up, but there had still been that charming, sweet guy underneath that first year or so.

As he faced her once more, red faced and wild, all traces of the man she'd fallen for were gone.

"You won't leave."

The cold, hard inflection in his tone was like a slap, but she steeled herself. This had been a long time coming, and she wasn't going to back down or cave now.

She was done being a doormat.

"I am."

"You have nowhere to go."

"I'll find a place."

"What about the money you owe me?" he asked cruelly.

She reeled back. Asher had helped her with some of the bills for her dad, but when she'd tried to pay him back, he'd told her she didn't owe him anything. That helping out someone you loved was just part of the gig.

Obviously, that sentiment had only been in effect if they were *still* in love.

Refusing to let him see her hurt, she gave him a curt nod. "I'll leave it on the table when I pick up my stuff." It would eat into her savings, but if it meant a clean break from him, so be it.

As if he finally realized she was serious, his face crumpled and he took a step toward her, reaching out to her. "Babe, I'm sorry. I know I have been a dick, I am a dick, but don't...don't leave me. I need you."

The tears in his eyes didn't affect her the way they always had. She knew that they were just a manipulation to make her stay; if he was really sorry, if he really cared, he would have changed long before today.

Rylie moved out of his grasp, shaking her head. "No, Asher. It's over."

She walked away from him and opened the door, refusing to give him any more time to change her mind, and stepped into the sunshine. Her stride grew lighter the closer she got to Dustin, who was leaning against his car, waiting for her.

Suddenly, Dustin pushed off his car, his face a mask of concern. Before she realized he was moving toward her, her arm was caught in a painful vise grip. She was swung around like a ragdoll, her head snapping at the velocity. When the world finally stopped spinning, she stared up into Asher's twisted features, too surprised to be afraid.

"You don't get to walk away from me, bitch!"

His hand was in the air. He was going to hit her.

Asher had never hit her. Shoved her, grabbed her, shook her... He was always sorry afterward, but never had he struck her.

And he never would.

No sooner had the thought crossed her mind, Rylie's knee came up, catching Asher in the jewels. She blinked as he fell to the ground, gripping his crotch and groaning.

Dustin gently eased her toward the car, his arm around her shoulder. "I'll call the sheriff." She didn't protest as he pulled his cell out and dialed.

She couldn't tear her eyes away from Asher rolling around and cursing her while Dustin talked to the dispatcher. When he finally hung up, she murmured, "I told him I was leaving."

Dustin's arm tightened around her. "Good. We'll get your stuff and get you the hell out of here. The sheriff's on his way."

She nodded. "That's probably a good idea."

Two sheriff cruisers pulled up just as Asher was climbing to his feet several minutes later. They must have been really close to get there that fast. While one of the deputies cuffed him and put him in the back of the car, Deputy Luke Jessup, Marley's boyfriend, came over. As he passed by the patrol car, his gaze fell on Asher and his expression was rather terrifying.

It made Rylie glad he was on her side.

The big man's frown was laced with concern as he stopped in front of them. "You okay, Rylie?"

She nodded slowly, watching Asher's angry face through the patrol car's window. "I'm okay."

"I hope you don't mind that I called Marley," Luke said.

Rylie winced, just imagining if Asher was still here when Marley arrived. "No, that's fine. Thanks. I should call Kelly too and let her know I'm not coming back to the office today."

Dustin shook his head. "I'll call her and Bill at Short and Sweet Movers. Have them bring over a truck and some boxes."

Rylie didn't know what to say. Gone was the smart-ass flirt, or the furious Hulk who had held Asher by the throat.

There were just too many layers to Dustin Kent.

"Thanks."

Their eyes caught and held, his blue ones so sympathetic that it made her more uncomfortable than his inappropriateness.

Luke broke the spell when he squeezed her shoulder. "I'm going to head back out there. We'll hold Asher until tomorrow, and it's up to you on whether you want to press charges."

"Thanks, Luke."

He left, and she walked inside, Dustin on her heels, talking on his cell phone. She glanced around the house. There wasn't much she wanted. Her books, her pictures, her clothes. She had a few things in storage, items from the duplex she'd shared with her dad that Asher hadn't wanted in the house, but she didn't even have a bed. And she didn't have enough money to pay Asher, put down first and last on a new place, and buy furniture. She'd just have to find a rental fully furnished or get used to sleeping on the floor.

Dustin finally got off the phone with the movers, and asked, "You got any trash bags?"

She turned to him, puzzled. "Trash bags? Yeah, in the cupboard, but why?"

"I figured we could at least bag up your clothes until the boxes get here."

The realization of all that had happened finally hit her, and her chest tightened as panic set in. "Yeah. Yeah we could. I was just thinking about what I was going to do after I get my stuff. I haven't even looked into any places, have nothing planned—"

"I've got a pool house you can use. Until you find somewhere more permanent."

Rylie choked on her laughter, until she caught the extremely serious expression on his face.

"You're kidding, right?"

"Why? It's empty, and you need a place to crash."

He wasn't wrong, but staying at his place, even in a separate dwelling? She'd be absolutely out of her mind to say yes.

Then again, what were her options? Staying on Marley's couch while Luke and her did it in the next room?

Rylie made a face. "How much is rent?"

"I don't need your money," Dustin said firmly.

"Then no way."

He cocked his head, and shot her a bemused look. "Did it ever occur to you that I'm just a good guy trying to do the right thing?"

He must have inferred by her expression that she did not.

"Fair enough, but the offer still stands."

Dustin headed toward the back of the house while Rylie was still mulling things over, but when he disappeared into her bedroom, she shouted, "What are you doing?"

"Helping you pack."

The image of Dustin rummaging through her underwear drawer sent her rushing after him.

* * * *

Dustin hadn't planned on spending the rest of the afternoon taping boxes and loading a moving truck, but by the time they finished, he was the one relieved. Relieved that Rylie was getting out of there and didn't have to see Asher again.

Unlike his mother, who spent thirty years with a man who had used her as a physical and verbal punching bag.

Dustin clenched his fist around the handle of the moving van's door, and slammed it shut. Once it was locked in place, he turned to face Rylie, who was being hugged hard by a distraught Marley. Marley was a tall, leggy blond with expressive green eyes that normally shot daggers his way. He'd never been interested in her, anyway.

Unlike Rylie. When Marley finally released her, Dustin studied Rylie's sweaty, red face, with a stripe of dust across the bridge of her nose.

It made her look young and adorable, but Dustin couldn't think like that anymore. Rylie was no longer someone to be flirted with and tormented.

She needed to be protected.

It was why he'd offered her his pool house. It was the one thing he could do for her that he wished someone had done for his mother. A safe place to get back on her feet.

"You call me if you need anything. Are you sure you have a place to go?" Marley asked.

"Yes, I'm fine, really."

Marley seemed resigned. He wasn't surprised that she couldn't even spare a greeting in his direction. It wasn't as though he'd always been the most charming fellow to her.

Once Marley was in her car and driving away, Dustin finally spoke.

"What now?" he asked.

"I just have to leave Asher a check."

"A check for what?"

Rylie leveled him with those dark eyes and his mind automatically compared them to hot, chocolate fudge.

Damnit.

"I owe him money, and I pay my debts. I'll only be a few seconds."

Dustin wanted to argue with her, but he just leaned against the moving truck and waited for her to come back outside several minutes later.

Several seconds ticked by as she stood in front of him, playing with the hem of her shirt. "He's never hit me before."

Dustin had a hard time believing her, but he didn't argue. "Okay."

"I just wanted you to know that he didn't. That I wouldn't have…have stayed."

The pain in her voice was so thick; his hands itched to reach out and pull her against him. But he resisted the temptation. It wasn't his place to comfort her. Not only did they work together, but he was possibly about to become her landlord.

Talk about a buttload of complications he did not need.

"I understand, Rylie. You don't have to explain any of it to me."

She sniffled, hiked her purse up on her shoulder, and when she lifted her chin, he could see the glassy sheen to her eyes, knowing she was probably holding back tears.

"I think I would like to stay in your pool house, if the offer still stands."

"It does." He waved at Mark, who was sitting in the cab of the moving truck. Once he got the signal, Mark headed out toward Dustin's place.

Rylie sounded as though she was choking on something. "Wow, you actually told them to take my stuff to your house before I'd even agreed?"

He clapped his hands together, ignoring the outrage in her tone. "Yes, yes I did. Are you hungry?"

Rylie shot him a suspicious glance and he chuckled. "Again, just a kind, concerned gentleman who figured if he was starving, then you must be too."

She seemed to weigh her answer before responding. "You would be correct in that assumption."

"Perfect. What are you in the mood for? Victoria is amazing—"

"Who is Victoria?"

He blinked at her interruption. "My chef."

Rylie rolled her eyes. "Of course, you have a chef."

Dustin walked ahead of her and opened the passenger door of his car. "I know what you're thinking. I'm just flashing my wealth and privilege around, but having Victoria makes sense. I can afford to pay her, she has gainful employment, and since my hours tend to fluctuate, I do not always have time to cook and clean. It's reasonable to assume I would have a whole staff employed, so I don't know why you're surprised."

Rylie just muttered to herself as she climbed into his car. "Are you taking me to Something Borrowed?"

"No, I figured we'd just head to my place and after dinner, unpack the truck. We'll carpool in the morning."

She sighed, but didn't argue. He opened his door and hopped behind the wheel.

"I do appreciate this and I promise that I will start looking for a place tomorrow—"

He shot her a dark look as he started the car. "Like I said, just trying to help."

"Well, I'll be the perfect guest. You'll hardly know I am there."

Single, sexy Rylie living less than five hundred feet from him?

What did I get myself into?

Chapter 5

Twenty minutes later, Rylie's wide-eyed gaze swept around the pool house, her jaw slack with shock.

"You look like you're trying to catch flies," Dustin teased.

Rylie snapped it closed, and shook her head slowly. "I thought your pool house would be...small."

"It's only two thousand square feet. My house is—"

"I saw the mansion; I don't need to know the dimensions."

Dustin clucked his tongue at her. "It's rude to interrupt."

"It's also in poor taste to brag." She slid her hand across the marble countertop in the kitchen. This home was gorgeous, modern, and way more than she could ever afford to rent. She wasn't sophisticated or complicated; she liked simple décor with a homey, country feel.

This was like stepping into one of those million dollar homes on the street of dreams.

"Touché. I guess talking about the size of my houses might give the impression I'm making up for something."

Rylie's cheeks burned as she caught his meaning. "Do you always have to go there?"

Dustin chuckled. "Sorry, old habits die hard. Sexual innuendos seem to be ingrained into my personality."

"Charming."

"Women usually think so," Dustin said, drawing an eye roll from Rylie. He clapped his hands and rubbed them together. "Okay, well, let's grab dinner and I'll help you unload the truck."

"You don't have to do that."

"I know, but I am, so no use arguing."

Rylie wasn't really planning on it. As awkward as it was to accept his help, she was emotionally drained and not looking forward to unloading her stuff alone.

"I'll take your help," she said with a smile.

"Good. Food first though."

"Agreed."

Dustin opened the sliding glass door for her, and they walked around the in-ground pool. The sun was still up at six in the evening, and so was the temperature. The blue water looked awfully inviting, but there was no way she was going to ask to use his pool. She already felt as though she was taking advantage of him.

He opened the back door of his house for her, and when his hand settled on her lower back, leading her into the dining room, she shivered.

"Are you cold?" he asked.

"No, that's crazy. It's still a hundred degrees outside."

"Yeah, but I keep the house at a cool sixty, so I figured maybe the change in temperature had gotten to you."

"I'm fine," she squeaked. She took a few quick steps and the warmth of his palm dropped away. She didn't like the flash of disappointment that crept unbidden to the surface at the loss of his touch. Rylie didn't want him or any man. She was going to swear off men indefinitely and focus on herself.

Rylie grimaced as she thought of her mother needing to focus on herself after she'd gotten sick.

I'm nothing like her. I don't have a responsibility to a child and a loving husband.

They walked into the dining room to find the long redwood table set with plates, silverware, and stemware. A bottle of wine was in the middle of the table and all around it were platters of food, enough to feed a professional basketball team.

"Wow, does she do this for you every night?" Rylie asked.

"No, she usually makes me several dinners I can reheat easily, but when I mentioned I'd have company, I guess she assumed it was romantic."

He held one of the dining room chairs out for her and she sat, her stomach growling as the smell of food reached her nose. She eyeballed the dish of mashed potatoes with cheese and bread crumbs on top.

"This looks so good."

Dustin took the seat across from her and waved a hand. "Ladies first."

Rylie was conscious of Dustin watching her as she scooped a small portion of the rich looking mashed potatoes onto her plate, then the green beans, and a chicken breast. She was trying very hard to be ladylike when she really wanted to pick up the dish like the Beast in the Disney cartoon and throw etiquette to the wind.

She had just taken her first exquisite bite when she noticed Dustin had piled his plate high, but wasn't eating. Instead, he was watching her. Intensely.

She swallowed the creamy potatoes and tilted her head. "What?"

"Nothing."

He took a bite, his gaze still on hers, and she knew he was thinking something.

"You want to say something to me."

Dustin shook his head and poured wine into his empty glass. "Nope. I just want to eat and get started on that truck."

Rylie let it go, slipping another mouthful past her lips. He held the bottle of wine out to her and she shook her head. Instead, she reached for a pitcher of ice water and poured it into the wineglass to her right.

"You afraid to drink around me?"

"I told you, I'm not a big wine drinker."

"Probably because you're used to the six-dollar shit."

Rylie resisted the urge to flick a spoonful of potatoes at him. "There you go, flashing your money around."

He quirked a brow at her, and she was beginning to resent that look. "Most women don't mind it when I wine and dine them."

"I'm not most women."

"So I've noticed."

The way he said it made Rylie wonder if he thought that was a bad thing.

* * * *

The meal had been excruciating, but not because he didn't like Rylie or didn't want to be around her.

It was the way she'd looked after that first bite of food. Her eyes had rolled up into her head, and he could have sworn she moaned a bit.

He wasn't about to point that out and embarrass her, but damn, it had been hot.

Too hot.

Now, they were outside the pool house gate, lugging boxes. It was dusk, with hardly any sun left in the pinkish-purple sky, and muggy. The T-shirt he'd changed into after dinner was now sticking to his back, and as he picked up the last box, he was ready to strip down and jump into the pool.

He walked through the sliding glass door and set the box down. Her stuff had only taken up about half the truck, but the books were heavy and made up about six medium-size boxes.

"You ever think about getting a Kindle or something and downloading all these paperbacks?"

She shook her head as she lifted a bag of clothing off the floor. "I like the smell and feel of real books."

Dustin wrinkled his nose. "Whatever you say."

She laughed from the bedroom, a husky sound that went straight to his dick. "I don't mind ebooks. I have an app on my phone for when I get stuck places and forget a paperback, but staring at a screen isn't the same."

Dustin preferred reading on his iPad, but to each their own.

He clapped his hands, then rubbed them together, speaking loudly, "Well, if you don't need any help in here getting settled, I was going to take a swim. Do you care to join me?"

The rustling in the back room stopped, and he wondered what her expression was at this moment. Was she disgusted, thinking he was asking her with nefarious plans in mind?

"No thanks, I'm really tired. I think I'm going to just get in my pjs and start a new book."

Probably best. He didn't know if he could handle seeing Rylie in a bathing suit, soaking wet and...

Shit, I need to just stop thinking. "Okay, well, feel free to use the pool anytime."

She walked out into the hallway wearing a T-shirt and sweats. Her hair was sweaty and pulled up in a haphazard bun, and she still had that little streak of dust he'd noticed hours ago.

Somehow, he found this look just as attractive.

She smiled shyly, clutching a book in her hand. "I really appreciate you letting me stay here, and I promise I won't bother you."

Dustin frowned, the urge to tell her he wanted her to bother him strong. He really needed that swim.

* * * *

Rylie finished washing her face and brushing her teeth ten minutes later, embarrassed when she'd seen how dirty and disgusting she was. Now, feeling at least halfway human, she sat down in the big, comfy chair in the living room, pushing her glasses up her nose. She wore contacts outside the house but at home, it was nice to give her eyes a rest.

Besides, if she started crying, she didn't want to deal with her contact lenses getting all funky.

It still hadn't really hit her that three years of her life with someone was over. She didn't regret leaving, but the ache was still there. She should have left sooner, when it started to get bad, but it was hard to let go of her first love and after losing her dad... Well, it was tough saying good-bye.

Rylie wiped at her cheek as she opened her new T.J. Kline romance, being careful not to break the spine. She'd just reached the part where the heroine was stuck hanging over the front seat of her car with her butt in the air when she heard a splash and looked up.

Outside the glass doors, she watched Dustin pop up over the side of the pool, and climb out, the solar lights illuminating what she'd already thought was underneath all his snappy suits.

Dustin was built. Like washboard abs, broad shoulders that nipped down into narrow hips, and firm, muscular legs built.

Rylie swallowed hard as he walked by her door to the end of the pool and dove in, disappearing from sight.

She shook herself, her cheeks heating as she realized that she'd been ogling him. She was supposed to be immune to men, completely swearing off the entire lot.

She was obviously one sick individual.

Trying to concentrate on her book again, she was distracted by every splash outside and when she read the same line three times, she finally gave up, slid her bookmark into place, and stood. She picked up her cell phone from the counter and dialed Marley, turning her back to the glass door.

"Hey, I was just about to call you. Are you doing okay?" Marley asked after the second ring.

"Yeah, I'm good. Swearing off men, of course."

"I don't blame you. I want to kick his ass—"

"Don't please? It's over now, and despite how it ended, it wasn't all bad. I just want to move on with no regrets."

"Good for you. So, where did you end up? Are you at the Love Shack Hotel?"

Rylie bit her lip. Marley was her friend and she loved her, but if she told her she was staying in Dustin's pool house, she would blow a gasket. Probably call Rylie crazy.

Which wouldn't be far from the truth, considering Rylie felt a little nuts.

"No, but don't worry, I'm safe. Just tired."

"You're being weird and mysterious. Please tell me you aren't living in your car."

"I'm not, I swear. I'm good."

"All right, I'll let you be mysterious today, but tomorrow is another story. Get some rest and we'll talk soon. If you need anything, call okay? Love you."

"I love you too."

Rylie ended the call and glanced over her shoulder. The motion activated porch light was off and it was dark outside, which probably meant Dustin had gone to bed.

After making sure the door was locked, she plugged her phone into the charger and set it on the nightstand in the bedroom. She'd already hung up her clothes and slipped the rest of them into the dresser against the wall at the end of the king-sized bed. She still had a ton of boxes to unpack, but she didn't want to get too comfortable. She didn't plan to be here that long.

Rylie pulled her iPad from the night stand drawer and shut off the light just before she crawled between the soft sheets. She sighed as the smooth fabric caressed her feet; Asher had always preferred flannel sheets, even in the summer. These were cool and smooth and probably cost a small fortune, nothing like the itchy, hot fabric on their old shared bed.

Pushing the bitterness back, she turned on an episode of *Who's the Boss* on Hulu and set the tablet on the nightstand, along with her glasses. Curling onto her side, she tried to relax, to just enjoy the show, hoping it would help her fall asleep.

After three episodes, she gave up and turned the device off. As she tossed and turned some more, flashes of Dustin crept into her mind. Hard. Wet. Shirtless.

Flopping onto her stomach with a groan, she mumbled aloud, "Stop thinking about him, idiot."

It didn't work, but it was worth a try.

Chapter 6

The high-pitched melody of Rylie's alarm woke her. She groaned as the sound exacerbated the heavy thud in her head. Reaching for the device to turn off the offending sound, it took her several seconds to remember where she was.

She cracked an eye open. The room was still dark, thanks to the blackout curtains covering the single window in the room. She yawned and stretched, wincing at the sore muscles in her shoulders and arms from all the lifting. As she lay on her back and stared up into the abyss, she swallowed hard.

She was single. She was on her own. And she had no idea what she was going to do.

The first thing I should probably do is shower and get dressed. Then coffee.

But getting out of the warm, comfortable bed she'd had so much trouble falling asleep in proved to be a challenge all on its own. When the sound of knocking on glass woke her once more, she realized she'd fallen back asleep. Pressing the button on her phone to light up the home screen, she cursed. She only had twenty minutes to get ready for work.

After climbing out of the bed, she rushed to the front of the house and found Dustin standing on the other side in the early morning light. He was already dressed in a navy blue suit, blue striped shirt, and gray tie.

If he hadn't already spotted her, she would have backed up slowly to inspect the damage on her hair.

Discreetly wiping at her mouth to check for any crusted drool trails, Rylie finally opened the door. Her gaze zeroed in on the steaming mug in his hand.

"I was coming to check on you. We've got to be out the door in twenty minutes."

"I know. Sorry, I didn't sleep well." She pointed at the beautiful, gorgeous cup of Joe and asked, "Is that for me?"

Dustin chuckled as he held the deliciousness out to her. "Yeah, I usually take mine black, but I added a little half and half and sugar for you."

She reached out and took the mug from him before sipping the wonderful elixir of life with a sigh. "This is perfect. Thank you."

"You're welcome," he said, his blue eyes twinkling with amusement.

Rylie realized he was giving her the once over, his grin widening even more, and figured she must look worse off than she suspected.

"I should go get cleaned up," she said.

"Sure, I'll just have Victoria pack you a breakfast burrito to go."

"She doesn't have to do that."

He shrugged. "It's already made. I guess I could force myself to eat another, if you really don't want it."

Her traitorous stomach growled loudly, and he laughed, proving he'd heard it.

"If it's already made, I will take it. I wouldn't want to be rude."

He saluted her with one hand against his forehead. "I'll see you up at the main house in fifteen minutes then. We don't want to be late."

She closed the door on him, and mimicked him as she walked down the hallway. *"We don't want to be late."*

Rylie set the mug down on the counter and grimaced when she saw the indentation marks on her cheeks and chin from the pillow she'd slept on.

I really need to stop worrying about what he may think of me.

She'd gotten cleaned up and dressed in record time. Sporting a blue dress with white polka dots, a wide yellow belt, and white wedges, she wrapped her wet hair into a bun on top of her head. She didn't have time for full makeup, so she just put on some mascara and lip gloss. She'd packed a change of clothes and her tennis shoes in her large, yellow and white striped tote in case they did some more scouting today, but she needed to wear her dress. It was like a suit of armor; it made her feel strong and confident.

Which were two things she could use a boost on today.

When she walked through the door of the big house a few minutes later with her coffee cup in one hand and tote in the other, she was greeted by a short, older woman with blue-black hair and a wide smile. She was wearing an apron covered in colorful hearts over a simple T-shirt and jeans. She was not what Rylie had pictured for Dustin's chef and housekeeper.

Was I really expecting her to look like Megan Fox and wearing a French maid outfit?

"You must be Victoria," Rylie said, holding her free hand out to her. "I'm Rylie. Your potatoes are wonderful! I need that recipe from you!"

Victoria took Rylie's hand in both of hers and squeezed. "Of course! I am so glad you liked them."

"I loved them." Rylie held up the coffee cup. "Do you happen to have a to-go cup for this?"

"Oh, yes, let me warm it up for you."

Rylie started to protest, but Victoria was too fast. She'd already put the mug in the microwave and was rummaging through the cupboard next to the sink.

"When Mr. Kent said he was having a guest staying in the pool house, I knew you were special."

"Why is that?" Rylie asked, surprised.

Victoria grabbed the cup from the microwave and poured it into a black travel mug. "Because none of Mr. Kent's usual *guests* stay in the pool house."

Rylie's cheeks warmed and she took the mug from Victoria with a snort. "You don't say?"

"Yes, but you know, it's none of my business what the man does. That's why I don't say anything. Not a word." Then, Victoria leaned over and lowered her voice. "I will say that most of the women who stay are not worthy of Mr. Kent. He is a good man."

Rylie had seen a bit of that man yesterday, and wondered if it was truly who he was, or just another image he portrayed to others. Was he the ladies' man? The jerk? The nice guy who offered his home to women in need?

The sound of Dustin whistling interrupted them. He stood in the doorway, jingling his keys.

"Come on, let's shake a leg. We have a lot to do to make up for yesterday."

"She hasn't even had her breakfast yet, Mr. Kent," Victoria scolded.

"She can eat on the way."

Victoria huffed as she pulled a pan from the oven and wrapped her burrito in tin foil. She slipped it into a paper sack and handed it to Rylie. "I'll see you tonight."

"Yes. Thank you for the coffee and the burrito," Rylie said to Victoria.

"It was my pleasure."

Rylie carried her treasures and tote as she walked toward Dustin, sticking her tongue out at him as she passed. His deep chuckle behind her sent a shiver down her spine and she hated it. She did not want to be attracted to Dustin Kent.

She was on a guy-hatis and needed it to stay that way.

* * * *

Dustin kept glancing at Rylie as they walked to his car. Although she wasn't quite as done up as she usually was, she still looked great and that pin-up style dress accented all her...attributes.

He really needed to stop thinking about her like that, but it was hard. *Pun intended.*

Dustin finally caught on by her angry stride that she was irritated, most likely at him for rushing her out the door, and attempted to smooth things over. "I can get your bag."

"I'm fine, it's not heavy."

Man, she was moodier than a bear with a sore paw. "You're kind of a grump in the morning,"

"Yes, lack of sleep can affect my mood. It's a normal human occurrence."

Dustin's eyebrows shot up at her retort. Rylie was usually so sunny it bordered on sickening.

She just broke up with her long-term boyfriend and stayed the night in a strange place. Cut her some slack.

Dustin thought about getting the door for her, but he'd have to race her for the door, since she was at least three steps ahead. He just tried for landlord-ly concern. "Was the bed uncomfortable?"

She stopped along the passenger side of his car and sighed. "No, it was very comfortable and the sheets were amazing. I just don't sleep well in strange places."

"Gotcha." Dustin climbed into the driver's side at the same time she got situated next to him. As he took the circular drive around to get out onto the highway, he glanced over at her. The paper bag containing her burrito sat in her lap, untouched. "Are you going to eat that?"

"No, I'll wait until I get to work. I don't want to get anything in your car."

Dustin didn't try to convince her it was fine; if he was being honest, he didn't really want to clean up scrambled eggs and bacon crumbs out of his car anyway.

"I appreciate your consideration."

"I don't eat in my car, so why would I do it in yours?" she said.

So, she liked to keep her car clean? That was something they had in common. Dustin appreciated order and control. He'd had so little of it growing up in his father's house. Like all his brothers before him, he couldn't wait to escape.

Only he'd come back after the old man had died, while they'd stayed gone.

"Victoria is nice. I can understand why you like having her around."

Dustin nodded. "Yeah, she's great. She's been with me since I came home two years ago."

"I'm actually surprised you came back here. I figured you'd take all that app money and settle in Aspen or New York. Somewhere a lot fancier than Sweetheart."

It was a move he had considered, but his mom lived here. Despite his frustration over her life choices, he loved her. His brothers used to give him hell about being a mama's boy, but he figured that his mom had been punished enough without having all her children abandon her.

"I've had fancy, and I figured that the people are the same everywhere. At least here I already know who my friends are."

"Should we get back to scouting locations today? There's only a short list for what's available, right?" he asked.

"Yes, because they want it small and soon, so our choices are limited. I thought the second week of November would be lovely. Tie in the fall colors and décor. Pray that the weather stays mild."

Dustin had never planned for a wedding and didn't intend to, but it seemed like a high-profile couple like this wouldn't be leaving all the details to two professional strangers. "I'm actually surprised that they didn't book a venue right away."

"They only got engaged a few weeks ago."

"Then what's the hurry? Is she pregnant?"

Dustin had meant it as a joke, but Rylie groaned loudly. "Please do not even suggest that to anyone else! Some of us need to work for their money."

That stung a bit. "I did work for my money."

He pulled into the parking lot of Something Borrowed, and parked right next to her car. When he killed the engine, she turned in her seat to face him.

"I didn't mean that you didn't work for your money, but you don't have to work now. You don't need to be at Something Borrowed, but I do. I need this commission and I just want to make sure you're taking this seriously."

"Of course I am."

She gave him a curt nod before getting out of the car, leaning in before closing the door to say, "Maybe give me a few minutes head start? I haven't told Marley I'm crashing with you."

"Technically, you're crashing in my pool house and not with me. If you were, we'd both be a lot happier this morning."

She slammed his door in response and he cringed, gripping the steering wheel with tight fists as the soft, floral scent of her lingered. He hadn't meant to say that to her, but the fact that she acted ashamed that she'd taken his offer to help stung. He'd told himself he'd stop needling her, but it seemed he was incapable of growth.

Dustin climbed out of his car and walked inside Something Borrowed. Rylie was nowhere to be seen, but that was probably a good thing. Obviously, the two of them living and working so closely was already making their tense relationship worse.

Maybe he should just ask his mom to host the wedding at the family winery. He'd resisted pulling those kind of strings, but if it kept him out of a car with Rylie today, why not?

Once he reached his office, he dialed his mother's cell.

"Hello, darling. How are you?" she asked.

"Fine, and you?"

"I was just getting ready to head out to lunch with Bev and Carolyn. Is there something you needed?"

"I was just curious if the ballroom had been rented the first weekend in November."

She paused briefly. "I don't believe it is, but I would have to check my book."

"Would you? I have a client looking for a venue and I thought it would be the perfect spot if the weather's bad."

"Of course, I'll call you when I get back. Anything else new?"

Besides the fact I'm letting Rylie Templeton stay in my pool house for free?

"Not a thing, Mom. We'll talk soon."

"Wait, Dustin," she cried, and he waited. "I was hoping you'd come over for brunch Sunday. It's been several weeks since you've been by and I know you're very busy, but I am still your mother. I miss you."

Dustin grimaced at the small guilt trip. "Sure, I'll try to make it."

"Thank you, honey. Okay, I've got to run. Talk to you later. I love you."

"Yeah, love you too. Bye."

Dustin hung up the phone, frustrated in more than one way. Without a definite answer from his mom about Castle Vineyards' availability, he'd have no choice but to spend the whole day in a car with Rylie. The sweet scent of her surrounding him. Watching her twitch about in that dress…

A knock on the door made him jump. Rylie poked her head inside. "Hey, you ready to roll? I've got five places lined up, so we need to get on the road."

The way she leaned in gave him a generous view of deep cleavage and he almost groaned aloud.

Time to be professional and deal, man.

"Yeah, I'm ready."

Chapter 7

Rylie's phone vibrated on her desk for what seemed like the hundredth time that day, but she just ignored it. She already knew that the calls were coming from Asher after the first angry voicemail and she didn't have time to deal with it.

Besides, it was almost time to leave and she was exhausted. Dustin and she had looked at three other vineyards before he'd gotten a call from his mom to let him know that the Castle Ballroom at his family's winery was available. Once they'd gotten back to the office, Rylie had e-mailed Tonya Rolland pictures of all the venues and available dates, including the link to the Castle Vineyards website. She figured she'd let her decide, but she had a feeling Tonya was going to love Castle; it really was the prettiest venue in Sweetheart.

Now she just needed to sit back and wait for her to respond.

Of course, she could easily do that from the comfort of Dustin's pool house, but after spending the whole day with him, she'd needed a break. Not because he'd been obnoxious or flirtatious, but because he'd been… pleasant. Even gentlemanly and…

Well, it kind of freaked her out.

Checking the time on her phone, she stood, rubbing her growling stomach. It was a quarter past six. There was a good chance she wouldn't even bump into him if she left right now. She needed to go by the store and grab groceries; as good as that burrito was, she didn't want to take advantage of Victoria or Dustin. She'd already gone by the bank to pull money for rent. Despite Dustin's assurances that she didn't have to, she couldn't just stay there for free. She needed to pay something.

Rylie picked up her purse from the edge of her desk and headed for the door. She saw Kelly's door closed at the end of the hall. She was probably in there with the company attorney, Christian Ryan, which was good. Rylie wasn't in the mood to talk about anything that happened yesterday and if Kelly caught her alone, she would check up on her. Right now, Rylie just wanted some quiet time.

Rylie walked down the hall, her tote over one shoulder. She'd changed back into her dress when they'd finished looking at venues, and she had taken down her bun, letting her long hair fall in loose waves over her shoulders.

She was just about to push the door open when she saw Asher's truck parked across the street. He was leaning against the side of it with a big bouquet of bright flowers in one hand.

Taking a deep breath, she steeled herself as she pushed open the door and headed straight to her car. Her wedges tapped along the pavement as she quickened her step.

"Rylie. Ryls! Wait a minute."

She didn't even look at him as she reached her car. "You need to go, Asher."

His tone was wheedling. "I just want to talk, baby. Give me five minutes."

"No!" she shouted, holding her tote against her front like a shield and finally looking at him. "No. I gave you three years of my life. I'm not giving you a second more."

His face paled. "You don't mean that."

"I do."

Her whole body trembled as his cheeks flushed red, and his dark eyes narrowed. He threw the flowers on the ground at her feet, then pointed at her menacingly.

"You're going to regret this."

Rylie felt a rush of strength. *I doubt it.*

She didn't say it aloud though. The last thing she wanted was to set him off again.

"Good-bye, Asher."

Rylie stared him down, refusing to turn her back on him again. She waited, her calm a façade; if he could hear the pounding of her heart, he'd know she was full of it.

"Hey!"

Rylie recognized Dustin's shout before she saw him coming out of Something Borrowed. Damn it, she'd thought he had left for the day and been too distracted by Asher to notice his car on the other side of hers.

Dustin held up his phone as Asher turned around. "I've got 911 already typed out and my thumb is hovering over the talk button. Just give me a reason."

Asher snorted. "The big protector."

Dustin's face darkened. "I'm not playing with you. Get the hell out of here."

Asher took several steps toward his truck, glancing back at Rylie. The dark look on his face sent a chill down her spine.

"You okay?" Dustin asked.

Rylie jumped, not realizing how close Dustin had gotten. She turned her attention away from Asher and swallowed hard, composing herself. "Yeah, I'm good. I guess I should start paying you to protect me. This is the second time you've come to my rescue."

"You were handling him. I was just backup."

"Well, it is appreciated just the same."

"You headed home?" he asked.

Home. Weird to hear him describe it like that.

"Um, off to the grocery store first, then back to the pool house."

Dustin frowned at her. "I've got food."

"Yeah, *you* have food. I'm already staying at your place, I'm not eating your food. Although, that reminds me." She rummaged through her purse and pulled out the envelope she'd filled with cash from the bank. "Here."

One dark brow raised, Dustin opened the envelope, and once he saw what was inside, he scowled. "What's this for?"

"For the moving truck and rent—"

He held the envelope back toward her. "I told you, I don't need your money."

"But I need you to take it so that I don't feel like I am mooching off you." When he looked as though he was about to argue, she added, "Please."

Dustin cursed and snapped the envelope closed. "Fine. And I'll keep you company at the store."

"Oh, you don't have to—"

"Humor me."

Rylie wasn't sure how her life had changed so much in two days, but having Dustin Kent want to tag along while she bought groceries had to be the strangest incident yet.

* * * *

Dustin had no idea why he kept offering to help Rylie, especially when this morning he'd wanted to keep his distance. It was as if he had no control over himself when it came to needing to protect her. She was getting under his skin and he hated it.

Well, most of him hated it.

He walked behind Rylie into the store, and when she started to pull out a cart, he intercepted.

"I'll push, you shop."

She moved out of his way with a huff. "You're bossy, anyone ever tell you that?"

"Occasionally."

She pursed her lips, but brought out a piece of paper from her purse. It amused him that she was old school about her shopping list. He usually sent a text to Victoria with what he needed from the store.

As they headed inside, along the front of the store, Dustin looked around and realized it hadn't changed much in twenty years.

"It's been a long time since I've been in here," he said.

"Really? Why? Because you don't do your own grocery shopping?"

It was said sarcastically, but he didn't take offense. "Exactly."

Rylie looked up from her list to roll her eyes at him. "Ugh, you're like one of those billionaires in the books I read."

"I take it that isn't a compliment." He followed her down the bread aisle as she tossed a loaf into the cart. Rylie shook her head.

"Depends. Some women love it. I've never been into it."

"Into what?"

"Pretty boys who don't know how to get their hands dirty."

Oh, you have no idea what dirty things my hands can do.

His one-track mind roared down a dangerous road and he had to bite the inside of his cheek not to say exactly what he was thinking.

She paused as she grabbed a package of bagels off the shelf. "Don't say it."

"Say what?"

"Whatever pervy comeback I set myself up for."

Dustin chuckled. "Ah, you know me so well."

"Mmhmm."

Dustin watched her fill her cart. Her forehead wrinkled as she crossed things off her list, and her all-business demeanor made him want to make her smile. To ease the tension he could see in her shoulders.

"You sure you're okay?"

"Yeah, why?"

"I was just thinking it can't be easy to have that guy showing up at work. Maybe you should talk to someone about getting a restraining order."

Rylie scoffed. "A restraining order is just a piece of paper that doesn't protect you if someone really wants to harm you."

Dustin agreed, but was surprised she didn't even consider it.

"Besides, I know Asher. He'll hook up with someone new this weekend and forget about me."

Dustin didn't believe that. He'd seen the way Asher looked at Rylie. No matter how screwed up the guy was, he cared about her.

Besides, three years was a long time to be with someone and just forget them in a weekend.

"Selling yourself a bit short, aren't you?" he said.

She didn't meet his gaze as she responded, "I'm being realistic. Men never have issues finding someone new after a break-up."

Well, this conversation wasn't helping to cheer her up. He thought getting her to talk about her problems might unburden her, but obviously, he was wrong.

They passed the toy aisle and Dustin saw a photo prop kit. He pulled it off the shelf, and opened it up while she was getting some stuff down the opposite aisle. Putting the mustache on a stick above his lips, he pushed the cart one handed until he was right next to her.

When she turned to him, her eyes widened with surprise before she laughed. A sound that warmed him all the way to his toes.

"Where did you get that?"

Talking in a thirties-detective voice, he said, "I'm sorry, miss, but I believe I mustache the questions."

"You are ridiculous." When she spotted the open package in her cart, she gasped, "Dustin! You can't just open this and not buy it."

"I have every intention of buying it," he said.

"What for?"

He handed her a pair of fat pink lips from the pack and pulled out his phone. "For our photo shoot."

She pointed the plastic lips at him like a sword. "I do not feel like taking pictures right now."

"You do, I can tell by the way you're smiling."

Rylie pursed her lips. "I'm not smiling."

He came up alongside her and held his phone up in proper selfie position. "If you don't play along, I am going to take awful random pictures and post them all over social media."

"You monster," she deadpanned.

"That's the nicest thing anyone's called me today." He held up his mustache and leaned toward her. "Ready?"

She sighed heavily, but he felt her arm press against his, and the sweet scent of her hair engulfed him as he took the picture.

Dustin checked the photo and showed it to her. "See! Perfect!"

"Nuh uh, my eyes look like they are bugging out of my head! Another."

It took three shots to get the perfect one, but when they did, Dustin's mission had been accomplished. Rylie was smiling, the stiffness in her shoulders completely gone.

For some reason, he wanted to continue this, and he found himself acting the fool the whole time they shopped. When he started juggling oranges, she wrestled them away from him, wheezing with laughter.

"You're going to bruise them, you idiot."

Dustin trapped her between his body and the orange display, putting the fruit back on the pile slowly. She stilled against him, her laughter dying as he stepped a little closer. When her face tilted up and her bright eyes met his, he leaned down, those lush lips calling for him to—

"Hey! You two stop that right now!"

Rylie jumped and Dustin stepped back, glaring to their left at Mrs. Needermyer. The nosy old woman's wrinkled mouth was pinched with disapproval.

"Rylie Templeton, you should be ashamed of yourself! You have a boyfriend."

Rylie's whole face was flushed scarlet as she addressed her. "We broke up, Mrs. Needermyer. And besides, Dustin and I were just playing around. We're friends."

Mrs. Needermyer looked as though she wanted to say more, but Dustin picked up an apple and bit into it, giving her a feral smile. Mrs. Needermyer drew herself up and pointed a finger at him.

"I'm going to tell your mother you're stealing food. I know you think you're above it all, but money does not make you untouchable."

He chewed slowly, and added a large gulp as he swallowed. "I never said I was and I'm not stealing. It's called sampling. I've got an idea though. How about you mind your own business you uppity, self-righteous curmudgeon?"

Both women gasped and Mrs. Needermyer turned her cart around with a huff, heading to the front of the store as fast as she could move.

When Rylie hit him on the arm, he glared at her. "What was that for?"

"You cannot talk to people like that!"

"Yes, I can. She deserved it, sticking her nose—"

"It doesn't matter what she was doing. I was handling it; insulting her was uncalled for. Didn't your mom teach you to be respectful of your elders?"

Dustin's temper snapped like a rubber band. He didn't need her sanctimonious lecture.

"It doesn't matter how old she is, she was out of line. If you want to let everyone walk all over you and run your life, then go right ahead."

He picked up his prop kit and took a vicious bite of his apple. "I'm not so desperate for people to like me that I'll take their shit."

He hated the hurt in her eyes, and the slight tremble in her lip, but this was who he was. He wasn't going to change for anyone.

"Enjoy the rest of your night."

Chapter 8

It was Saturday, and Rylie was fuming. Dustin hadn't been into work the rest of the week. He'd told Kelly that he had a virus and was sick in bed. But Rylie knew better. He wasn't sick; he was pouting. If he was sick, then she wouldn't have seen Paula Kramer sneaking out of his house this morning with her heels in her hand and her hair looking like she'd spent all night with Dustin Kent's hands in it.

This had nothing to do with the fact that he'd been avoiding her since his blow up at the grocery store, or that his bedroom was a revolving door. They had stuff to get done. He was her partner, for better or worse.

So his butt was going to work even if she had to drag him out of the house and lock him in the trunk of her car.

She marched up the steps to the house and knocked on the door. Victoria opened it several moments later, a wide smile on her face.

"Ah, Rylie, are you hungry? I can make you whatever you like."

"Thank you, Victoria, I'm okay. I was actually wondering if Dustin was up yet."

Victoria appeared slightly uncomfortable as she said, "Mr. Kent is still in bed, I'm afraid. He has been under the weather."

I bet.

"Do you mind if I just go up and have a chat with him? It's about work."

Victoria's eyes twinkled. "Are you sure you don't want me to warn him?"

"Oh, no, I think the element of surprise is best. Where is his room?"

"Top of the stairs, second door on the left." Victoria picked up her purse and car keys. "Just give me a two-minute head start. That way, he can't fire me for not trying to stop you." She pulled an innocent look and said, "'I had no idea she was going up to your room, sir. I'd already left to run your errands.'"

Rylie laughed softly. "Good call."

Victoria saluted her, and Rylie waited until she heard the front door shut before she started for the stairs. Artistic photographs and paintings adorned the white walls instead of family photos, and the second floor felt sterile and cold. She opened his bedroom door and stopped dead in her tracks.

He was naked. Buck naked, on his stomach with the sheet tangled just below his round, gorgeous ass.

Rylie hadn't expected to find him so exposed. She almost turned tail and ran, but something caught her attention. His bare back was exposed and as the sun streaked through the gap in his black-out curtains, she saw the white crisscross scars on his skin. Her heart squeezed as she counted dozens of them.

She took an involuntary step closer and before she knew it, she was standing next to the bed, looking down at the right side of his face. The muscles were relaxed, his lashes thick, and his mouth open slightly as his breathing came out hoarse and deep.

God, he really was such a beautiful man and he had obviously suffered. No wonder he had a hard time making connections with people and could be such a giant pain in the—

"Watching someone sleep is fucking creepy, you know that, right?"

His deep voice startled her so much that she lost her balance and started backpedaling. Her heel hit a knot in the wood floor and it snapped off with a *crack*, sealing her fate. She toppled backward and crashed into a table in the corner before she reached the floor. The skirt of her dress had flown up, as the cool draft on her bottom proved, and she wanted to sink into the floor.

Well, I did see his rear end. Only fair he sees mine.

"Jesus, Rylie, are you all right?"

She could hear the laughter in his voice as his feet padded across the room, but she refused to look up. She had already seen enough of him.

"Yes," she groaned. Her hip was throbbing as was her arm. When Dustin squatted down next to her and took her chin in his hand, she tried to fight back the tears as he raised her gaze to his.

"No, you aren't."

She squeaked as he slipped his arms around her shoulders and behind her knees and lifted her straight up from the floor.

"Stop, you're going to hurt yourself!"

"Shut up," he said gruffly.

He carried her over to the bed and sat down with her on his lap. She tried to wiggle off, very much aware that he was naked, but he tightened his arms.

"Chill. I'm just checking to make sure you're okay."

"I'm fine, really, I just—"

His fingers slipping off her broken shoe stalled her words. She gulped as he took her ankle gently and turned it in a circle.

"Does this hurt?"

She shook her head, unable to meet his gaze, she was too embarrassed. She stared at his mouth, instead.

Big mistake.

"My heel just caught something. I'm not hurt. Although I think I destroyed the table."

"I don't care about the table." His hand rested on her calf and she blushed as she felt something hard poking her butt.

"I was… I was just coming to tell you that I need you to come back to work."

"Didn't Kelly tell you? I've been sick." To emphasize his lie, he fake coughed.

Her gaze finally snapped up to his, and she scowled at the mischievous gleam in his eye. "You are not. You're just avoiding me and it's stupid." With a heavy sigh, she took the leap first, and said, "I am sorry for lecturing you on how you spoke to Mrs. Needermyer. I understand how frustrating she can be. You are a grown man and I shouldn't have overstepped."

He tilted his head, as if considering her. "Hmm, and for hitting me?"

"I am sorry for that too. It was immature. I will try to fight the urge."

"Then apology accepted."

Rylie waited, and when he didn't reciprocate, she poked him in the shoulder.

"Hey, I thought you were going to stop assaulting me!" he said.

"It was just a poke. And it's your turn."

He scowled. "For what?"

"For calling me a doormat and stomping out of the grocery store like a big baby."

"I didn't—"

"You did! You were a complete asshat. Not at all acceptable."

Dustin's lips twitched. "Your apology for lecturing me is slowly losing credibility."

"Well, it was embarrassing, and to be honest, it hurt my feelings. I thought we were having fun."

She hated how vulnerable she sounded, but it was true. She'd been feeling so stressed after Asher had shown up, and Dustin's goofy antics had eased it. She'd started to remember why she'd initially seen something in him when he'd first began working at Something Borrowed.

But his reaction to Mrs. Needermyer and Rylie's chastening had just confused her again. She'd been taught not to talk that way to her elders. That didn't make her a doormat.

His thumb grazed her chin and her gaze met his.

"I *was* having fun, but I'm still an asshole. Nothing's going to change that. I don't pretend to be someone different. You can't change or save me."

Rylie swallowed hard at the intensity in his blue eyes. "I'm not trying to save you, but I don't believe that's *all* you are."

At her soft admission, his nostrils flared, and he stared at her lips. "You should go."

"But you need to come to work—"

"Right now you are sitting on my lap, you feel really good, and your mouth is too close."

She blinked at him. "Are you saying you want to kiss me?"

His blue eyes turned nearly black and her thighs clenched in reaction to that look. *Lust. Dustin wants me.*

"Yes. Yes, I want to kiss you. Everywhere."

Rylie's heart slammed against her breastbone and she found herself tempted. Oh so very tempted.

Then she remembered the girl sneaking from his house this morning and she pushed herself off him, putting distance between her traitorous body and his.

"You are a pig. You really can't keep it in your pants for more than a few hours?"

He leaned back on his hands with a grin, but she refused to look down. "It seems to have escaped your notice, but I'm not wearing pants."

"Oh!" She picked up her broken shoe and limped out of his room.

The unbelievable nerve of him. Propositioning and teasing her. And she'd started to think he might be a decent guy.

"See you at work, sweetheart," he called after her.

Rylie grit her teeth, resisting the urge to turn around and throw her broken heel at his head. She was going to have to call the realtor and find something else to rent. There was no way she could stay here anymore and not kill him.

*   *   *   *

A half an hour later, Dustin stood in his shower, letting the hot water rain down on him as he stared at the tile floor, emotions churning in his gut.

God, he was a dick.

He really hadn't meant to be, but when he'd first come awake to find her hovering over him, he'd been on alert. He knew she could probably see everything.

His ass. His back. The scars.

Dustin's hand came up to finger one of the raised lines on his shoulder. They weren't his scars; he wasn't claiming them. They belonged to his dad.

He'd never told his mom or his brothers about them. He'd wondered if his brothers shared similar marks across their skin from the buckle of their dad's belt, but he didn't ask. Like the nights his mom had screamed and cried from his parent's bedroom, it wasn't something they talked about.

He'd refused to break for the old bastard though. There had been a couple times that he'd prayed his dad would just kill him. That was something his dad couldn't make them cover up or hide and at least his mom would be safe.

Women didn't ask him about the scars and if they did, they were not so politely asked to leave.

The one therapist he'd gone to had asked him why he didn't blame his mom for the abuse, and he didn't have an answer. His dad had never hit him when she was home. He often wondered if she knew, or if his dad had done it this way to hide it from her, knowing that Dustin wouldn't say anything. It had started at twelve, and he'd been too old to go crying to her, especially when he knew she got it worse.

But when he was fifteen, he'd had enough. He'd shot up six inches and put on about fifty pounds of muscle over the summer. One afternoon, his dad had come after him for mouthing off, and he'd been ready.

Only he'd almost put the old bastard in the hospital he'd beat him so bad. Dustin had told him the next time he touched him or his mom, he wouldn't get back up off the floor.

His father hadn't had him arrested, maybe because he'd known that his dirty secrets might come to light. His father had taken off to their beach house in Mexico and when he'd come back several weeks later, Dustin had moved into the guest house. He'd spent the last three years he lived there barely speaking to his father.

If he had continued to hurt Dustin's mom, Dustin had never seen it, so she'd either hidden it well or his dad had taken his threat to heart. Dustin didn't talk about what happened with anyone, so when Rylie had stood over him, watching him sleep and seeing his scars, he'd been struck down with a vulnerability he'd never known. And he'd hated it. He'd felt powerless and he'd wanted his power back.

And the only way he knew how to do that was with anger, sarcasm, and sex.

But Rylie had run. He'd seen the flare of interest; she couldn't deny that she wanted him, but she was just so damn *good*. Way too good for him.

He hardly remembered fucking Paula last night. She'd just been available and he'd wanted someone. Anyone.

Rylie wouldn't be a convenient lay, but that didn't stop him from wanting to push her skirt aside earlier and slide up into her. He could still feel the curve of her ass in his lap, the warmth of her skin coming through the fabric of her skirt.

Dustin reached down and gripped his aching cock in his hand. Her lips, so pink and lush, just a few inches from his. He'd almost done it too, but something had held him back.

Respect. He respected Rylie, even liked her. He wouldn't touch her. Wouldn't use her.

Think about her when he was jacking off? He could do that.

He pumped his dick several times, imagining what she looked like under the hot pink dress she'd been wearing. Was she the type of girl who wore matching bra and panties? He imagined she was.

When he finally found release, he took several deep breaths, knowing deep down that this would never be as good as the real thing.

Too bad, asshole.

This is as close as he'd ever get.

Chapter 9

Later that night, Rylie got wasted, which she never did, especially at a client's wedding. She was the epitome of responsible, but after this morning with Dustin and the flowers she'd found on her car today after lunch, she'd needed a drink.

Or five or seven. She'd lost count after a while.

She didn't know what to do about Asher. He'd left flowers and a note that read *I need you* on her windshield. He hadn't signed it, but she recognized his handwriting. She'd told Dustin she didn't need a restraining order, that they didn't work, which was true, but Asher wasn't taking the hint and she didn't know how to make it any clearer that it was over. She was emotionally drained and stressed.

And then there was Dustin. He'd come into work after their interlude and acted as though nothing had happened. She had no idea how he could do that, but it was maddening.

Thus the liquor to chase her troubles away.

They'd already seen late night talk show host Anderson Grady and his barely legal bride, actress Gwendolyn Thomas, into their limo and most of the guests were trickling out. There had been a guy in the corner giving her the eye most of the night, but when she hadn't given him any signal, he'd moved on to one of the other bridesmaids.

Which was perfectly fine, because she was over men. As far as she was concerned, the entire male species could go suck a dick!

Rylie made her way to the parking lot, and climbed into her car, but she knew she couldn't drive. Hell, she could hardly walk.

After retrieving her phone from the middle console, she dialed Marley. When it went straight to voicemail, Rylie ended the call, then squinted at her phone screen. She scrolled through her contacts, trying to make out the blurry names.

She stopped on Dustin's, and she hesitated. The last thing she wanted to do was ask for his help, but she didn't really want to sleep it off in her car and have someone see her looking like a hot mess. And there was no way in hell she was calling Kelly or Asher.

With a sigh, she hit the green phone icon and waited for him to answer. It rang several times and by the fourth, she almost hung up.

"Hello?" he said.

She opened her mouth to say hi, but that wasn't what tumbled out. "I just want you to know that you behaved abomibly...adomably... You were a meanie pants and if I wasn't out of options, I wouldn't be calling."

Several beats of silence before he spoke. "Rylie? Are you drunk?"

"Stupid question. Course I am drunk. Thus, the call." She knew she was slurring but couldn't seem to fix it. "So, will you or not?"

"Will I what? You haven't asked me anything, just insulted me."

She huffed in frustration. "I need a ride. Can't drive."

The line went silent and she called loudly, "Hello? Did you hear me?"

"Ask me nicely," he said.

Rylie snorted. "Butt Ass."

His deep laughter echoed through the phone. "Did you just call me butt ass?"

"Maybe." He continued chuckling, and she said, "I like your laugh. Have I told you that?"

"Okay, I am definitely coming to get you; you're being nice to me now. Where are you?"

She looked around, trying to piece her location together through her fuzzy brain. "In the parking lot of a church."

"Which church?"

"Too many questions. You're hurting my head."

She heard tapping, as if he was texting, and the phone went quiet for several moments. Or longer. She might have dozed off before his loud voice woke her.

"What?" she moaned.

"I said I know where you are and I'm on my way. Just stay on the phone with me."

"I'm not having phone sex with you if that is what you are asking."

A bark of laughter exploded from the phone. "Who knew that sweet little Rylie Templeton got pervy when she's had a few."

"Corression," she slurred. "I was telling *you* not to be a perv."

"My bad. So, why did you get shit-faced anyway?"

"I needed one after the week I had."

"Sounds like you had more than one."

"You would be correct, monsieur." She giggled and leaned her head back against the head rest when the world spun. "I always wanted to go to France. Learn to bake from a real French pastry chef."

"Sober up, and I'll take you."

"Pshah, whatever." She closed her eyes. "I always imagine France with a pink sky and fluffy white clouds above my head. And everyone sings like in the opening of *Beauty and the Beast*."

"Yeah, no, it's not like that at all."

"You've been?"

"Yeah, I've been."

"Bastard."

"Wow, you also get hostile when you've had a few."

It was suddenly so hot. She leaned her head against the cool glass of her car window, sighing in relief. "I'm just jealous. I've never been anywhere. I'm so boring."

"I wouldn't say that. I find you pretty interesting."

She scrunched up her face, keeping her eyes closed. "Ha. Dirty man."

"How was that dirty?"

"I don't know, but it was. I can feel it in my bum."

"I think you mean gut, sweetheart."

Psychedelic lights were swirling behind her eyelids. "Mmmm hmmm."

"You falling asleep on me?" he asked.

"Dah," she mumbled.

"I'm two minutes out. Lock your doors."

She didn't know how long she was asleep, but when her door was yanked open, she screamed as she tumbled out. Dustin caught her with one arm before she hit the ground.

She glared up at both of his faces. "Dude, haven't you ever heard of knocking?"

"I did, but you were passed out. I told you to lock the door," he said.

"I forgot."

"Okay, drunk girl. How about we get you some coffee and you can go home to sleep it off?"

Rylie's stomach twisted painfully and bile rose in her throat. "Uh oh."

"What uh oh?"

She pulled away from him in time to fall to her knees and vomit the contents of her stomach. The tea length skirt of her peach colored bridesmaids' dress saved her knees from the sharp rocks of the gravel parking lot. Not her palms, though, which throbbed as the hard points dug into her skin.

Rylie felt warm hands rubbing her neck and back as she heaved. When the sick feeling finally passed, she rolled to sit on her butt against her car, not even a little sad that the dress would most likely be streaked with dirt and oil.

"Feel better?" he asked as he squatted down in front of her.

"Tired."

"Well, come on. I think I have some wet wipes and mints in my car."

"Middle console," she murmured, her eyes closing.

She heard the car door open and a few moments later, Dustin was wiping a wet towelette across her mouth and chin.

She sputtered and held her hands up weakly. "I can do it."

"It's already done. Here, chew on this."

She looked down at the white piece of gum in his hand and took it before slipping it past her lips. The sour taste in her mouth disappeared, and she almost sighed aloud as she perked up a bit.

He took her hands and helped her to her feet. She was still a little unsteady, but with his assistance, managed to sink into the seat of his car with a modicum of grace.

He slid behind the wheel and shut the door. "You want that coffee now?"

When she turned her head to look at him, the dome light gave him an almost halo effect.

"You're an angel."

He laughed again and she smiled. *I really do like his laugh.*

"Maybe I'll keep you drunk. You're a bit like a Sour Patch Kid. First you're sour, then you're sweet when you've got the beer goggles on."

"Mmm, rum and coke glasses, actually. Open bar."

"No wonder you're sick."

She couldn't process what he meant so she just shrugged. "I'm sick cause I don't really drink and I seeded my limits."

"I think you meant *exceeded*, but I think it's cute when you mispronounce things."

She glared at him with one eye open. "A nice man would not make fun of me in my current condition."

"Sweetheart, I think we both know I'm not that nice."

She opened both of her eyes again to look at his profile. "You came and got me. That makes you kind of nice."

"Well, thank you. You're going to turn my head with compliments like that."

"As long as it isn't while you're driving, that's okay," she mumbled.

His pleasant chuckle was the last thing she heard before she passed out again.

* * * *

Dustin parked the car in front of Love on the Corner gas station and leaned forward so he could see Rylie's face. She was dead asleep and there was even a trail of drool running from the corner of her mouth to her chin.

It's really weird that I find that adorable, and not grotesque.

Dustin locked the car doors and went inside the gas station. He waved at Maggie Welton, who had been hired after Marsha Hornsby had quit the month before to run off with a truck driver. He only knew that because nobody could keep a secret in this town.

He filled two large cups with a combo of white mocha and caramel lattes. It tasted good to him, and he added a couple packages of doughnuts to the purchase.

Maggie was working the cash register, and she flashed him a wide smile. She was a couple of years older than him, and was a tiny little thing. She had married her high school boyfriend, and had two children she loved to talk about. Every time he saw her, she was showing someone pictures of them on her phone.

"Hey, Dustin! Big plans tonight?"

"Just heading home, Maggie. How is Mike and the kids?"

She beamed at him. "They're great. Makayla is in kindergarten and I cannot wait until they are both in school full-time so I can get normal daytime hours. Working nights is killing me."

"I bet."

She rang up his items and he swiped his card.

"Hey, I heard that Rylie Templeton is living with you," she said in a hushed tone.

Dustin paused as he was putting in his pin. "Where did you hear that?"

"Oh, you know this town. People talk. They say that she dumped Asher for you."

Dustin hit the green button on the power pad and clicked his tongue. "You shouldn't believe everything people say. Rylie's just renting my pool house. We are coworkers. That's it."

"Hmm. That's too bad. Rylie is a nice girl. She'd be good for you." Maggie lowered her voice again and asked, "Do you know why her and Asher did break up?"

Cause he's an abusive dick head.

"No idea. It's none of my business, but I'll tell her you asked after her when I see her. You have a good night now."

"You too."

Dustin walked out the dinging door and went around to the passenger side. If Maggie looked out and saw Rylie in his car, he didn't give a shit. Sweetheart's citizens gave the term "nosy neighbor" a whole new meaning. He tapped on the window and Rylie jerked awake. "I come bearing gifts. Want to unlock it?"

She opened it, reaching up to take his purchases. She seemed more alert thanks to her little nap. Which was good considering a couple times she'd groaned and he'd been afraid she was going to hurl again. The last thing he needed was puke to permeate the carpet of his car.

She looked into the bag and grinned sloppily. "Doughnuts?"

Dustin shrugged a little sheepishly. "It sounded good."

"Oh yeah."

He headed around the front of the car to the driver side. He took a drink of his coffee as he walked, wincing as he burned his tongue. He forgot how hot the powdered coffee and water combos were; it had been so long since he'd had one. Probably high school.

He preferred his Colombian dark roast.

Once he was behind the wheel, he turned to Rylie. "Home then?"

She shrugged. "I'm not really tired anymore."

"Wanna head up to Buzzard Gulch and take a walk?"

He had no idea why he'd suggested the old mining town. It was dark and secluded. Creepy. Maybe because it was just another connection between them. They were renter and rentee, coworkers, business partners.

The only relationships they hadn't formed were friendship and lovers.

"Sure. I could use the fresh air," she said.

Dustin put the car in gear and they headed out of town, up the hill that led to the ghost town the Kents had owned until recently when Marley, Kelly, and Rylie had convinced him, *forcefully*, to split the deed and work on restoring it for a wedding venue. They hadn't started the renovations. They were still in the planning stage, but Dustin was excited about it.

"Why did you decide to work at Something Borrowed?" Rylie asked.

Dustin shrugged. "Just looking for something to do."

"But you don't have to. If I didn't have to work, I wouldn't. I'd just bake and read all day."

"Believe me, it gets boring having no purpose. That's why you see rich people on that TV show, *Shark Tank*, getting involved in other people's businesses and such."

"But why a professional groomsman? Why not something tech-y? That's what you studied, right?"

Dustin hesitated, knowing he couldn't tell her the entire reason. There was no way straight as an arrow Rylie would appreciate him admitting to writing a tell-all about Something Borrowed. "The money's good and I look smokin' hot in a tux."

"Oh, geez, we need to find a witch to shrink that big head of yours."

Dustin parked in front of one of the partially burnt buildings, and flipped on the dome light before he reached across to grab his package of doughnuts. "If you were being honest, you'd admit it."

"That you look smokin' hot in a tux? You're all right."

"You mean *all right all right all right*?"

"Ugh, no! That is a terrible McConaughey impression."

"I thought I delivered it." He opened the package of doughnuts and took a big bite of one. He could feel the powdered sugar sprinkle over his chin.

"You're going to get that all over your car," Rylie said.

"I'll have it detailed tomorrow." He took another bite and groaned. "God, it has been a long time since I have had a doughnut. I forget how good they are."

"I make better ones."

He quirked his eyebrow at her in the dome light. "Really?"

"Yep. Different flavors too. I make this lemon one dipped in a sugar glaze that is so good. I don't make them often because one time I ate all of them and Asher…"

She trailed off and he had a feeling her ex had been a dick about it.

"I used to stress eat as a kid," Dustin said.

Rylie laughed. "Bullshit."

"No, it's true. In elementary and the start of middle school. One time, I got this D on a test and I was so stressed about telling my dad, that I ate an entire cake I found in the refrigerator that they had bought for a party they were going to. Turns out, he was so pissed about the cake, that the D didn't even faze him."

Rylie grabbed a doughnut from the box he held. "How did you get past it? Overeating, I mean."

"I shot up six inches the summer after eighth grade. Started running and swimming. Exercise and getting stronger became my substitute. Turns out, it's easy to replace one addiction with another."

"Ha, not for me. I am allergic to running. I do like swimming though. I love dancing, too, and Marley got me into yoga. I like to try different programs, I just wish I was more consistent about it."

"Well, you could always go with me in the morning. I usually run five K starting at six."

"Eff that! I'd go one mile and collapse!" she said.

His eyes scanned her smiling face, the oval shape and wide brown eyes. His gaze dipped a bit to her breast peeking over the top of her peach colored bridesmaid gown and he couldn't stop the noise of appreciation from rumbling from his lips.

"Whatever you're doing, I think you look good."

Her cheeks flamed. "Thank you."

The car grew hotter than the coffee, and Dustin opened his door. "Bring your coffee and doughnut and let's walk."

The night had cooled, signaling that fall would be there soon. Dustin popped the last bite of his doughnut into his mouth and looked around the run-down buildings. The old mining town included a saloon, a general store, a hotel, a bank, and several other buildings that had lost their identity years before. The saloon had been nearly destroyed in a fire just a month ago, and the rest of the buildings needed a lot of work. New roofs, floors, windows. But their renovation goals were to keep the town as close to its original state as possible with a few modern conveniences.

The moon was three quarters full, and bright enough to light their way as they walked down the dirt road between the two rows of structures.

"I am so glad my bride let us wear flats tonight," Rylie said next to him. Her enunciation had improved, and he figured she was slowly sobering up.

"Why did she?"

"Because she was only four foot eleven inches and even with heels on, the rest of her bridesmaids towered over her."

"Yikes, that is a short woman. I'd break my neck trying to kiss her."

Rylie laughed. "Oh please."

"What?"

"Don't act like you don't like short girls. Guys love that shit. It makes them feel big and powerful."

He shot her what he hoped was a wolfish grin and waggled his brows. "I like women of all shapes, sizes, and heights. I don't discriminate."

"I've noticed," she grumbled.

"Are you jealous?" he asked, turning to walk backward so he could see her face in the moonlight.

She scoffed forcefully. "No. I just think you could show a little discretion about who you give yourself to, is all."

"It's just my body. It's not like I fall in love with every girl I sleep with." Rylie threw up her hands. "That makes it worse. You should feel something if you're being that intimate with someone."

He would never understand some women's hang-ups about sex. "Intimacy is living with someone and sharing a life with them. I don't do that."

"Why not?" she asked.

"Just not interested. I like my space and my freedom. I like not having to answer to anyone else."

She stepped up onto the boardwalk and hopped along the creaking wood planks. "Not all relationships are demanding or hard."

"Oh yeah? How many have you had that weren't like that?"

Her silence was his answer.

"See? Why put yourself in a position where someone else is making you miserable?"

Rylie stopped on the stoop of one of the unnamed buildings and swung around one of the porch beams, leaning toward him. "Real love isn't like that. You have hard times and you have to work at it, but you're happiest being around that person."

He reached out to put his hands on her waist, afraid the beam was going to collapse and take the whole building down. "All I heard was hard and work."

She let him lift her down back onto the dirt street. "So, what, you're just going to be a bachelor forever? Sleeping with every woman you meet, whether she's available or not?"

Something about her tone rankled him and he released her to cross his arms over his chest. "You got something to say?"

"You sleep with engaged women."

"I do?"

"Sonora Star. I know you hooked up with her. Marley told me."

Ah, is that why her attitude toward him had changed? "And?"

"And? It's wrong."

Why was it those two little words made him feel lower than a snake? His defenses shot up, and he tried to act cool. "They're the ones cheating. Maybe if their fiancé was keeping them satisfied, they wouldn't come to me."

He couldn't tell if her face was red, but her eyes were flashing in the moonlight. "That is a cop out! If they are that miserable, then they should break up or get a divorce. Not destroy someone who they once imagined building a life with."

"Maybe they aren't ready to leave. Or they aren't sure what they want."

Why am I even arguing with her? I'm just riling her up.

Which was true, and it turned out her voice rose another octave the more riled she became. "It's one thing to have fantasies but to actually cheat with another person is wrong, and if their partner in crime knows that they are attached, then they are just as bad, in my opinion."

It seemed on this subject, Rylie wasn't afraid to call it how she saw it. He'd have been almost impressed if her ire and disgust weren't directed at him.

"Wow, how does it feel, Rylie?"

Her head cocked to the side. "How does what feel?"

"How does it feel to be morally perfect?"

Now her hands were getting into it, flailing about as she said, "I don't think I'm perfect! This is just something I feel strongly about."

"Yeah, I got that. But it's not exactly your business what I do, is it?"

She didn't respond right away, then sighed. "You're right. I'm sorry. It isn't any of my business who you hook up with."

Dustin frowned. He didn't like the hopeless tone in her voice when she said it, as if he was beyond redemption.

What happened to not caring what people thought?

The funny thing was, he kind of did care...about Rylie. About how Rylie saw and thought of him.

Not because he wanted her, but because he liked her and valued her opinion.

He had no idea when that had happened, but he found himself saying, "If it makes you feel better, after Sonora, I've taken a vow to stay away from attached women."

The flash of a smile was so full of joy, it was almost too bright to look at her face. "It does."

"Good."

Chapter 10

Dustin parked his car on the back side of Castle Vineyards and climbed out. Before his dad had died, he'd had no desire to ever return to this place.

He didn't mind it anymore though, especially since his mother had removed anything and everything that reminded her of his father.

He couldn't really blame her. There wasn't a single thing about the man he could remember ever finding redeemable. He was able to fool everyone in the town of Sweetheart about what a great guy he was, but his children and wife knew he was a monster.

Dustin took the steps up to the main house and walked inside. "Mom?"

"In the dining room!"

"The formal or the family?" he called.

"The family, of course."

He chuckled. "Of course."

People who thought the house he owned now was huge had never been inside his childhood home. Eight bedrooms, two dining areas, and three living rooms plus a game room, not to mention the six bathrooms made it almost double the size of his three thousand square foot home.

He made his way down the hallway toward the family dining room, ignoring the pictures of him and his brothers in their youth. As he stepped into the room, he found his mother sitting at the head of the table, drinking coffee and reading the *Sweetheart Gazette*. Her blond hair was swept back into a classic up-do, and she wore a pink dress with a white sweater.

"Hello, Mom. How are the ins and outs of Sweetheart?"

"Well, let's see. Peter Lynch was pulled over for another DUI last night. Oh, and Sissy and Daniel Stewart are expecting their first child." She snapped the paper closed and leveled him with a heavy stare. "And apparently, you have a live-in girlfriend."

"It's not like that. Rylie needed a place to stay, so I am renting her my pool house. It's strictly business."

"Is it?" His mother said those two words so coyly that he stiffened. "Because from what I understand, the two of you were seen late last night at the gas station on what looked suspiciously like a date."

"First of all, as my mother, you should really know by now that I don't date. Secondly, I was just her designated driver. We stopped off to get coffee and I drove her back to the pool house where I left her untouched." Dustin poured himself a cup of coffee. "Now, are you satisfied that you got the whole story?"

His mother shot him a disgruntled glare. "I swear, I don't know what is wrong with you and your brothers. I am not going to live forever and I would love to have at least one daughter-in-law and a few adorable grandbabies to spoil. Is that too much to ask?"

"Well, Mom, if we're being honest, I think that most of us realize we'll be really shitty husbands considering the example we had."

She dropped her cup onto the saucer, and some of the black coffee spilled over the side.

"That's not funny, Dustin."

He paused while scooping a slice of quiche onto his plate. "I was being serious."

She appeared genuinely surprised. "Why would you think you were anything like your father? Not one of you would ever..." She cleared her throat and when she spoke again, it came out hoarse. "You are all good men and I expect any woman would be lucky to have you."

Dustin shifted in his chair, uncomfortable with her praise. He didn't really think that marriage would turn him into an abusive prick.

It was the settling down in general that scared the wits out of him.

"I don't think any of us have met a woman that makes us want to settle down."

"From what I know of her, your Rylie Templeton is a nice girl."

"She isn't mine."

"Just the same, maybe you ought to take a second look at her. Finding a pretty girl is one thing, but a woman who is good and kind is another."

Dustin gave his mother a sour look. "Have you seen Rylie, Mom? She is gorgeous."

"Then you've got the whole package within your grasp."

Dustin sighed. "Is this why you invited me to brunch? To play matchmaker?"

"No, actually. I want to get rid of your father's boxes, but I don't want to donate them locally. I was hoping that maybe you could drive them into Sacramento or something and drop them at the Goodwill?"

Dustin lost his appetite. Not because he didn't want her to get rid of his dad's things; hell, he'd burn them if she'd let him. It was that they couldn't seem to have one conversation where the old bastard didn't make an appearance.

"You know they will come pick the stuff up for you, right?"

"I know, I just wasn't sure if you wanted to look through it first. The other boys have, but you've never checked to see if there is something you might want."

Dustin set his fork down with a clink. "Let me be very clear. There is nothing I want from that man. I don't need to look through boxes of shit that are just going to stir up a bunch of memories I'd rather forget. All right?"

"Of course, Dusty, I didn't mean—"

"It's Dustin. Has been for a long time."

The rest of their brunch was eaten in silence and he took several calming breaths. He shouldn't have snapped at her, but asking him if he wanted anything from that son of a bitch…

Then she'd called him Dusty. He hadn't been Dusty since before his eleventh birthday. Not since the boy he'd been had been beaten and tortured out of him.

You need to be a man. Stop hiding behind your mama's skirts, you little candy ass wimp.

Dustin wiped at his mouth and stood. "The quiche was great Mom, but I've got some stuff to do today."

He could tell she was hurt, but he couldn't stay there another minute. He needed something to distract himself and banish the ghost of his father from his mind.

He came around the table and kissed her cheek. "I'll come see you again soon."

* * * *

Rylie had gone to the same church her father had been taking her to since she was a little girl, and as she left, she cruelly thought it was about time that Pastor Dan retired. He was just so…boring. She'd almost fallen asleep twice during his sermon about the dangers of online dating.

Of course, her exhaustion had nothing to do with drinking too much or the late-night walk with Dustin Kent.

As she parked in front of the Sweetheart Cemetery, she tried not to dwell on his promise to stay away from attached women. There were plenty of single women in town for him to hook up with, and there was absolutely no innuendo that she was even in the top ten of his hook-up list.

Not that she wanted that anyway. She was happy without a man mucking up her life.

She got out of her car and walked across the green grass between the tombstones. When she finally reached her father's plot, she sat down, holding a fresh bouquet in her lap.

"Hey, Dad," she said softly. "I know you've been watching everything that's been happening, and I'm sure you're upset, but I'm okay. Really."

There wasn't a sound or a breeze that gave her some sign her dad was listening, but she knew he was there. He was always with her.

"I'm staying in Dustin Kent's pool house and I know what you're thinking, but he's really not a bad guy. I think he's just been through a lot and learned that the only way to survive bad stuff is to be a total jerk and keep people at arm's length. He didn't have to help me, but he did. And that's why I am going to give him a real chance to be my friend. No preconceived notions."

She picked up the dead flowers from last week and replaced them before standing. "Same time next week? I love you. Miss you, Daddy."

Just before she turned, she noticed the headstone next to his was starting to get overgrown and she grit her teeth. Bending over, she pulled out the obstructing plants and put them in the plastic bag she'd brought for garbage. When the words on the gravestone were uncovered, they read, *Here lies Willow Anne Templeton. Beloved Wife and Mother.*

Rylie turned her back on the lies and headed back to her car. She wasn't going to let this one thing ruin her day.

An hour and five minutes later, she knocked on the back door of Sierra Animal Rescue, and waited for one of the kennel technicians to answer. Sundays were her favorite day of the week. She got up early, went to church, and then stopped by the cemetery to say hi to her dad. She changed out the flowers by his headstone, and traded in her church clothes for a pair of jeans and a T-shirt. After visiting her dad's grave, she always needed a pick me up, which is why she went to the rescue. Spending a few hours with adorable dogs and cats always brightened her spirit.

The door was pushed open and Tayler Gibson smiled at her. "Hey, Rylie! The dogs were just asking where their special treats were."

Rylie laughed and handed the basket of freshly made dog biscuits over to the other woman. "I would never disappoint the fuzzbutts."

They moved inside and walked down the hallway until they reached the end of the kennel area. A white tub with clear liquid sat at the edge of the concrete with a blue bleached-stained towel on the other side.

"What's with the tub?" Rylie asked.

"We had a puppy come in with parvo today, so we're just being cautious."

"Oh, no! Poor baby. Is he going to be okay?"

Tayler's lips flattened. In her late thirties, Taylor's hair was in a crew cut, and her blue eyes were filled with shadows. Rylie didn't know how she was still running the rescue; after some of the things Rylie had seen as a volunteer, it tore her up inside.

"Mya took him to the vet, but he was pretty emaciated, so we're not sure if he's going to make it yet." Rylie's eyes filled with tears, and Tayler squeezed her shoulder. "I don't want to make you sad; I know this is your happy time."

Rylie sniffled, wiping at her watery eyes. "Thanks. Is Raider still here?"

At the mention of Rylie's favorite dog, Tayler snorted. "Yes, and he'll probably be here until you decide to take him home. I swear, that dog only tolerates the rest of us. When people try to visit with him, he just ignores them."

Rylie didn't want to be thrilled by this news, but she secretly was. Raider was special, and she'd wanted him from the first time she'd seen him. "I'm still looking for a place that allows pets. There aren't a lot of rentals in Sweetheart."

Tayler frowned. "You're looking for a new place? What about Asher?"

"Oh, we broke up. I am staying in a friend's pool house until I find something permanent."

Tayler's face brightened. "Well, good for you. I didn't want to say anything, but I never liked that guy. You can tell there is something really wrong with a person who doesn't like animals."

"Thanks, Tayler. If you hear of any rentals, can you let me know?"

Tayler nodded. "I'll keep my ear to the ground if I hear of any place that takes pets. Does it have to be in Sweetheart?"

"Well, not too far outside. I don't want a long commute."

"Understood. You go have fun and I'll take these to the other residents."

Rylie smiled and slid the homemade peanut butter treat she'd made especially for Raider from her back pocket. She stopped just outside his cage and said, "Hey, buddy, did you miss me?"

At the sound of her voice, the muscular pit bull bounded to his feet and let out a series of booming barks. His long thin tail wagged straight in the air and his gray body wiggled with joy.

Rylie's heart warmed as he ran for the door of the cage. The burns on the left side of his face and ear had healed months ago, but the hair would never grow back there. She grabbed his leash off the gate and after unlocking the heavy metal door, stepped inside. She kneeled and was immediately drowned in doggy kisses. Laughing, she wrapped her arms around Raider and kissed him on the side of his head.

"I missed you too, bud."

Rylie had fallen in love with the dog the first time she'd seen him. He'd been locked in a cage in the infirmary, growling at anyone who came near. He'd been brought in by a Good Samaritan who had seen a bunch of boys light the poor dog on fire. The man had put out the flames and rushed him to the rescue. They'd been keeping him on antibiotics and pain meds while he healed, but he didn't trust anyone and they had to sedate him in order to treat him.

But Rylie had seen past his aggression, recognizing the fear in his eyes. He'd had his trust completely broken and needed to learn that not all humans were evil.

So, she'd come in every morning before work after Asher had left, sat outside his cage, and talked to him. Sometimes she even read him stories. Several weeks passed and when she showed up, Raider's tail would wag. He started taking biscuits from her and soon, the staff was following her lead. He stopped growling and the first time Rylie took him into the yard, she learned that he loved to chase a ball.

She'd begged Asher to let her adopt him, but he hadn't wanted a dog. She'd started slowing down her visits after that, knowing she couldn't have Raider hurt. Yet people kept passing him over because he was aloof with everyone but her.

Rylie sat down and let Raider climb across her lap and roll over for belly scratches. "You are such a big goofball."

His upside-down smile never failed to delight and cheer her, and she leaned over to kiss his nose.

"Do you want to hear about my week before we go play ball? I gotta warn you, it's a bit of a doozy."

Raider woofed softly in response and Rylie took that as a yes.

Chapter 11

On Monday morning, Rylie was organizing her folder for the Rolland/Marconi wedding when Wendy Harrington knocked on her doorframe. Wendy had been hired as Kelly's assistant this summer, and seemed to be working out. Something Borrowed had a high turnover. Kelly usually hired women home for the summer from college, women who were just looking for something temporary until they found something in their field of study. Rylie knew that Wendy had a degree in business and was saving up money to go back to school for her masters.

"Hey, Kelly wants to see you when you get a second."

"Sure." Rylie stood up and came around the desk.

"Oh, I love that skirt!"

Rylie looked down at her black lace pencil skirt with a nude underskirt. It was one of her favorites, but she hardly wore it, afraid of snagging it.

"Thanks. I love your dress." Wendy was wearing a yellow dress with a square neck and a full skirt that hit just below her knees. The style was 1950s and adorable on her slight frame. Her red curls were pinned back from her face and her freckles darkened as she blushed. Rylie thought she was sweet, if sometimes a bit too forward.

"Thank you." Wendy danced from foot to foot for a few moments and Rylie could tell there was something else she wanted.

"What's up? You seem nervous."

"I was just wondering… I know it's none of my business, but I heard that you were staying at Dustin Kent's place."

Rylie figured that people were going to find out eventually, but she hadn't told anyone… So how had Wendy known?

The movers.

No one could keep a secret in this town.

"Yeah, I am. Temporarily."

Wendy's eyes widened. "Really? I didn't think he did that sort of thing." This conversation was slowly crossing from curiosity to nosiness.

"We're just friends, and I'm only staying in his pool house until I find a place of my own."

"Oh. Sorry, I didn't mean to pry," Wendy said, sheepishly.

Sure you didn't.

Apparently, she wasn't done because Wendy gushed, "It's just... He's just so hot, but I didn't want to step on any toes if I asked him out."

Rylie still managed to smile, even as her jaw tightened. "Nope, my toes are good. Go for it." The sudden need to get away from the perky redhead overcame Rylie and she added, "I better go before Kelly gets antsy."

"Okay, thanks. See you later."

Wendy walked out ahead of her, turning into Dustin's office.

Wow, she didn't waste any time.

Rylie headed down to Kelly's office. When she passed by Dustin's, he was focused on Wendy, who was leaning over his desk. He didn't notice Rylie, and she hated the flirtatious smile he was bestowing on the other woman.

She had no reason to be irritated, though. Rylie had been avoiding him since he walked her to the pool house door on Saturday night. Partly because she'd been embarrassed for the way she'd behaved. She almost never drank, especially not to the point of puking.

Then there had been the way he'd told her he was staying away from attached women, as if he cared what she thought of him. It had caused butterflies to erupt in her stomach, getting caught in her chest until she'd had trouble breathing past all the flutters. The last thing she needed was another reason to like him.

Of course, she'd panicked at her reaction to him. If there was ever a guy who had heartbreak written all over him, it was Dustin.

So, she'd run, hid, and avoided as best she could. It seemed the only course of treatment for the insanity that had obviously taken over her body.

Rylie stopped just outside Kelly's office and watched her boss pore over several documents on her desk. Kelly seemed caught up in whatever she was reading, so Rylie knocked on Kelly's doorframe gently.

Her boss glanced up and stood, waving at her. "Come in and shut the door."

"Sure." Once she'd done as Kelly asked, Kelly sat down and Rylie took the chair across from her. "What's up?"

"How are things going with Dustin?"

You mean besides the fact that I'm softening around him like a marshmallow over a fire? "Fine."

Kelly watched her closely. "He pulling his own weight?"

"Yeah, he's doing great. In fact, I was going to grab him so we could go order the flowers and such."

Kelly tapped her perfect French tips on her desk several times before she nodded. "Okay then. I just wanted to be sure and touch base with you. You go do that and let me know if there are any issues."

Rylie cocked her head. "Exactly what do you think Dustin is involved in?"

"I don't know. Just a feeling I have."

"Then why not just fire him?" Rylie asked.

"You know what they say about curiosity…just call me a kitty cat."

Rylie laughed and stood up. "Whatever you say, boss."

She left Kelly's office and wondered what was worth the stress of keeping Dustin around if Kelly didn't trust him. It was too weird.

She stopped in the doorway of Dustin's office. Wendy was gone, thank God. The last thing she wanted was to walk in on the two of them getting to know each other better.

In the biblical sense.

She leaned against the doorjamb and it took several moments before he looked up and beamed at her, officially knocking the wind out of her with just a smile.

Oh boy.

"Hey. You just going to stand there?"

"You looked like you were concentrating. What are you writing?" she asked, taking a step into his office.

He tapped his keyboard and shut his laptop before she got too close. "Just an e-mail. You ready?"

"Sure. I have all of the pictures and mock-ups Tonya sent me, so I thought we'd start with flowers."

He stood up and pulled his blue checked vest down over his pristine white shirt. Today his tie was navy blue and his slacks charcoal gray. He always looked like he was ready for a *GQ* shoot, which was something Rylie could appreciate. She loved clothes and enjoyed looking nice.

"After you," Dustin said with a wave of his hand.

She walked in front of him out the door, conscious of the fact that the tight pencil skirt felt like it was molded for his perusal.

She casually checked over her shoulder, but there was no quick glance away or guilty look. He grinned at her, as if he knew exactly what she was doing and her face warmed.

He jogged ahead of her and opened the front door. As she stepped out, he leaned over, his voice low. "I was."

She slowed her pace, glancing up to meet his gaze. "You were what?"

"Checking you out."

Mortified, she was tempted to take off her black ballet flat and hit him with it. "Do you like embarrassing me?"

"Embarrassing you? No. Flustering you? Absolutely."

She angrily yanked his car door open, setting off the alarm. When he hit the button, quieting the blare, she spoke through gritted teeth.

"What is the difference?"

"One is mean. The other is just so I get to see that pretty pink blush stain your cheeks."

"Oh!" She climbed inside, and held the folder against her chest protectively. "Isn't there anyone else you can torment?"

"Sure, but you're my favorite."

No. No. NO! The way he said it was *not* supposed to make her feel warm and gooey. "Lucky me. What about Wendy?"

"What about her?"

He seemed genuinely confused so she elaborated. "She was asking about you. Said she was going to ask you out."

One of his dark eyebrows lifted as his smile widened. "Are you jealous?"

She tried to laugh, but it sounded a little forced, even to her ears. "Absolutely not. I just think you shouldn't get involved with people you work with."

He leaned into the car, but she refused to look at him. When his mouth grazed her ear, she jerked as he whispered, "What if there is someone that you try to stay away from but you just can't help yourself?"

"Oh, you're such a tease." She pushed him away, shutting the door on his laughter.

He went around the back of the car and got in a few moments later, still chuckling. "Okay, I'll behave." He started the car and put his hand on the back of her seat. When he turned to look out the back window, his thumb grazed her bare shoulder as he backed up, and a tingle spread across her skin, down to her breasts. Her nipples hardened, and she was thankful she was wearing one of her thicker bras so he couldn't tell.

"You call that behaving?" she said.

He switched gears to drive and shot out onto the street. "What?"

"Touching me."

"Total accident, I swear."

He wasn't smirking, but she still had a hard time believing him.

* * * *

Dustin held the door for Rylie when they reached Pocket Full of Posies Flower Shop, thinking that she smelled better than the overpowering scents coming from inside. Once he was surrounded, he sniffed a bit, feeling a sneeze coming on. Normally he wasn't allergic, but he also didn't stand in the middle of a hundred different flowers in an enclosed space every day. Kenzie Olsen came out of the back, her blond curls kept out of her face with a purple bandana. Once upon a time, she'd been hot and heavy with his brother, Charlie, but they'd broken up right before Charlie had left for school. Dustin had never asked why they called it quits, but it really didn't matter. He'd always liked her.

"Hey, Rys. I'm so excited to be working with you." She hugged Rylie hard, and pulled away to give Dustin a wide grin. "Hey, kid! It's been a long time." She gave him a tight embrace and pulled away, smacking his cheek lightly. "Good to see you. You're into this wedding stuff too, huh?"

Charlie and Kenzie were five years his senior and the full two years they'd been dating, Kenzie had always called him *kid*. Apparently fifteen years and several inches did not break the habit.

"Hey, Kenz. What can I say, there's just something about a wedding."

"Uh huh." Kenzie turned her attention back to Rylie, obviously knowing who the expert was. "So, what do you have for me?"

Rylie opened her binder and pulled out several pictures of bouquets and centerpieces. They all had white roses with silver ribbons, pearls, and green leaves placed strategically between them to give the floral arrangements just a touch of color.

Dustin thought it was boring as hell, but what did he know about wedding themes and color schemes? He was just there to look pretty and nod.

"Your bride doesn't like a lot of color, does she?" Kenzie asked.

"Not from all of the things she's sent me." Rylie pulled out two printed photos from her folder and placed them on the nearby counter. "This is what her gown looks like and the bridesmaid's dresses she wants. We're headed to the dress shop next to order them."

Dustin didn't really care, but he just happened to look down and see simple silver gowns in a shiny material. He made a face.

"You got something to say?" Rylie asked.

He realized she'd caught his expression, and he cleared his throat, uncomfortable. "Nothing."

"No, tell me."

He shrugged. "I just think that the colors are wrong for a fall wedding in November. It seems bland."

Rylie nodded. "I agree with you. Plus, that dress is going to look terrible on me."

"That dress would look terrible on anyone with curves," Kenzie agreed.

Dustin could almost see the gears in Rylie's head turning as she plotted. "Maybe we can change her mind about the color scheme?"

"What do you have in mind?" Dustin asked.

He waited as she looked around the shop, her eyes lighting up when she spotted something. She pulled out a white rose with burgundy tipped petals. "What if we used these with silver pearls? And a burgundy ribbon with silver trim?"

Kenzie was practically bouncing from foot to foot, obviously inspired. "I can do a few sample bouquets this afternoon and send you pics. Then you can send them to her and see if they change her mind."

Dustin stepped back as they started spitballing ideas back and forth, his gaze landing on a vase in the refrigerated glass case full of lavender roses. They were gorgeous and matched the exact shade of Rylie's off-the-shoulder shirt.

Why he'd noticed that, he had no idea, but he found himself clearing his throat.

"How much is this display?" he asked.

The women's conversation hushed as Kenzie checked to see what he was looking at. "Sixty dollars plus tax."

There was no way Rylie would accept them from him at that price. He stayed quiet as Kenzie promised to make the mock-ups and send Rylie pictures that afternoon. Dustin pulled out his wallet as Rylie headed for the door.

"Are you coming?" she asked.

"In a second. I'll meet you by the car."

She shot him a curious glance, but left the building.

"What's up, kid?" Kenzie asked.

Dustin didn't bother telling her not to call him that. If it hadn't fazed her when he was a kid, he doubted she'd pay him heed now. "Do you have a single purple rose I can buy?"

She cocked her head to the side, studying him thoughtfully. "In the back refrigerator. The price tag on the dozen too much for you?"

"No, but it would be for the girl I gave them to."

Kenzie's eyebrows shot up as her gaze shot toward the door. "I see."

Man, did his face get really warm. "It's not like that. It's an apology, for me being a jackass."

Her expression clouded and her mouth twisted into a frown. "Must run in the family. I'll be right back."

Kenzie disappeared before he could ask her what she meant. He forgot about it until after she'd already rung him up and sent him out the door.

When he walked over to Rylie, who was leaning against his car, he hid the rose behind his back.

"What are you doing?" she asked.

He held the rose out to her. "For you."

She stared at the rose, hesitating. "Why?"

"It's an apology rose. I'm sorry for giving you a hard time, and I'll try to be better from this point forward."

She still seemed unsure, but she took the long stem with a small smile. "Thank you."

His hands flexed as she brought the bud to her nose and inhaled softly, closing her eyes. He watched at the petals brushed her lips and he found himself envying a stupid flower.

"You like it?" he murmured.

She opened her eyes, the chocolate depths warm and happy. "Lavender roses are my favorite, but they are so expensive, so I never buy them."

"It's not up to you to buy your own flowers."

"Well, it is now," she said, lightly. "Asher always gave me assorted bouquets when he...after we'd fight. I don't know if I ever told him I love these. Probably." The shy, sweet smile she sent him was like arms wrapped around his chest. "I appreciate the gesture. Thank you."

"You're welcome."

Dustin opened her door for her, and as she stepped inside, he jogged around the back. He didn't know if it was her reaction to his rose or the fact that he'd guessed her favorite flower, one that Asher had never known about, but he was suddenly in a very, very good mood.

He climbed in and then buckled up. "Where to now?"

"I think we should go to the bridal shop and see if we can find any alternatives to the dress she chose. From the measurements of these bridesmaids, I think they'd also appreciate something a little more flattering."

"Should we call Tonya?"

She shook her head. "I want visuals for her to fall in love with before we contact her."

"Works for me."

Chapter 12

Dustin wasn't big into women's fashion, so he'd fully planned to head down the street to grab them some lunch while Rylie handled this.

But just as he was ready to head out the door, Rylie had insisted he stay. "I need you to take pictures of the dresses and e-mail them to me."

Before he could protest, Rylie disappeared into the racks of bright colored silks, satins, and taffeta and one of the saleswomen was ushering him toward the viewing area. He gazed over his shoulder at the front door as it got smaller and smaller.

Now, he found himself sprawled in one of the overstuffed chairs, playing some puzzle game on his phone while he waited for her to come out of the dressing room.

"Okay, this is option number one," Rylie said.

He looked up to find her stepping onto a raised podium. The dress she was wearing was a deep wine color in a flowy fabric that came up over one shoulder. The color made her skin look creamier and brought out the golden highlights in her hair.

Rylie waved her hands up and down like she was a game show model. "So, this is an empire waist dress in a chiffon, and they have several different styles for the top... Why aren't you typing?"

He blinked at her. "What?"

"I thought you'd take the picture, and then e-mail the picture and description to me."

He set his phone aside and leaned forward with his elbows on his knees. "You do realize that I am a guy, right?"

Jasmine, one of the sales girls, giggled as Rylie blushed. "Yes, of course I am aware."

"Then how about I just take the pictures and you can write your own descriptions later?"

She sighed, as if he was being a pain in her ass, but conceded. "Fine. Here is this one."

He took a picture but frowned down at it.

"What's the matter?" she asked. "Do I look bad?"

"No, the dress is good, but you aren't selling it." He got up and turned his iPhone around to show her the picture. "See? No smile. No excitement. Nada. If I were Tonya, I would stick with the original dress because you are doing nothing to make me *want* this dress."

Rylie put her hands on her hips. "How exactly do you want me to sell it?"

He stroked his chin as if considering, then twirled his finger. "Spin."

"Excuse me?"

"Spin around and show me if the skirt flows up."

She frowned at him, but did as he asked. The ankle length dress didn't lift far, but it rippled as she moved.

When she stopped, he gave her a thumbs-up. "Pretty good. Now this time, try smiling."

Her smile was wide and strained. He shot her a look that said he clearly wasn't impressed and she huffed. "I feel ridiculous."

Dustin sighed dramatically. "Do I need to show you?"

"Um, sure?"

He called Jasmine over and gave her his iPhone, squeezing her hand as he did. "If any pictures or videos of me end up on the internet, I have an army of lawyers who will destroy you."

The poor girl gulped.

Dustin pulled a dress off the rack, walked into a dressing room, and closed the curtain.

"What are you doing?" Rylie called, laughter evident in her voice.

Dustin smiled. The sound was like music to his ears.

"I am showing you how to sell a dress."

"Wait, are you putting it on? You just gave me crap for asking you to write down a description and you are actually going to *wear* a dress?"

He ignored her. When he had the dress on, he opened the curtain and glided out.…

To several more salespeople in the audience, covering their mouths with their hands. Rylie's eyes were as wide as saucers.

Undeterred, he sauntered over to her and struck a pose. "Lesson the first. You should always be having fun."

"You're nuts!" Rylie laughed.

Dustin reached for her hand and helped her down from the podium. "No, I am just comfortable with my masculinity and have absolutely no issue putting on a dress if it will make you relax."

The dress he'd put on was just below his knees, which he figured meant the dress was probably supposed to land around the average woman's ankles. When he spun, the skirt came up, and Rylie squealed with laughter. Dustin caught Jasmine's eye and signaled for her to take pictures of Rylie's glee. When he took her hand and spun her around, she didn't stop giggling and he grinned.

Finally, she came to a stop and he put his hands on her shoulders, giving them a tiny squeeze. "Now, if I can strut my stuff in this breezy scrap of cloth, you should be able to make me want whatever you try on next. You just got to work it.

Rylie covered his hands with hers. "Put me in, Coach and I won't let you down."

Mesmerized by the twinkle in her eyes, he almost forgot that they weren't alone. But when several titters around them halted his desire to kiss her, he stepped back with a grin.

"That's the spirit."

* * * *

An hour later, Rylie was still struggling to breathe. She'd never laughed so hard as when Dustin had come out in that seafoam green spaghetti strap dress, his broad shoulders and muscular arms at odds with the delicate fabric. Even as she'd tried on other dresses and styles, he'd kept the scrap of cloth on, just to tease her.

When he'd done several model turns across the floor after her third option, telling her to "vogue," she'd thought she'd fall to the floor and never be able to get up again. If he hadn't caught her around her middle and pulled her against him, she would have.

As it was, when her mirth subsided, she'd found her gaze held by his too blue eyes, and she wasn't thinking about the dress or his ridiculous antics.

She was wondering what it would be like to have him dip his head and kiss her.

Another flash from Dustin's iPhone had broken through her disturbing thoughts. Now that they were walking out of the store, going through all the pictures, she realized it had been a really long time since she'd had so much fun.

"Ew, delete that one!" she said.

The picture in question had her with her mouth open like a braying donkey, one eye wide and the other in a slit. She looked like Quasimodo from the animated version of *The Hunchback of Notre Dame*.

"No way, that is Instagram worthy."

She leaped onto his arm as he held the phone out of reach. "No! If you do, I will annihilate you."

"Oh, I'm so scared," he teased.

"Please don't," she said, all serious now.

He brought his arm down and she watched as he deleted it. "There. See. Not such a bad guy."

"Thanks." He brought up the next picture of her in a dark green Cinderella style gown complete with poofy tulle skirt. "You think it's too much?"

"No, but this one…" He swept until he found what he was looking for. "This one is it for me."

The dress was a wine-colored chiffon with an empire waist and off-the-shoulder sleeves. It had been her favorite as well.

"Can you just e-mail me the best ones and delete the rest? Except the silver one she wanted. I want her to see it on, so she can compare the others to it."

"You think I should send her this one?"

He lifted his phone so she could see it was one of him in the seafoam green gown, giving the camera his best Blue Steel.

"Oh my God, if I didn't think it would get us both fired, I'd double dog dare you."

"Hmmm, fair enough. That does give me an idea though," he said.

"What?"

"First—lunch." They stood outside the little drive-up diner, Runaway Burger, and he pointed to a picnic bench. "Snag that table while I get us food. You like everything on your burger?"

"Yeah, with curly fries and a root beer. I left my purse back at Something Borrowed, though."

"Don't worry about it. It's on me."

She didn't like him paying for things, especially since she was already living in his pool house for way less than he could be charging her.

"Fine, but I get the next one."

"We'll see."

She rolled her eyes at his response and sat down. Rylie hoped that once she talked to Kelly, and then Tonya, they would both get on board with the alternative color scheme. At least this would give Tonya some options; if she hated them all, they could go back to the original dresses and bouquets. It was her wedding, after all.

An empty building across the street caught Rylie's eye. It used to be a doughnut shop once upon a time, but when the grocery store expanded, adding in a bakery, the shop had gone out of business. The big front window was covered in cardboard, probably from having a rock thrown through it or something, but for a second, Rylie imagined what the shop would look like with a coat of pink paint and a new display window. And in white stencil, with little flowers along the side, it would read *Rylie's Gourmet Bakery.*

Dustin disrupted her fantasy by placing her basket of food in front of her. "All right, here we go." He sat across from her, and after double checking the drinks, set her root beer to her right.

"Thanks." Rylie didn't look at the empty building again. It was stupid to think about opening a shop here. There was already a wedding cake designer, and even though Kelly and Marley had talked about having Rylie handle the cake orders for Something Borrowed, that hadn't happened yet.

Besides, it wasn't as though she had the right kitchen for it anyway.

"Is the burger not good?" Dustin asked.

Rylie realized she'd zoned out for too long and laughed. "Sorry, just thinking."

"About?"

"Just how things can change so rapidly. You think your life will go one way, and then you find yourself living in some rich mogul's pool house, planning other people's weddings, and basically wondering where to go from here."

"Well, that is heavy subject matter. One that does not need to be solved today. Which brings me back to my idea. Truth or dare."

She chewed the fry she'd just popped into her mouth, sure she'd misheard him. "Huh?"

"Let's play truth or dare. It's the perfect way to get to know each other."

"I don't need to get to know you anymore than I already do."

He winced. "Ouch, but I'm going to ignore that. I'll start. I want…truth."

Rylie eyed him over the lid of her drink, considering. "Have you ever had a real relationship?"

"Define real."

"More than six months."

"No. Your turn. Truth or dare."

There was no way in hell she was picking dare. "Truth."

His expression turned sly and she wondered if dare would have been a better choice.

"Did you or did you not think I looked sexy in the dress?" he asked.

Rylie almost choked on the French fry she'd just taken a bite of. "That's a stupid question."

"Why?"

"Because you know you'd look sexy in a trash bag."

Rylie slapped her hand over her mouth. She hadn't even thought about it; the response had just come out.

Dustin grinned. "Now we're getting somewhere."

Rylie made a face at him. "This is dumb and inappropriate—"

"Oh, come on, don't be a chicken." His blue eyes danced with an obvious challenge, but she wasn't going to take the bait.

She opened her binder up and flipped to the entertainment page. "Tonya wants a cover band—"

He slapped the binder closed, almost trapping her hand. "Uh uh, we're on lunch and the game is still on. I choose truth."

Rylie leveled him with an exasperated look. "Fine. What are all of those scars on your back?"

The way Dustin stilled made Rylie instantly regret letting her temper get the best of her.

"I am so sorry. I shouldn't have asked that. It was out of line and none of my business."

Dustin went back to eating, an awkward silence circling them. Rylie wished she'd just played along. That she could take it back.

After what seemed like hours, Dustin wiped his mouth with a napkin and put it on top of his leftover food. "You done?"

"Yeah," she said.

He picked up both of their baskets and dumped the contents in a nearby trash can. She caught up with him on the sidewalk, and they'd walked several feet back to the car before Rylie spoke, wanting to make up for her rudeness.

"I used to make out with Tommy Wynn behind the concession stand sophomore year."

Dustin stopped walking and turned to her with a blank expression. "Where did that come from?"

"I just shared a deep dark secret about myself with you. Letting you get to know me."

"Okay... Didn't Wynn come out in high school?" he asked.

"Yes. For a long time, I thought he'd come out because of me. He finally sat me down at a party and told me he'd been struggling with who he was for years, and he'd figured since he'd liked me as a person, then maybe he'd feel something different with me. He's engaged now to a successful civil rights attorney, and they live in L.A. with their two spoiled rescue pups. If you ever want a pick me up, their Instagram is adorable."

"Good for them." They started moving again, and Dustin wrapped his arm around her shoulders. "So, what does making out entail? First base? Second?"

She tossed his arm off with a disgusted laugh, relieved that he'd seemed to forgive her.

"Wouldn't you like to know."

Dustin nudged her arm with his. "I would, which is why I asked."

"Is second base feeling me up?"

"Usually."

"Then we rounded third."

Dustin's expression was so stunned she burst out laughing.

"You almost made it with Tommy Wynn behind the concession stand?" Suddenly self-conscious, she nibbled her lip. "Why do you say it like that?"

"Nothing. I was just thinking that I might have jumped to conclusions about you. You might just be a bad girl after all."

Rylie elbowed him in the side. "This is the twenty-first century. It's called exploring my sexuality."

They'd reached his car, when he started to speak. "Wanna explore your sex—"

She covered his mouth with her hand, giggling. "Damn it! I need to stop setting myself up for your little innuendos."

Dustin looked at her intensely, and gooseflesh rose as she felt his soft lips press against her palm. She leaned back against the door, her legs suddenly weak. He wrapped his fingers around her wrist and pulled her hand away from his mouth. Slowly, he took each of her fingers and pressed a burning kiss onto every tip. Each caress sent electric shocks down every nerve ending, shooting through her arms, legs, breasts…

Straight between her thighs.

He placed her open palm against the side of his face and she slid it over the scratchy surface before she really thought it through.

"Rylie."

The deep groan of her name snapped her back to reality and she pulled away. She couldn't do this. It was too complicated. Too crazy.

"We should get going. Lots more to do."

He stepped back, smiling ruefully. "Whatever you say."

Chapter 13

On Friday afternoon, Dustin was sitting in his office listening to some of the bands and DJs that Rylie had given him to review when his cell phone rang. He checked the caller ID and when he saw it was his agent, he swiped to answer.

"David, good to hear from you. Did you like the chapters I sent?"

David Brown was at one of the top literary agencies in New York and a total bulldog. He knew how to get the best deal for his clients and could smell a hit before he even pitched it.

It was why Dustin had gone with him in the first place.

"Hey, Dustin, I was just getting ready to walk out the door, but I wanted to call and tell you personally, that yes, absolutely, I loved every second of them. This is gold, baby, and with this, you are going to hit the best seller list."

Dustin grinned as he leaned back in his chair. All week he'd gone home and when he sat down at his computer, the words had just flowed. He'd sent in fifteen thousand words to David this morning and was surprised he'd read it that fast.

"It's not too reality TV?" Dustin asked.

"Are you kidding me? The characters alone make me want to keep reading. I mean, that one bridesmaid, Rachel? Man, what a downer, but in the best way possible. The girl is just tragic and you know how readers love an underdog."

Dustin frowned at his description of Rylie's character. He hadn't meant to make Rylie seem like a drag. He'd thought he'd made her out to be kind, fiercely loyal, and tough.

"Sorry, David, but what do you mean about Rachel?"

"She's like one of those quiet kids that gets bullied and eventually, they just explode. The way she kisses everyone's ass so they will like her, come on, only people with no respect for themselves do that."

Dustin cleared his throat, trying to beat down the anger directed at David and himself. "Okay, well I'm glad you liked them, but I think I'm going to rework them a bit. I'll send you the edited versions with my next installment."

"Sure, sure, it's your book and I can't wait to read them. Have a great weekend, bud."

"You too."

Dustin ended the call with a groan. God, he didn't want to go back and rework those pages, he just wanted to keep moving forward with the story.

But he couldn't shake the sound of David's laughter at Rylie's expense and he hated it. Even if it was the fictional character Rachel and only loosely based on Rylie, Dustin couldn't do it.

His phone rang again, and it was Rylie this time.

"Hello?"

"Hey, so, what are you doing tonight?" she asked.

"It depends on if what you're going to ask me to do is boring or stupid."

"Ha. Ha," she said. "I was going to ask if you wanted to come with me to check out Hickory Ridge."

"Hickory who?"

"They are one of the bands Tonya asked us to check out. They are playing at The Pine Cove Tavern in Placerville at eight. Are you in?"

Pages to fix or hitting a bar with Rylie. Tough choice.

"I'm in. What time do they go on?"

"Nine."

"I'll grab you at eight."

* * * *

Rylie wasn't sure what to wear to check out a country rock band, but she figured jeans and a tank top that read, *Boots, Dirt Roads, and Country Music* would be okay.

She sat in the passenger seat of Dustin's car, twisting a curl from her pony tail around her finger. She still wasn't sure why she asked him to come; he'd already told her that he wasn't a big fan of hillbilly music. But she'd heard this band's version of "Your Love Amazes Me," which was Blake and Tonya's song, and she had a really good feeling about them.

Dustin parked across the street in the dirt parking lot, and they walked over to the wood building. There were some motorcycles parked outside and a few groups smoking out front and along the side. As they passed by a couple of bikers pulling in, someone let out a high-pitched wolf whistle. "Damn, baby, you got a mirror in those jeans because I can see myself in them from here!"

Rylie didn't even bother turning around, because if they were talking to her, she might be tempted to flip them the bird and if they weren't, well, she'd be just a tad bit embarrassed for assuming.

Dustin put his hand on her back to guide her through the doors. The bouncer in the opening gave them the nod and Rylie found herself hit with a cloud of stale cigarettes, booze, and perfume. She wrinkled her nose just as Dustin leaned over to say loudly, "That's a pretty unique aroma they've got going on."

Rylie laughed. "I was just thinking the same thing."

"Want a drink?" Dustin asked.

"Yeah, but I'll come with you. There is no way I want to be left alone in this place."

"You afraid the big bad wolf will get you?"

"More like I'm afraid I'll take a barstool and break it over the wolf's head."

Rylie could hear Dustin chuckling over the music of the current band as he led her over to the bar. They still had twenty minutes until Hickory Ridge started, but Rylie wasn't sure she could stand the lead singer's caterwauling another moment.

"What are you drinking?" the bartender asked.

"I'll have a Heineken. Rylie?"

Rylie really wasn't interested in drinking ever again, but she hated beer almost as much as wine. "I'll take a Mai Tai, please."

"Sure thing."

Rylie turned and leaned back against the bar, watching the band. "They really are terrible, aren't they?"

Dustin leaned close, probably so she could hear him better. "I'd rather listen to a man screaming while having his balls removed without anesthetic."

Rylie choked on a laugh. "Geez, that's a bit graphic, don't you think?"

He shrugged, and it suddenly occurred to her he was wearing a Hurley T-shirt and jeans. She was about to say something about his casual dress when the bartender came back with their drinks.

Once they had moved back into the crowd, Dustin asked, "Would you rather move closer to the stage?"

"Not right now."

Rylie took a sip of her fruity drink just as a couple of guys bumped into her, knocking her back into Dustin, who caught her with his hands on her hips. Her drink sloshed over the edge onto the floor and she cursed. "You okay?" Dustin asked, his warm breath on the side of her neck.

She stilled at his proximity, her whole body turning to Jello as she realized his hands were still spread on her hips. "Yeah, just have sticky drink all over my hand."

Dustin let her go just as the two dumbasses almost backed into her again. "Hey!"

The one with blond hair and gages in his ears smiled apologetically. "Whoa, sorry about that, sweetie. It's a little crowded in here."

"Yeah, I know, but you should be more careful."

His friend, who was wearing one of those loose-fitting beanies over his long brown hair nodded. "You're right. We're a little drunk, but we should watch where we're going." He held his hand out to her. "I'm Eric, and you are?"

She switched her drink to her dry hand and gave him her wet, sticky one. "Rylie. And this is..."

Rylie turned to introduce Dustin but he had disappeared.

Gages nodded toward the bar. "If you're looking for your friend, he's over at the bar making friends."

Rylie followed where he was looking and spotted Dustin chatting up a tiny blond in a red halter top that showed off abs that she'd only seen in fitness videos.

When he laughed at something the other woman said, Rylie politely excused herself, and made her way over to stand next to Dustin.

"Dustin? I thought that was you!" she squealed. "How is it going? Say, did you ever manage to get that thing fixed?"

Rylie could tell blondie was hanging on her every word when Dustin asked, "What fixed?"

"You know. Your micro penis," she whispered loudly. She addressed the other woman now with a sympathetic tone. "Poor thing has lived his whole life with this itty-bitty weenie."

When she held up her pinkie to elaborate, Dustin grabbed her hand and yanked her away.

Rylie had no idea what had come over her, but seeing him laugh at another woman's joke had rubbed her wrong.

They'd just entered the middle of the crowd when the band stopped and a man came out on stage. "Thanks, Electric Thunder. And now, please give a warm welcome to Hickory Ridge."

Rylie would have clapped, but it was a little hard with her drink in her one hand and Dustin's fingers wrapped around her wrist. She stared up into his glittering blue eyes and swallowed. She didn't expect him to get so mad.

"Here come the guys we've been waiting for," she said weakly.

"Where do you get off?" he asked.

"Excuse me?"

He let go of her wrist. "I left you with two guys salivating over you and didn't say one thing. Some girl comes on to me and you announce to the whole bar that I have a tiny dick?"

"It's a micro penis, which is a legitimate, medical condition—"

"Yeah, only I don't have it. So what in the hell made you think it was a good idea to tell a complete stranger I did?"

The band started playing a slow song and all the people around them started coupling up. The two of them stood there, a foot apart, not moving or speaking.

When a guy nearby started to ask her to dance, Dustin snarled at him, "Back off, we're talking."

Rylie took his hand and dragged him a few feet away, afraid the other man might take offense to his temper.

"I'm really sorry I embarrassed you. I don't even know why I did it, except I didn't want you to ditch me and leave me here. In case you haven't noticed, this place is kind of a meat market."

"I wouldn't have left you here, all right? As far as I'm concerned, this is a work thing and if we came together, we're going to leave together."

Rylie gave him a tentative smile, but his scowl didn't ease, so she tried a different approach. Sinking to his level.

"I said I was sorry. Besides, you and I both know that you don't have a small…thing, so why do you care if some random chick you're never going to see again thinks you do?" Downing half her drink, she added, "If it makes you feel better, I will go chat up some random dude and you can tell him that I stuff my bra."

Dustin's gaze shifted down. "No one would believe that."

"That I'm lousy in bed?"

He shook his head. "I don't want to get even. I know why you did it."

"And why is that?"

Dustin took her drink and set it on one of the tables. "Because you didn't want to have to share your dance partner."

Before she could get her bearings, Dustin was twirling her into his arms and dancing her out onto the floor.

"What are you doing?" she laughed.

"If we're going to listen to some shitty band, we might as well have some fun while we're doing it."

Rylie didn't argue, especially when she liked being in Dustin's arms more than she should have.

Chapter 14

Dustin realized two Saturdays later during his morning run that he hadn't had sex since Paula, which had been the longest he'd gone without in years. Most of his sex partners knew his stance on relationships and didn't mind, so the number of partners he'd had wasn't as extensive as most people suspected. But it was strange that he hadn't even thought about it.

Correction, he'd thought about it, non-stop. Just not with some faceless girl.

With Rylie.

He pumped his arms as the house came into sight and he picked up his pace. Working with Rylie lately had been good. No awkwardness or snark. He'd even managed to behave and keep most of his sexual innuendos to a minimum. Tonya had taken their suggestions to heart and called Kelly to thank her for assigning them to her wedding. Rylie had been so excited she'd thrown herself into Dustin's arms and hugged him tight.

Of course, she'd pulled away as soon as she realized what she'd done, but he'd played it off as no big deal. Only he could still feel the squish of her breasts against his chest, her hot breath on the side of his neck...

Get a grip, Dustin. That is a dead-end road.

He had to admit that they made a pretty good team. They'd gotten every major detail for Tonya Rolland's wedding hashed out, including the band. It was the fastest a wedding had ever come together, and Kelly had given them each a bonus for their hard work.

Still, despite how well they were getting along, Rylie avoided him at home. He'd invited her to join him for meals, but she would tell him she was fine. He didn't know if she was afraid to be alone with him in a place that wasn't work, or if she had just been faking it, pretending to enjoy his company, but he was getting a little tired of her rejecting his edible overtures.

Codi Gary

He came through the door, sweat pouring down his face and back. He had almost made it to the front step, but Victoria caught him.

"Oh, Mr. Kent! Can you please do something for me?"

Dustin walked into the kitchen, where Victoria was busy in front of the stove.

"What's up, Victoria?"

"Will you mind walking that package down for Rylie? It came yesterday, and I forgot to give it to her. I think it's her date outfit."

Dustin picked up the brown box, scowling down at the label. "Date outfit?"

Victoria covered her mouth with one hand, looking horrified. "Whoops! She asked me not to say anything. And I swore I'd take it to my grave, but it slipped my mind. You just forget what I said, Mr. Kent. You know how much I hate to gossip. Pretend you never heard that."

Like hell I will.

"Who's the guy?" he asked, trying for casual even as his fingers dug into the sides of the box.

"Now, what did I just say? I am not about to gossip about Rylie's date." Victoria shot him a sly glance. "But I think he's from Pleasant Valley."

Dustin snorted. So, she treated him like a leper, but said yes to some rando from PV? Who was the guy?

It's none of my business.

"If she wants the box, she can come up here and get it. I'm not FedEx."

He started to put the package down, but Victoria thrust her spatula so hard in his direction that eggs flew off the end and smacked him in the cheek.

"Where are your manners? She is your guest and she is going through a rough time. This date is the first thing she has been excited about since she got here, and I am glad for it. So, hop to it or you can cook your own meals."

"Actually, she pays rent, so technically, she's a tenant." Dustin quirked his eyebrow at her. "And you do realize you work for me, right?"

"Yes."

"And that I can fire you?"

She snorted as she turned back to his breakfast. "Ha, but then you would have to train someone else to your likes and dislikes and that annoys you."

She had him there.

"Also, you love me," she said.

Dustin didn't say those words to anyone, but of the handful of people he was fond of, Victoria was one of them.

"Fine, I'll take it to her."

"That's a good boy."

He shut the door on her praise and jogged down the steps to the pool house. He had to knock on the door several times before Rylie finally came stumbling into view and he grinned. He probably shouldn't tell her that she moved like a zombie off *The Walking Dead* before she had her caffeine fix. She tended to be a bit cranky in the mornings.

It took two tries for her to get the door open, but when she did, she looked at him with one squinted eye.

"You know it's my day off."

His gaze passed over the messy hair, threadbare T-shirt with a kitty on it, and her little plaid pajama shorts. "I do."

"Then, for the love of frosting, why are you knocking on the door at seven forty in the morning?"

He held up the box and shook it at her. "Victoria said you might want this."

Suddenly, she was awake and reaching for it. "Give me."

He held it out of reach. "What's in it?"

She hesitated half a second before her chin jutted up. "A dress and shoes."

"I helped you pack and move. You have plenty of dresses and shoes."

"A woman can never have enough dresses or shoes." Apparently, she got tired of jumping for it and just groaned with her arms out. "Will you please just give them to me?"

"Depends. Are you going to model for me?"

"No."

"You're no fun." He passed her the box, watching her hold it to her chest like a precious treasure. "What's the occasion?"

Her expression turned wary, and he thought she was going to lie to him. "I… I have a date tonight."

"You do? Who is the lucky guy?"

"Just a guy. You don't know him."

"Oh, you never know. I know a lot of people."

"Not this one."

Hmmm, he was curious why she was so convinced. "How'd you meet him?"

"Oh, God, you aren't going away, are you?"

"Nope." He stepped into the pool house before she could stop him. "Want me to put on some coffee so you're at least awake for my interrogation?"

"There isn't going to be an interrogation and why are you shirtless? And all wet and drippy?"

"I went for a run."

Rylie gripped her nose, her eyes twinkling. "Did you put on deodorant first?"

"Are you saying I stink?"

"Um, yeah."

He lifted his arm and sniffed. "I do not." When she broke into giggles, his face split into a wicked grin. "So, you got jokes, huh?"

He grabbed her before she could escape and wrapped his arms around her, rubbing his sweaty body and hair all over her, wherever he could reach. She screamed, squealed, and laughed, sometimes all at once, until he was so weak with mirth that he let her escape. She wiped at her face with her hand, and then grabbed a towel from the counter before rubbing it everywhere.

"You're such a jerk."

"Oh come on, admit it. You like my sweat."

"No, I don't."

He caged her in against the kitchen counter, his voice lowering. "Actually, I don't just think you like it. I think that you love it."

"You're insane. If I had a weird fetish, it would not be having your sweat rubbed all over me."

He knew what he was doing was dangerous, but he couldn't resist leaning closer. Her brown hair was loose down her back and a little wild. He reached up to tuck the strands behind her right ear, and whispered against the shell.

"Are you sure? Not even if I was naked? And under the right circumstances?"

Her breath caught and his heart sped up at the sweet sound. He pressed closer and felt the hard buds of her nipples through her shirt against his chest. His cock hardened against the basketball shorts he wore over his boxer briefs, something that was going to be all too obvious if he backed away from her.

"What kind of circumstances?" she asked, softly.

There was no way she hadn't caught his meaning. Either she was curious about what he would say or she was baiting him. What she didn't seem to realize was that he was more than ready for the challenge.

He lifted his left hand off the counter, trailing it across the velvety skin of her arm, from her wrist to her bicep. "The kind that have me stripping off this adorable shirt, and finding you braless and beautiful underneath. Then I'd put my thumbs into the side of your shorts and push them all the way down to your ankles. Your panties—"

"What if I wasn't wearing any?"

He might have thrust against her; he couldn't be sure. "Even better."

Dustin's mouth touched the side of her neck, just under her ear, and she let out a soft moan.

"Then what?"

He stilled, his mouth hovering over her skin. She was encouraging him. She'd been keeping him at arm's length for months, but here they were in his pool house kitchen, and she wanted him to talk dirty to her.

His hands settled on the curve of her hips. He brought her lower body tighter against his so she could feel what her teasing was doing to him. When she didn't jerk away, he growled, and nipped lower, just above her T-shirt collar. She pushed her own hips forward, pressing closer, and he pulled the shirt down, kissing the newly exposed flesh even as he kept talking.

"After that, I'd drop my shorts, and lift you up onto this counter. And as soon as my cock was free of my briefs, I'd put it inside you. In and out. Slowly, swirling my hips until you came."

Rylie's breathing was coming in short, tight pants, and he was so turned on he wanted to follow through. Hell, he wanted to carry her all the way back to the bed and make the walls shake.

The faint sound of music drifted down the hallway, and she stilled. "That's Marley. She's coming over with breakfast and we're having a girls' day."

God, he didn't want to stop. Didn't want her to come to her senses and for this, whatever it was, to end.

"What time is she coming?"

"She was going to call when she was on her way," Rylie said, breathlessly.

Feeling bold, his hands slid up under her shirt, running his thumbs across the skin of her waist. "I should probably get out of here then, before she shows up."

"Probably."

He pulled away, staring down at her. "I really want to kiss you right now."

Rylie's brown eyes doubled in size. "I haven't brushed my teeth."

"I don't care. I smell like BO."

She shook her head. "No you don't. I was only kidding. You actually smell really good."

The way she said it, husky, almost guttural, was the hottest sound he'd ever heard.

"Rylie—"

Her phone started ringing again. Her face was so full of regret it made him feel slightly better when she pulled away.

"If I don't answer, she's going to freak."

With great effort, he stepped back. "Then you better get it."

She went down the hallway. Before she could come back, he walked out the door. Not because he didn't want to pick up where they'd left off, but because he knew they shouldn't. Rylie was dating someone. She'd been with the same guy for three years. She wanted monogamy and marriage and the whole shebang.

And he wasn't the guy to give her it.

* * * *

Rylie sat in the massage chair as the girl at her feet finished up her pedicure. When she'd told Marley how nervous she was about the first date she'd had in three years, Marley had planned this girls' day complete with getting their hair, nails and toes done. After this, they were getting their eyebrows waxed and heading back to the pool house.

When she'd had to admit to Marley where she'd been staying, her friend hadn't been happy at first. But she'd explained everything Dustin had done for her, and Marley had grudgingly admitted that maybe he wasn't all bad.

It was a step in the right direction, and Rylie was going to take it. She wanted her friends to know Dustin the way she did.

Why? Why do I care what Marley thinks of Dustin?

Because Dustin was her friend? He'd gotten a bum rap that wasn't all deserved?

"I can't wait to see your new dress," Marley said, drawing her from her thoughts.

Right, her dress. The one for the date she no longer wanted to go on.

Okay, that wasn't totally true. She had been excited about it. Will Younger owned a mechanic shop in Pleasant Valley and had been changing her oil for years. When he'd asked her about Asher, and she'd told him they'd broken up, she'd been surprised when he'd asked her if she was dating yet. She hadn't considered how long before she started trying again, just kept saying she was swearing off men. Surprisingly, when Will had asked, his green eyes alight with interest, the yes had just tumbled out.

Of course, that was before Dustin had pinned her to the side of the kitchen counter and talked dirty to her. She hadn't even known she liked dirty.

Until now.

"Rylie? You okay? You've seemed out of it all day," Marley asked.

"Oh, I'm fine. Just thinking."

The woman doing her toes put the clear coat on and took her hands to help her up.

"What are you thinking about?" Marley asked.

"Nothing, just my date."

Marley gave her a look that clearly said she could smell the bullshit Rylie was slinging. "Is Asher still bothering you?"

Rylie didn't want to talk about Asher. She'd had to block his number after he'd sent her twenty-eight text messages, one after another, all about whether or not she was living with Dustin. It had been her fault for trying to explain that she was just renting from him; that had only seemed to make things worse.

"No, not for a couple days now."

"I wish you would just file a restraining order on his ass."

Rylie sat down in the chair the woman indicated and slipped her feet into the dryer. "I think if I just avoid him, he'll get tired of trying. Asher never liked to put in much effort when we were dating."

The other woman finished with Marley's toes and when she helped her into the chair next to Rylie's, Marley gave her a hug. "I am so sorry you are going through all this."

"It's okay. Dustin has been really great about it." At Marley's disgusted face, Rylie protested, "I'm serious. He's not a bad guy. He's actually pretty great, he just likes to hide it."

"Yeah, beneath a layer of slime and sleaze."

Rylie didn't respond, and Marley shot her a sharp look. "Do you like Dustin?"

"I just said he was a good guy—"

"No, I mean, do you *like* him?"

"Of course not," she said. Was it a lie if she wasn't sure? She was attracted to him, and obviously wanted him, if this morning's antics were any clue. Was it anything more than lust, though?

"Why don't I believe you?" Marley asked.

"Because you are a distrustful person?"

Marley tapped her newly painted red nails against her lips. "Hmmm, no, that's not it."

Rylie did not want to analyze her feelings for Dustin today. "So, after this, it's eyebrow waxing and then we're done?"

Marley took the change in subject easily. "We're not just getting our eyebrows done."

"We're not?"

"Nope. You're getting back into the dating game. You need to be prepared."

"I shaved my legs this morning…" Rylie's voice trailed off as she realized what Marley had planned. "Uh uh, hell to the no!"

Marley cackled gleefully, like she was a supervillain revealing her evil plan. "Yes, yes! This is happening."

"If I get waxed down there I won't be able to walk for a week!"

"You'll be fine, seriously… And your date will appreciate it."

Rylie glared at her. "He won't be seeing it. At least, not tonight."

An image of Dustin lifting the skirt of her dress and finding her groomed flashed unbidden through her mind. What did it say that she couldn't imagine hooking up with Will on the first date, but she had no trouble fantasizing about Dustin getting all up in her business?

Marley seemed to think her silence meant she was mad at her. "Okay, well, it was just a thought. I know that getting my hair and nails done makes me feel pretty and getting a special wax gives me this weird confidence—"

"Fine, I will do it. Just stop talking."

Marley grinned and whispered, "*Slut*."

"Shut up."

Chapter 15

Dustin grabbed a water from his fridge and watched out the window as Marley's car took off down the driveway. It was just after five-thirty and Dustin felt like a stalker, standing there staring at the pool house so intently.

Victoria came into the kitchen behind him, and said, "Okay, Mr. Kent. Your dinner is in the fridge, and I will see you on Monday."

He turned, hoping Victoria didn't think he'd been spying on Rylie. "Thanks, Victoria."

When Victoria walked toward the side door, he said, "Where are you going?"

"I want to see Rylie's new dress. It's a woman thing, you wouldn't understand."

Dustin stood there as she closed the door, thinking that he very much wanted to see Rylie in her new dress.

And then he wanted to see it on the floor.

God, he needed to get the hell out of here and drink something. Picking up his cell phone, he noticed a missed call from his brother, Charlie. That was weird. He hardly heard from any of his brothers, unless it was around the holidays or his birthday.

He hit the voicemail button and held it to his ear.

"Hey, little brother, it's me! I'm in town and on my way to your place. I'm going to crash with you instead of mom, in case I want to relight some old flames. See you in a few!"

Dustin checked the time the message was left. Thirty minutes ago. Shit.

Dustin looked out the window again in time to watch his big brother slide open the pool house door and step inside.

He ran out the side door and down the stairs. He didn't want Charlie walking in on Rylie changing or Rylie to think his brother was an intruder.

Well, he kind of was, but Dustin didn't want him getting whacked by a frying pan.

When he stopped outside the glass door, he found Victoria and Charlie with their backs to him.

Looking at Rylie, who was as shiny as a new penny.

The golden highlights through her brown hair had been touched up and she'd applied a dark shadow to her eyelids that made her brown eyes pop. He couldn't really see the dress with his brother and Victoria in the way, so he knocked on the door.

Rylie glanced over Victoria's shoulder and when she saw him, she smiled. Victoria gave her a hug before opening the door for Dustin.

"Isn't she lovely?"

Dustin's gaze traveled from the black, strappy sandals that laced up her calves and showed off the sparkly purple polish on her toes. The black dress was tight, hugging her curves with a pendulum ruffle breaking up the waist. With her loose curls and glossy lips she was more than lovely.

She was nut-punchingly gorgeous.

"Hey, bro, you forgot to mention you had a renter," Charlie said, coming over to slap him on the back. "Guess I shouldn't have assumed you'd take me in."

"Yeah, that was stupid of you. Maybe next time give me a little more warning than a half an hour." Dustin didn't mean it though. Of his three older brothers, Charlie was the one closest to him in age and his favorite.

His brother's black hair was overly long, and his T-shirt showed that he'd been bulking up since the last time he saw him.

"Well, it's a good thing you have a big ass house with fifty other rooms then." Charlie shot Rylie a killer smile. "It was nice to meet you, Rylie. Since I'll be staying a while, I look forward to getting to know you."

Dustin's jaw clenched. The last thing he wanted was for Rylie to get to know his very charming brother.

"It was good to meet you too."

Charlie took off out the glass door before sliding it closed behind him. When it was just Dustin and Rylie, he cleared his throat.

"You're beautiful."

"Thanks."

"That dress is… Well, it's definitely something." What the hell was wrong with him? He didn't have problems talking to women.

"Really? I was afraid it was too tight."

"Yes. I mean, no, it looks perfect. Sexy." He ran a hand over his hair and groaned. "I mean, your date is going to love it."

"Will. He'll be here in a few minutes."

"Will, huh?"

She sighed, seeming to realize she'd given him an in. "Will Younger. I've known him for a while. He's nice."

Nice. Of course Rylie would go for a nice guy after that asshole Asher. The opposite of what she'd had.

Definitely not a womanizer who'd almost nailed her in this very kitchen.

"Well, I hope you have a good time." What the hell else was he going to say? This morning was something that shouldn't be repeated; he'd already decided that. Didn't mean he wanted to hang around and watch some other guy salivate all over her.

There was a knock on the glass door and he realized it was too late. On the other side stood a stocky man with sandy hair and a nervous smile. The way he kept pulling at his collared shirt made Dustin think he would probably have been more comfortable in a T-shirt and jeans for his date.

Rylie opened the door, and he couldn't see her face.

Just the way her dress hugged her round, delicious ass.

"Hey, Will. This is my coworker and landlord, Dustin."

Dustin's eyebrows rose at her description. She wasn't lying, but he'd started to think there was more to them than just that.

Though it made sense she wouldn't want to introduce him as a friend. Friend carried implications when it was between a man and a woman.

Will stepped inside with his hand out. "Nice to meet you."

Dustin took it, noticing the stains and rough callouses on the man's hands. This was the type of guy Rylie wanted. Someone who worked with his hands.

"Good to meet you. Where are you two headed?"

Will slid his hand out to rest on Rylie's lower back and Dustin hated it. "I thought we'd go to dinner and see where the night took us."

"Sounds like fun. I'll let you two get to it. I have an unexpected guest to deal with, anyway."

Dustin walked past them outside, but turned when Rylie said his name. "Thanks."

Dustin had no idea what she was thanking him for. Not mentioning their little interlude this morning? That he'd been civil to Will?

"You're welcome."

What else was he going to say anyway? *Don't go?* What was the point? The only thing that happened between them was some close calls.

That's all it needed to be.

* * * *

Charlie had talked Dustin into heading into town for a drink at the Shotgun Wedding Bar and Grill. Charlie had already tossed back three shots of Jose, and didn't seem to be slowing down.

Dustin wasn't stupid; his brother didn't just pop into town for no reason. "You going to tell me what this impromptu visit is all about?"

Charlie leveled him with blue eyes identical to his. "Sure, let's trade stories. What is up with that stone-cold fox living in your pool house?"

Dustin nursed his beer, not wanting Charlie to get any ideas about Rylie. "Nothing. She was in a bad spot and I said she could rent the pool house until she found something else."

"Yeah, but you don't get involved with women and you definitely don't let them stay with you."

"She's not staying with me. She's in a separate living space."

Charlie waved at the bartender, indicating he needed another round. "Fine, semantics. The point is, you've never even hung around a woman for more than a couple of days, but this one you're playing the hero for."

"She's my coworker."

Charlie snorted.

"Fine, she's a friend. Or something close to it."

"Now we're getting somewhere." Charlie took his shot, and hissed between his teeth. "I guess that means it's my turn, huh? Well, I told my boss to shove it, right before I walked out the door and never went back."

To say Dustin was shocked was an understatement. Charlie had gone to NYU and graduated with a master's in architecture. He'd been working at a large firm for the last eighteen months, and as far as Dustin had known, Charlie was happy.

"Why?"

"Ah, that is a long story for another time. For now, all you need to know is I'm seeking a little help getting back on my feet, Brother. Got an extra room for me?"

"Sure. For a price," Dustin said, grinning.

"I just told you I was unemployed."

"I don't need your money."

Charlie watched him suspiciously before his brother's eyes flared wide. "Hell no!"

"You don't know what I'm going to ask for."

"Yeah I do, and I'll stay with Mom before I let you get your grubby hands on her!"

Dustin smiled, amused his brother still called his original '68 Camaro SS a "she." "Please? I'll take good care of her."

"You just stick with your modern candy ass cars and stay away from my baby."

"Jesus, your baby? You have got to get laid, man," Dustin said. His thoughts immediately strayed to Rylie and her date and he grimaced. Rylie wasn't the type to bring a guy home on the first date, was she?

"That's why we're here. I'm on the prowl."

Dustin gave Charlie a skeptical glance. "If you drink much more, you're going to be on the floor."

"Please, I am thirty-two. I can hold my"—he burped—"liquor."

Charlie turned on the barstool and after several seconds, he elbowed Dustin in the side. "Dude, is there a reason why Asher Reid is staring at me like he's trying to kill me with his mind?"

Dustin looked over his shoulder and saw Asher pounding back a beer, slamming the mug down on the table when he caught Dustin's gaze.

"I think he wants you, Charlie."

"The hell you say? Asher's gay?"

Dustin shook his head. "No, he's Rylie's ex. Not really pleased with me right now."

"I would say not from the way he's glaring at you. Why'd they break up?"

"He's a dick." Charlie raised an eyebrow, and Dustin muttered, "Like dad."

Charlie stiffened. "You serious?"

"That's what I got from the little I saw."

Charlie grabbed his refreshed shot off the bar and tipped it back. Then he stood up and shouted, "Yo, Ash! You keep looking at me like that and I'm going to give you what you're asking for." He cracked his knuckles as the bar went dead silent. "Something to chew on."

Asher stood up, but several of his friends grabbed his arms and yanked him back down.

Dustin was so floored he froze for a second before he grabbed his brother by the shoulder. "What the hell are you doing?"

"He's the one picking a fight. I'm just giving him what he wants."

"It's directed at me, not you, idiot."

"Well, I'm looking for something to hit. Besides, you're my bro. Nobody dicks with you but me."

Rod, the bartender, slammed his hand on the bar behind them. "You're cut off, Charlie. You two settle your tab and get the hell out of here. I'm not having you stir up shit in here."

"We're gone, Rod." Dustin tossed down a hundred, and guided his brother out the door. Charlie gave Asher two middle fingers and a full-on tongue-hanging-out-of-his-mouth face that would have scared Gene Simmons.

Once they were outside, Dustin pushed Charlie toward the car. "If I wanted to knock the guy out, I would have done it myself."

Charlie's eyes narrowed in the lighted parking lot. "Then, why don't you? Why are you sitting around like a pussy letting that guy dog you?"

"Because I don't care what that dumbass thinks of me. Not everything has to be solved with your fists. You'd think living with Dad would have taught you that."

Charlie's face turned an ugly shade of red that in the parking lot light appeared orange. "Fuck you, Dustin! I learned not to take shit from people."

"You're thirty-two years old and you walked out on your job because you lost your temper. Sounds like you need to grow up, *Brother*."

Suddenly, Dustin found himself in a headlock, but even though his brother was bulkier, Dustin was fast and squirrely. He slipped out of Charlie's grasp and when his brother threw a hard right, Dustin easily dodged the clumsy move.

"Knock it off, Charlie."

His brother ran at him with his arms wide, and as fast as Dustin was, he couldn't get out of the way of his brother's tackle. Dustin hit the ground hard, the breath whooshing out of his lungs as Charlie's fist connected with his jaw. Lights exploded in Dustin's vision and then it all went red as he knocked Charlie off him and tried to pin his brother. Dustin and Charlie rolled around the parking lot, fighting for the upper hand, when the high-pitched chirp of a police siren broke it up.

Dustin climbed to his feet first, and when he tried to help his brother, Charlie shook him off.

Luke Jessup stepped out of the cruiser in his sheriff's uniform, and nodded at Dustin. "Everything okay?"

"Yeah, Luke, just a little brotherly bonding," Dustin said, shooting Charlie a meaningful look.

"Definitely. Been a long time, and I just wanted to show Dustin I could still take his ass down, just like when we were kids."

Luke crossed his arms over his wide chest. "How about you take the wrestling matches home? Less likely to get run over that way."

"Absolutely, Luke," Dustin said.

Once Luke climbed into his cruiser and was backing up, Dustin pointed a finger at Charlie. "I'm taking your ass to Mom's house."

"Bite me, you candy ass—"

Before he realized it, Dustin's fist flew and cracked his brother across the cheek. In slow motion, Charlie spun around and hit the ground out cold. He shook out his hand, disgusted with himself and Charlie. He hadn't hit anyone since he was in high school…the last time his dad had come at him and he'd knocked his ass out too.

With a resigned sigh, he slid his arms under Charlie's armpits and dragged him around to the passenger side of his car.

"You're lucky I love you. Dumbass."

Chapter 16

Just before eleven, Rylie stepped out of Will's truck and let him walk her to the door. They'd gone to dinner at a little Mexican restaurant in Placerville and then to a movie. Will had reached for her hand halfway through, but hadn't pushed for anything more. Rylie liked that about him. He wasn't pushy, bossy, or demanding.

And yet, Dustin, who embodied all those things, wasn't far from her thoughts all night.

"I had a nice time," she said, truthfully. Dinner was pleasant, and Will was funny and sweet.

"Me too."

They stopped outside the glass door and Will leaned over, brushing her lips lightly. It wasn't earth shattering, but still...

"Can I call you?" he asked.

Rylie nodded, despite the tiny voice that whispered through her, *why bother*? It was clear that she didn't have any chemistry with Will, but she didn't want to hurt his feelings.

Or think about who she did have it with.

Will's smile flashed in the porch light. "Well, good night then."

"Night."

He got into his truck and she stepped inside the pool house before locking the glass door behind her. She hobbled back to her bedroom, wincing with every move. She should have known better than to go out in shoes she hadn't even broken in yet. Her feet were aching and she could tell several blisters had popped up.

Rylie flipped on the bedroom light and then sat down on the bed. She unlaced the heels and hissed as she pulled them off and saw the angry blisters on the back of her ankles and the side of her foot. Once the heels had been kicked to the side, she reached behind and unzipped the tight dress, peeling it down her body with a deep, relieved breath. Standing in her bra and underwear, she stretched out her back and thought about the pool outside and the adjacent hot tub. It might feel good to soak in the hot water... And she had bought that cute new suit from Torrid on clearance. Quickly she changed into the two-piece, pulling the black tankini with little white and red hearts down over her stomach. The ruffle at the bottom was adorable and the simple black high-waisted briefs were flattering, at least, in her opinion. She went to the bathroom to get a better look, and finally, piled her hair on top of her head with a pony tail holder so it wouldn't get wet.

After she'd washed her face clean of makeup, she went back outside. Gooseflesh rose on her skin as the cooler air touched her. The lights in the pool gave the water an aqua tint, and when she put her toe in, she was delighted to find the water warm. Dustin must heat it when the weather turned colder.

She stepped into the water, gritting her teeth at the initial sting of her feet. Several seconds ticked by and the pain eased. She glided through the water with a sigh, loving the peaceful chirp of crickets. An owl hooting. The sound of a car coming up the drive.

The crunch of wheels on gravel startled her and she lifted on her tiptoes to see Dustin's car pulling in next to hers.

Rylie ducked down when she heard his car door opening and closing and footsteps against the ground. Another door opened and heavy grunting. Dustin came into the light, dragging something...no, someone, toward one of the lounge chairs. He hefted, who Rylie recognized as his brother, Charlie, onto the chair and stood over him for a moment, his arms crossed.

When he started for the stairs that led up to the main house, she realized he hadn't noticed her. She'd lucked out....

"You aren't going to leave him there, are you?" she called.

He stopped and turned her way. His clothes were rumpled and his hair mussed. When he stepped into the light above her porch, Rylie licked her lips at how out of sorts he was. When he was dressed to the nines he was hot, but this?

This was sex on a stick.

"Believe me, this is the least he deserves." He cocked his head a second at her, then walked into the pool house. Before she even launched a protest, he was back with a large throw blanket. He spread it out over Charlie's sleeping form, and grinned at her as he came around the side of the pool to where she was. "But I guess it would be pretty shitty to let him freeze."

"I think so. What did he do?"

Dustin kicked off his shoes and socks, then bent over to roll up his jeans. "He got drunk and obnoxious. Tried to start a fight. Called me a rather nasty name."

"Wow. And you still let him crash here?"

"Well, considering I punched his lights out, I felt like I owed him at least that." He'd sat down on the edge of the pool and casually stuck his feet in. Rylie's jaw dropped.

"Oh my God, is he okay? Did you take him to the hospital?"

"Of course. They said he was fine, he'd have a black eye in the morning and a hell of a headache, but he'd live. He passed out from all the shots he took down."

Rylie winced. "Ugh. Been there."

"I know." Even in the dim light, she could see the twinkle in his eye and she blushed.

"And we never have to talk about it again."

"Fine by me." Quiet descended over them for several beats, and then he asked, "So, how was your date with Phil?"

She rolled her eyes at his obvious dig. "Will."

"Yeah, Will."

"It was good."

She had a hard time meeting his eye and he must have noticed because he asked, "But?"

"No but. I had a nice time. He's going to call."

He sent a little splash of water her way with his feet. "You don't sound thrilled."

"Of course I am. I mean… He's employed. He's funny. He's kind."

Dustin pretended to snore.

"You're a jackass."

He grinned at her, the glow of the water rippling across his face. "Oh, come on. Even you have to admit you're making it sound like good old Will is applying for a job."

"He kind of is. Relationships take work and I don't want to make any more mistakes." Swallowing past the lump in her throat, she added softly, "I can't afford to allow my heart to make all the decisions for me."

Dustin slid all the way into the pool, clothes and all, and stalked toward her. She held her hand out to ward him off, but he took her arms gently.

"I agree with you. You should make rational choices when it comes to who you date, but that's not always possible."

Her heart skittered as one of his hands lifted and his thumb traced the curve of her cheek.

"You are the kind of girl who wants forever, but you shouldn't have to settle for it. You deserve passion."

She couldn't turn away from the intensity on his face. "Passion burns out and fades. It's not what lasts."

He leaned closer to her, his voice a low rumble. "Even if you don't have passion with the guy you end up with, you should have it. At least once."

"I... I've had passion."

"Really? Please don't tell me with Asher or I'm going to fucking drown myself."

She couldn't lie to him. Rylie had been excited and flattered by Asher's attentions and enjoyed their sex life at first. But it had never been overwhelming, all consuming.

"Fine. I haven't."

"You should. Even if it doesn't last, you should know what it is like to get swept off your feet."

Before Rylie knew what was happening, Dustin had his hands on her ass and was lifting her half out of the water against him.

Literally off her feet.

"So, why not me?"

"Why not you?" she squeaked.

His mouth found the crook of her neck and he whispered against her wet skin. "Let me give you passion. One time. No strings." His lips brushed the spot below her ear and her whole body quaked. "If the answer is yes, then just kiss me, sweetheart. I'll do the rest."

* * * *

Dustin could have blamed it on the beers he'd had earlier in the night, but he hadn't even gotten a buzz. It could have been the smell of pine on the breeze or the fact he'd gone without and he was just horny.

He knew it wasn't that though. It was Rylie. The way she smiled. The way she laughed. The curves of her body and the fact that she didn't try to turn him into the prince of her dreams. She knew who he was and still saw something good there.

When he realized she wasn't moving, hadn't even said a word, he lowered her to her feet and pulled away.

"Sorry. I don't know what I was thinking. Forget I said anything."

"Then why did you say it?" she asked.

Why did she sound pissed off? "What?"

"If you didn't mean it, any of it, then why did you say it?"

He had no idea if this was an opening or if she was really that clueless. "Because I want you, Rylie. I thought I'd made that pretty clear this morning."

When her hand floated below the surface of the water and slid under his shirt, resting against his stomach, he sucked in a breath.

"No strings?" she whispered.

Was this really happening?

He covered her hand with his, flattening it across his skin.

"Not a single one."

She kept looking up at him, and he resisted the urge to haul her against him, to make up her mind for her, but he wanted her to decide. He wanted her to choose.

Me. I want her to choose me.

"Well, then..." She stood up on her toes and when her mouth was mere inches from his, she breathed, "I guess I should kiss you."

The feather light press of her lips on his was all he could handle. With a growl, he bent over, cupping the back of her head. His mouth opened and he thrust his tongue between her lips. She slipped both arms around his waist and met his kiss with fervor, pressing her body flush against his.

They stood in the water, their hands traveling over each other's bodies as their mouths melded, exploring and learning what sent their blood pressure soaring. He almost lost it when Rylie cupped his ass through his wet jeans and ran her tongue along the column of his neck.

Hauling her up and guiding her legs around his waist, he made his way toward the stairs.

"What about your brother?"

"He's fine."

She giggled, her arms wrapped around his neck as she stared into his face. "We should bring him inside the pool house."

He stalled at the bottom of the pool steps, his jaw on his chest. "I'm not bringing him inside with us—"

"Shhh, calm down. I figured he could sleep it off on the couch inside and we'd... We'd go to your room."

Dustin didn't want to tap the brakes on what was happening between them, too afraid that she was going to change her mind.

Rylie stroked his cheek, as if she could read his thoughts.

"I want you, Dustin. That's not going to change in the five minutes it takes to make your brother comfortable."

Just in case, Dustin planned to make it two.

He let her slide to her feet and climb out ahead of him. He got a good look at her cute little bathing suit as she went over to open the sliding glass door. When she walked back over, she said, "Do you need me to get his legs?" He lifted his brother up and dumped him over his shoulder, grunting at the dead weight. "I'm good."

The heat in her eyes as she watched him carry Charlie inside would be worth any neck or shoulder pain tomorrow.

Once Charlie was placed onto the couch and covered with a blanket, Dustin took Rylie's hand and led her out the door, taking long strides up the stairs. "Ouch, slow down. I've got blisters."

Dustin stopped halfway up, and glanced down at her feet, although it was hard to see. The moon barely lit the world around them, let alone the ground. "How did that happen?"

"New shoes. Hadn't broken them in yet."

Dustin gave her a deep, tender kiss. "I'll doctor you up when we get inside." "And then?"

After kissing her again, he grinned. "Then, I'm going to make you forget about everything else but me."

Chapter 17

Rylie sat up against the headboard of Dustin's bed, a stack of pillows behind her back. She was wearing nothing but one of Dustin's old T-shirts and a pair of boxers; her bathing suit was hanging up over his shower drying. He'd teasingly told her she didn't need to wear anything, but there was no way she was going to sit naked while Dustin put a band aid on her blisters.

He came out of the bathroom with a first aid kit in his hands, but Rylie was having a hard time looking away from anything but his shirtless, powerful upper body.

As if he had no idea he'd rendered her catatonic with his pecs and shoulders, he sat down on the bed by her feet.

"Okay, feet on my lap so I can get a look."

He lifted her leg up in the air and she shifted uncomfortably. She was self-conscious he'd be able to see up the leg of the boxer shorts.

But when she tried to lower her leg, he held tight to her foot. The boyish grin he shot her made her stomach do a back handspring with a twist.

"Just hold still and I'll give you a sucker afterward."

The way his eyes twinkled made her think he wasn't talking about candy and she relaxed. Pervy Dustin she was used to.

"I can do it myself, you know."

"Maybe if you're a contortionist, which I fully support by the way. However, it will just be faster and easier if I do it for you." He flipped open the lid to the kit and pulled out an ointment. "Besides, I really don't mind."

Once he'd applied the Neosporin, the relief was almost instantaneous. She sighed and sank back into the pillows behind her as she watched him put band aids over every one of her blisters.

"You're good at this. First aid, I mean. You should have been a doctor with this kind of bedside manner."

"I'm sure my mother would have loved that, but since my eldest brother went that route, I figured one doctor in the family was enough."

He cleaned up everything and took the first aid kit back to the bathroom. She heard the faucet going and had no idea what she was supposed to do. She'd never really been in this position before. Should she pose herself in a sexy way?

She tried lying on her side, her head propped up on her hand, but she felt like an idiot. The water turned off just as she decided to let her hair down. She set the hair band on the side table as he came into the room, flicking off the bathroom light.

Dustin stood just five feet away, and as she stared into his blue eyes, watching them darken, she lost her ability to breathe. It was as though the air in the room disappeared, and she felt lightheaded.

Then he crossed to the wall and turned off the bedroom light, making the room pitch black. Her breath started coming in quick spurts until the bed dipped under her as he climbed up.

"Rylie…"

"Yeah?"

"Are you scared of me?" Fingertips grazed her neck and cheek, and she swallowed.

"No, of course not. That's ridiculous."

"Then can you slow down and take a deep breath? Otherwise you're going to pass out."

She laughed breathlessly, but tried to do as he said.

"Sorry, you must think I'm such a freak."

"Not the word I'd choose." His breath fanned across her chin just before his lips grazed it. "I think you're sexy."

"Right."

She yelped as she was jerked down, flat on her back on the bed.

"Are you calling me a liar?" he teased darkly.

His hands were sliding up under the T-shirt she was wearing before she could respond, her heart pounding so hard and fast she could hardly hear what he was whispering as his mouth dipped and pressed against her stomach.

"I've thought of you right here so many times. Although, in my fantasies, you aren't wearing my clothes. You're completely naked."

The T-shirt inched up her body, exposing her breasts to the cool air and then to his warm, wet mouth. She arched off the bed with a cry as he sucked her nipple inside, swirling his tongue around the hard nub until it tingled not just there, but lower, right between her legs.

"Lift up," he commanded and she did. Her back came up and her arms went over her head as he slid the T-shirt up and off.

She tried to hold him, desperate to bring him closer so she didn't feel so exposed, but his weight was gone and she heard the soft pad of his steps away from her.

"Dustin? Where are you going?"

"I just want to see you."

"Wait!"

He opened the curtains and although it wasn't much, it was enough to have her pulling back his covers and climbing under them.

His rich chuckle drew closer. "You don't have to be shy, sweetheart. I want to see all of you."

"You can see me just fine," she said tartly.

The light caught the side of him as he bent over and she realized he'd slid his boxers down and was now completely naked, just a few feet away.

"What about you? Can you see me *just fine?*"

"I've already seen you," she said.

"So you have." He climbed under the covers and over her. His hard cock pressed against her lower abdomen, and as he took the lobe of her ear between his teeth, all her inhibitions seemed to fly out the window. Now, all she wanted to do was yank her borrowed boxers off and have nothing between them.

"Did you like what you saw?" His hips moved against her, the hot length of him stroking her. "Rylie?"

He was hardly touching her now, his mouth hovering over her skin, but his pelvis pressed harder against her.

"Yes. Yes, I liked what I saw."

"Good."

And then his mouth was traveling, kissing the inside of her elbow, the side of her breast. The blankets she'd covered herself with slid lower as he moved, dipping just below her belly button. His hands tugged the flannel cotton shorts down her hips and then his mouth was there, kissing over her, pausing just before reaching the apex of her thighs.

She was just about to ask what was wrong when she felt his finger trace the outline of the heart design she'd had shaped during her wax earlier.

"Rylie Templeton... I think I was really, *really* wrong about you."

"What... What do you mean?"

He pressed a kiss right in the center and she cried out.

"I think deep down, you've been dying to be bad."

His tongue slid up her seam, circling her clit and she panted, breathlessly admitting, "Only since I met you."

It was like a switch had been hit and he stopped talking, opening her to his mouth with his fingers. She flattened her feet against the bed, curling her toes into the sheet and mattress. Her calf muscles ached as he tongued her clit in hard fast circles, his fingers moving in and out of her with every flick, building up a wonderful pressure that had her begging for release.

Rylie reached above, holding on to a pillow as her orgasm swept from her hairline, her fingers, her toes, traveling into the center of her body. When all the tremors collided, she arched off the bed with a scream. Dustin didn't stop, didn't ease up until she was no longer shaking.

"That was...was..."

She couldn't form a coherent thought, even when she heard a drawer by her head open and close. The rip of a foil package echoed along with their heavy breathing and when his hands gripped her outer thighs and lifted her until his cock rested against her, she caught her breath.

"It about to get better. I promise."

* * * *

Dustin didn't wait, couldn't if he'd wanted to. He pressed into Rylie's core, felt the give of her muscles as she took him all the way in and once he was fully encased in her warmth, he let out a shaky breath. His eyes closed as he rocked his hips against her, barely pulling out before he was back.

Her hands came up, sliding over his shoulders and biceps and he opened his eyes to look at her. The shadows of the room danced across her face, and he watched her lashes flutter, her mouth curve into a little *O* as his body picked up speed.

"God, you feel so fucking good, Rys. I knew you would. From the first time I saw you walk past my office in a pair of those heels, your skirt dancing around your legs, all I could think of was bending you over my desk, lifting that dress up, and making you scream."

He didn't look away as her eyes rolled back, as her muscles clenched down on his dick, milking him.

His sweet little Rylie liked dirty talk.

It was the push he needed and he groaned harshly as he came, the sound of her cries drowning him out as he jerked against her again and again until he was finally spent.

Catching himself on his elbows, he leaned over her to kiss her eyelids and cheeks. It wasn't until he reached her lips that he realized his were wet.

With her tears.

"Rys? Why are you crying, honey?"

"I don't know," she gasped.

"Did I hurt you?"

She shook her head. "It was wonderful."

Satisfied that she was okay, he smiled down at her. "So…better?"

"Better than better."

"Good."

He kissed her again before climbing to his feet and heading into the bathroom to dispose of the condom and clean up. He came back into the room, and grabbed a couple of waters out of the mini fridge he kept in the corner. He crawled back into bed and handed her one.

"Thanks." She set it on the night stand and climbed out of bed. The light outside highlighted the curve of her hip and ass and his hands itched to reach out and cup it.

She disappeared into the bathroom and he downed the whole bottle of water, feeling completely satiated and relaxed. Normally, he either fell asleep after sex, or he sent the woman he was with home and then he passed out.

Tonight, he was wired. In the best way possible.

Rylie came out of the bathroom and seemed to be searching around in the dimly lit room.

"What are you doing?"

"Trying to find your boxers and T-shirt."

"What for? Frankly, I like you just as nature intended."

Her outline stilled and her head cocked to the side. "This was supposed to be a one-time thing. No strings. I figured I wasn't supposed to stay."

He sat up and got a hold of her hand, then tumbled her onto the bed. When he had her sprawled on top of him, his hand traveled down to the hip he'd been admiring, giving her a light tap.

"Considering my brother is currently passed out in your rental, I figured we'd have a sleepover."

"Are you sure—"

He cupped the back of her head and brought her mouth down to his. If he was being honest, he wasn't ready to say good-bye. The sex had been incredible and the night was young. Their one-time thing could last until the morning.

He finally let her up for air, stroking a hand down her cheek.

"If you're up for it, I thought maybe we could try again in an hour or so. I think with a little more effort on my part, I could do better."

She turned her head and caught the end of his thumb between her teeth, before kissing the tip gently. "You think so?"

"Definitely. I'm willing to try at least."

"Do or do not, there is no try."

He stared up at her with his mouth hanging open. "Did you just quote Yoda?"

"Perhaps." He kept watching her until she was squirming against him. "Uh oh. Did my nerd roots turn you off?"

"Actually," he said, both of his hands coming up to grip her butt. "I was just thinking I don't think I'm going to need an hour to get it up."

She laughed. "What do you mean?"

"I don't know, but there is something about a stacked, sexy girl who can quote *Star Wars* that just does it for me."

"Do you want to hear it in my Yoda voice?"

"No, that's going too far."

When she rolled off him, laughing uproariously, he took full advantage. By the time her mirth had melted into throaty moans, he was ready to go again.

Chapter 18

Dustin woke up slowly the next morning, stretching out his arms and legs, curling his feet until his toes cracked. Last night had been incredible, better than anything he'd ever imagined. After the third time, Rylie had curled up on top of him, her head on his chest, and told him he was amazing before falling fast asleep. He'd crashed with a smile on his face.

His eyes popped open as he realized he was alone. He turned over, then sat up, searching the room for any sign that Rylie might just be in the shower, but the boxers and T-shirt she'd borrowed were gone.

To say he was disappointed would have been an understatement.

Why? You told her it was just a one-time thing. No strings. Booty calls don't usually stay for breakfast.

Still, he was at least hoping for a little morning delight.

He climbed out of bed and took a quick shower, hoping to find Rylie at the pool house before he took off. Once he was dressed for a run, he made his way downstairs to find Charlie at the kitchen table. Charlie looked up at him with bloodshot eyes, his cheek puffy and purple, and a delicious looking yellow cake doughnut in his hand.

"What are you doing?" Dustin asked.

"Drinking coffee and eating the doughnuts your *tenant* left for you." Charlie licked his lips, and smacked them loudly. "You know, just throwing this out there, but if I had a beautiful, sexy woman who could bake like this living only five hundred feet away, I'd be taking advantage of my good fortune."

Dustin spotted the basket on the counter and walked over to check it out. Inside there were two doughnuts left and a little envelope with his name on it. He picked it up and noticed the torn seal.

With a growl, he turned and waved it at his brother. "Did you read this?"

"Noooo," Charlie dragged the word out sarcastically. "I would never snoop through your shit."

"Asshole." Dustin pulled out the little card with flowers.

Good Morning!

I made these for you as a thank you for everything you've done. Enjoy!
Rylie

As far as morning-after-amazing-sex notes, it was pretty bland, but when he took a bite of one of the doughnuts, it was like his mouth exploded. He might have even moaned as the tart yet sweet flavor took over his taste buds and danced down his throat.

He looked out the window and saw that Rylie's car was gone. He'd noticed that she took off most Sundays, but hadn't thought to ask where she went. At first he'd assumed she just went to church, but she usually didn't get back until the early evening.

I'll just have to plan something special tonight. For the doughnuts.

Holding a doughnut in each hand, he faced his brother. "How many were there before you helped yourself?"

Charlie licked his fingers obnoxiously. "I lost count after eight."

Dustin took another bite and said around the crumbling pastry, "I should have let you freeze to death."

"You effed up my face."

"You had it coming. Do you even remember last night?"

Charlie had the nerve to appear sheepish. "It might be a little foggy."

"You tried to start a fight with Asher Reid, got us kicked out of Shot Gun, and then, proceeded to wrestle with me in the parking lot."

Charlie rubbed a hand over his day-old stubble. "Fine, maybe I did deserve it."

"Yeah. You did. Now, are you going to tell me what's really going on with you? Or do you just want to keep drinking and eating your problems away?"

His brother pointed to the cupboard next to the sink. "The rest of your doughnuts are up there. I only had two and hid the rest."

"That's mature." Dustin opened the cupboard after he finished his second one, and decided to save the rest in a Tupperware. "You can talk while I put these away."

Charlie sighed loudly behind him. "Fine I didn't quit. I was fired. My boss hired his son and the little shit stole the design I was going to pitch off my desk. When I went to Mr. Hendrix and called his kid out, he told me to let it go and I said he wasn't doing him any favors by covering for the bastard. So, he fired me. Then, he blacklisted me with every other firm in the city. He fucking ruined me because he was too big of a pussy to admit that he'd raised a little no-talent asshole."

Charlie took a drink of his coffee before continuing. "Anyway, my lease was up on my place so I… I came home. I didn't know what else to do and I'm just pissed. I should have just let it go, let him have the design, but I couldn't."

Dustin poured his own cup of coffee and came to the table. "No, you couldn't. There is nothing wrong with standing up for yourself, Charlie. I'm proud of you, big brother."

"Yeah, it's great. Except now, I'm screwed."

Dustin grinned. "Maybe not."

"What?"

"Kelly, Marley, Rylie and I are restoring Buzzard Gulch and turning it into a premiere wedding venue. How would you like to be the lead architect on the project?"

Charlie's eyebrows hiked up. "My benevolent little brother is offering me a job?"

"Hey, I want the best for this project and you're here. You're a genius when it comes to buildings and it pays well. And it will give you time to figure out your next move."

Charlie cleared his throat, then nodded. "Okay. I appreciate it."

"Then it's settled. You want to go for a run with me?"

Charlie groaned and grabbed his head, as if just the thought was painful. "Hell no."

"Okay, but I guess I could grab you one of those day-old breakfast burritos with the greasy sausage and onions if I make it to town? I heard foods with lots of fat and oil are good for hangovers."

Charlie turned green around the gills. "Fuck you."

"I love you, too."

* * * *

Tayler opened the door. "Rylie! I meant to call you yesterday and forgot. Are you still looking for a place?"

"Yeah, I am," Rylie said as she stepped inside.

"I might know someone looking for a tenant. A friend of mine has a little house on a couple acres outside of town, closer to Somerset. I could give her a call."

Rylie was torn. She really did want her own place again, somewhere she could have a pet and make it her own. But that also meant moving away from Dustin.

And surprisingly, that was the only con she could come up with.

It's not as though we're together. Besides, his brother is there now. He probably can't wait to get rid of me.

"That would be wonderful. Thank you," Rylie said.

"I'll do it right now. You go do your thing."

Rylie snagged one of the biscuits from the basket and handed it to Tayler. "For the other pups."

"You are such a doll."

"Thanks, Tay."

Tayler disappeared down the hallway and Rylie headed down the row of kennels until she stopped outside of Raider's.

"Hey, handsome! You ready to come out and play with me?"

Raider jumped up and woofed, the sound echoing through the metal warehouse and creating a chain reaction. All the other dogs started baying and howling, and Rylie held a finger up to her lips.

"See what you started." She unlocked the gate of his kennel and stepped inside. Once it was secure again, she sat down and let him climb into her lap, laughing as he flopped over onto his back for belly rubs.

"You are such a nerd butt. Yes you are."

He launched himself up and gave her a half dozen doggie kisses that left her spluttering and trying to hold him off. "Ugh, baby, you need a dental bone!"

"So, I got big news," Tayler said from the other side of the kennel gate.

Rylie gave Raider his treat, and looked up at Tayler from her position on the ground. "Wow, that was fast."

"Well, I may have put in more than one good word for you, and told her about Raider. Shelly has a soft spot for him, too, and she'll rent you her place if you'll adopt Raider."

Rylie's heart started racing. "How much is rent?"

"Six fifty plus utilities. Two bedroom, two bath."

With the bonus Kelly had given her, she could easily afford it, plus with the commission she'd get from the Rolland/Marconi wedding…

"Could I see it today?" she asked.

Tayler held up a slip of paper. "Yep. She's expecting your call."

Rylie couldn't believe that anyone would rent a house with property for that cheap. "You must have put in a *really* good word."

"You bet I did. You two deserve a home together after all you've been through."

Rylie was really lucky with the people in her life. Tayler, Marley, Dustin...
The thought of telling Dustin she was leaving made her sick to her stomach. Would he even care?

Remember no strings attached? You guys are just friends. Don't blow that by having feelings.

* * * *

That evening, Dustin and Charlie went over to their mom's for dinner. Dustin was hoping with Charlie home there would be less focus on him and what was happening with his life, but no such luck.

"Charlie, what do you think of Rylie?" his mom asked slyly.

"She gorgeous, sweet, and she can bake. What's not to like?"

Charlie shot Dustin a knowing grin. Dustin wished he could kick his brother in the shin, but he was too far away.

"Well, apparently, your brother isn't interested."

Charlie covered his mouth with his napkin and coughed. "Bullshit."

Dustin fingered his steak knife, calculating the accuracy if he threw it at Charlie's smug face.

"What's this now?" his mom asked innocently.

"They hooked up last night."

Dustin stood up. "Dude, outside. I am going to give you a matching bruise on the other side."

"Dustin sit down. Your brother is just messing with you."

"He acts like a ten-year-old," Dustin snapped.

"Sit. Down," she said firmly.

Dustin sat, still shooting daggers at his brother.

"Why don't you bring Rylie by for brunch next Sunday? I'd love to meet her."

"It's not like that, Mom. We aren't dating. It was a one-time thing."

His mother's smile faded. "Oh, Dustin."

"What?"

"Dumbass," Charlie mumbled.

"Why am I the dumbass? You dumped Kenzie and she is awesome. The best you're ever going to find."

Charlie stood up menacingly and his mom shouted, "Now that is enough! Why can't we get through one meal without someone storming out or wanting to kill each other?"

"I don't know, Mom," Dustin said sarcastically. "Maybe because we all have unresolved anger issues from being beaten by Dad for years."

The words had tumbled out before he could stop them and they hung in the air like poison.

His mother seemed to visibly shake as she stood. "I am sorry that I couldn't protect you boys. I did the best I could at the time, but I love you with all my heart and I am so sorry."

"Mom, I—"

She left the room and it was just Charlie glaring at him accusingly.

"What? You're going to tell me he never hit you?"

"No. He hit me all right. Mom and me letting him wale on us for so long was the only reason he didn't take the strap to you sooner."

"Is that supposed to make me feel better? Why didn't we just leave?"

Charlie shook his head. "Because Mom signed a prenup. If they ever divorced, Dad got any kids from their union and if he wasn't around to parent us, then we went to the next Kent relative. Mom tried to find a lawyer who would take her case, but he had money and power and she was scared that she would lose us if she left. That he would make it look as though she kidnapped us. Our father was a bastard, Dustin, but he was a smart bastard."

Charlie came around the table and squeezed his shoulder. "I get you're still angry, but you've got to figure out a way to deal with it or it will eat you up inside. You don't want to end up like him, do you?"

Dustin let that sink in as Charlie left the room.

Dustin headed down the hallway toward his mother's room, and as he stood outside the door, he could hear her sobbing. Slowly, he turned the knob and found her on the bed with her face in a pillow.

He didn't say anything until he'd sat down on the bed next to her. "I guess I blamed you more than I thought."

She sniffled behind him. "You have every right to. I should never have married him."

Dustin turned her around and smiled sadly at her. "But without him, you wouldn't have four terrible sons who refuse to give you grandchildren."

She laughed a little and he put his arms around her, lifting her against him, and for the first time, he realized how slight his mother was. She'd never been particularly strong, but now that he thought about everything she'd endured and how she'd still gotten up and carried on, he realized his mother had done the best she could. Could she have done something different? Maybe, but there was no point in wondering what if. He needed to accept what had happened, to all of them, and move on.

"I'm sorry. I know you lived in hell for years longer than any of us, and I never knew why you stayed."

"One thing I learned from your father is that money is a terrifying thing if you don't have it and worse if you do."

He squeezed her. "I'm okay with never talking about him ever again."

"I think you should talk about him. And me. Maybe go to therapy."

"I tried that and it didn't really work."

"Then talk to someone you trust." She pulled away from him and cupped his cheek. "Don't hold all that pain inside, sweetheart. I did that for twenty-five years and it ate me up inside. It's only been the last two years that I've found my joy again. It's time you found yours."

Chapter 19

When Dustin got back from dinner with his mom and brother, he'd expected Rylie to already be home. Instead, it was almost nine when she pulled up. He waited fifteen minutes and picked up the cheesecake he'd defrosted, stacking the freshly washed and cut strawberries on top, and then tucking the whipped cream cylinder under his arm.

Whistling as he took the steps down to pool house, he was very much aware of his racing heart and the nervous flutters in his stomach.

Why are you freaking out? It's just two friends having dessert.

Except if she was just a friend, or one of his booty calls, he wouldn't be this out of sorts…would he?

He knocked on the glass door and watched as Rylie came down the hallway in a camisole and plaid pajama pants, her face free of makeup, and her hair thrown up in a bun.

She pulled open the door with a shy smile. "Well, this is a nice surprise. What do you have there?"

He held up the stuff in his hands. "Dessert. You up for it?"

"I'm always up for dessert." He shot her a look full of heat, and grinned when she blushed. "I didn't mean that in a dirty way."

"Too bad," he murmured, waggling his eyebrows. His nerves were slowly starting to ease being this close to Rylie. Why had he been scared to see her? Things were just the same as they ever were; sex didn't have to change that.

Rylie rolled her eyes at him. "I'll get the plates and forks."

"I need a knife to cut this thing, too. Unless you want to just eat it straight from the box."

She set the fork, plates, and knife onto the table with a shake of her head. "And contaminate the whole thing? What if you want to take some home for your brother?"

"That douche can starve. He got into the doughnuts you left me."

"Oh no! I said they were for both of you. He didn't eat them all, did he?"

Dustin set the cheesecake and berries on the table, keeping a hold of the whipped cream. "No, he left me a couple."

"Did you like them?" she asked.

"I loved them. I could have downed them all, but I wanted to savor them."

"You have more willpower than me...which is why I only kept two."

When Rylie handed him the knife, he asked, "How big do you want it?"

"Normal-sized is fine."

He slipped her slice onto one of the plates. "Berries and cream?"

"Please. You even got the good cheesecake." She scooped off a little on her finger and slipped it between her lips, wrapping them around the digit with an appreciative little moan. "I'm impressed."

Dustin tried to ignore the excitement that one little action had stirred up in his pants. "Impressed I can defrost a frozen dessert?"

"Definitely."

He chuckled. "Thanks?"

"You're welcome."

They sat down and ate their desserts in silence, Dustin trying to come up with something to say besides, *"So, you want to head back to the bedroom for round two?"*

"I'm glad things aren't weird," Rylie said.

"Why would they be?"

"You know... Sometimes when two people who are friends have... become intimate, their relationship changes. Things become tense and awkward, and I'm just glad that isn't us."

"I'm not feeling awkward at all." He opened his mouth to continue, to tell her that he was thinking that maybe it didn't need to be a one-time thing.

But then she blurted, "I found a place to rent today."

Dustin froze, trying to sound casual when it felt like he'd been kicked in the gut. "You did? Where?"

"It's a little two-bedroom outside of town. It needs some work and updating, but the owners gave me a really good deal on rent as long as I handle the upkeep on my own. And I can have a pet."

"I didn't know you wanted one." He was so thrown he didn't even recognize the monotone of his voice.

"Yeah, I've wanted one for years, but Asher wouldn't let me."

"Why didn't you ask me? I'm nothing like Asher." His tone was harsh, and he hated that he was getting emotional about this. He didn't get attached to women.

She blinked at him. "Of course, you aren't, but this was only supposed to be temporary. Besides, I thought it would be presumptuous to ask to have an animal when I'm not even paying you what this place is worth."

Dustin didn't know why he cared that she hadn't mentioned wanting an animal, but it stung him. Actually, the fact that she sounded so excited about leaving did. Maybe it was because she'd snuck out on him this morning with a half assed note and no good morning love session, but did she have to sound so damn delighted?

She was frowning at him now and he couldn't blame her. "I thought you'd be glad to get your pool house back. And with your brother here now, I figured one less person in your space, cramping your style—"

"What style is that?" he asked.

"You know, dating and all that."

"Believe me, if I'd wanted to bring someone home, you being here wouldn't have mattered." Dustin stabbed a fork into his cheesecake. He knew he was acting like a complete asshat, but he didn't know how to rein his emotions back in. "So, when do you move?"

"I…I…was going to pack up this week. I'll probably be gone by the weekend." She set her fork down and reached across the table to take his hand. "Are you seriously upset about this?"

He pulled his hand back. "No, why would I be? You were right. I got what I wanted from you and you got what you wanted. It was a mutually beneficial agreement."

He knew he was letting her think the whole goal of letting her stay here had been just to get her into bed, but he couldn't seem to shut up. It was like someone had hooked up a fireman hose to his mouth and stupidity was spraying from his lips at a hundred miles an hour.

Rylie's face lost all color and the skin around her jaw tightened. "For the record, I wasn't using you. I accepted your offer, but I gave you money and—"

"Like you said, this place is worth more than six hundred a month."

Why the hell am I being such an ass?

Her eyes shone with unshed tears. "Why are you being a jerk about this? I thought you'd want me gone."

"Why? Have I made you feel unwelcome? Like I wanted you out of here?"

Rylie shook her head slowly, confusion clouding those beautiful brown eyes. "No, you've been wonderful. It's just that I know you like your space and your women, and having to explain my presence probably affects the latter."

"Like I said, if I wanted to bring someone home to fuck, they wouldn't care who was sleeping in the pool house."

Dustin watched the confusion and hurt melt away, replaced by fury. "Right. I forgot that you are God's gift and women would sell their soul to be with you."

"I'm sure some have."

"You're a jackass," she snapped. "Get out."

"It's my pool house."

"That I'm renting, per our verbal agreement, which means that you need to leave." When he didn't move fast enough, she picked up a handful of her cheesecake and threw it at him, smacking him right in the chest.

It would have been comical if he didn't know that the tremble in her lip meant any second now, she was going to crumble.

I just need to apologize. Two simple words.

He got up from the table, a thousand things perched on the edge of his tongue, among them an apology, but they wouldn't come. Instead, he just turned and walked out, cursing himself the whole way home.

* * * *

Hours later, Rylie sat up with a start, groggily glancing around the darkened bedroom. It felt as though she'd just fallen asleep, and after picking up her phone to check the time, she realized it wasn't far off. It was just after one in the morning, and after Dustin had left, she'd tossed and turned until at least eleven forty-five.

She still couldn't figure out what was wrong with him. She'd expected calm acceptance, maybe a little giddiness. She'd hoped for disappointment that she was leaving, but not anger. Not treating her like she didn't matter and he couldn't wait for her to disappear.

The sound of squealing tires and spraying gravel outside made her jump. Thoughts of Dustin pushed aside, she fled the comfort of the bedroom for the front of the pool house. Sleep still clouded her consciousness, which is why she didn't notice the window at first. Not until a sharp shard of glass sliced into the bottom of her foot, so deep she was sure it scraped bone.

She screamed and stumbled to the side, gripping the counter as she lifted her foot up off the ground.

"Rylie!" Dustin shouted from outside, just before the motion light flicked on.

How did he get here so fast?

Noticing the shimmering slivers glittering in the light, she hollered, "Don't come in here! There's glass everywhere."

Dustin and Charlie stopped outside the frame of the glass door, which had been obliterated by something.

"What the fuck happened?" Charlie asked.

Dustin stepped inside before Rylie could protest again and she heard the crunch under his feet. Rylie hobbled back to where the light switch was, and once she flipped it, she gasped at the carpet Dustin stood on in his sneakered feet. With the light shining in, it hadn't looked that bad, but now she could see it everywhere. Whatever had shattered the window had worked like a bomb, projecting glass every which way.

"Are you hurt?" Dustin growled, advancing around the counter toward her.

Wincing at the throb in her foot, she lifted it to get a better look and had to crane her neck to see. A shard of glass stuck out about a quarter of an inch, embedded deep in the tissue of the sole of her foot. Blood oozed around the edges, covering her pad and toes like thick, red paint.

"I stepped on it," she said faintly, already woozy.

Dustin kneeled and lifted her foot. "Charlie, call the cops. Tell them to send paramedics."

He grabbed a towel from the counter and gave her a grim look. "This is going to hurt, but just stay still, okay?"

She nodded, closing her eyes, but as he slid the glass out, she screamed. It was so much worse coming out, as if it was ripping apart her tissue, shredding it to pieces.

"I know, honey, I know." After he set the glass on the counter, he pressed the towel against the bottom of her foot. "I think you're going to need stiches. That son of a bitch went all the way in."

She bit her lip as he pressed against the wound. "Did… Did you see what did it? What broke the window?"

"No." He stood up and lifted her onto the edge of the counter. He tied the towel around her foot. She winced at the pain, but his fingers stroking her forehead as he brushed her hair back from her face made her feel slightly better.

"What were you doing down here?" she asked.

"I heard the tires squealing, and came down to check on you. We'd made it to the bottom of the stairs when I heard you scream."

"I… I woke up, but I didn't know why. Not until I came out here."

Dustin wrapped his arms around her and she hugged him close, burying her face in his neck as the dam of tears broke. She had woken up to a nightmare of fear and pain and she had no idea why. Who would break the glass door?

She was still crying when Charlie came up beside them.

"The cops are on their way, but I found this on the floor. Figured you might want to see it before they do."

Rylie pulled back in time to see Dustin take something from his brother, a small rectangle. On the back in black sharpie was a single word.

WHORE.

The blood chilled in her veins. "What is it?"

Dustin handed it to her, and when she turned it over, her stomach churned.

It was a photo of Dustin and Rylie in the pool last night. They were kissing, her arms locked around his shoulders. Seeing one of her most treasured, intimate moments captured and used to terrorize her brought bile up the back of her throat.

"It was tied to a brick. It's what he used to smash the window," Charlie said.

"He? Who?" Then it struck Rylie who Charlie meant. "You think Asher did this?"

"It doesn't matter," Dustin growled.

"Of course, it matters. If he did do this, then he destroyed your home because of me. This is my fault—"

His arms tightened around her. "This is *not* on you. The door can be replaced. We need to get you to the hospital and get your foot taken care of."

"You're going to want to stay to talk to the cops," Charlie said.

Rylie's head was spinning too fast to follow the rest of their conversation. Asher hadn't bothered her since the flowers. She'd ignored every call, had told him that nothing he said would get them back together. There was no reason for her to follow them. To take pictures and break a window. None of it made sense.

"Hey, hey. You okay?" Dustin asked, peering into her face.

She shook her head, just before everything went dark.

* * * *

"I can't believe I fainted," Rylie said hours later.

Dustin grinned as he carried her up the stairs of his house. He'd held Rylie as she passed out, terrified she'd hit her head on the counter. Then he'd taken her back to the bedroom and laid her down on the bed to wait for the paramedics. He'd stayed with her, checked the cut on her foot and though it was deep, the bleeding had stopped.

Once reinforcements had shown up, Rylie had come to as the EMT was examining her wound. They'd offered to drive her to the hospital to get her stitches, but she'd balked at the expense of an ambulance ride. He'd offered to pay and of course, that had only earned him a scowl.

He'd driven her to Marshal Hospital in Placerville, and after several hours of waiting, and a lot of hand squeezing, they'd headed back here. Dustin was shocked she hadn't passed out again after they'd given her a pain med in her IV. She'd been loopy but awake the whole drive.

"I was impressed with your constitution. I almost lost it when they were sewing up your foot."

"I was just glad I couldn't feel or see it." She laid her cheek against his shoulder with a sigh. "These pain meds they've got me on are magic."

Dustin set her down on his bed and pulled the covers back so she could get in. She turned on her side, and he was able to get the blankets over her without hurting her foot.

Tucking the comforter under her chin, he said, "When the pharmacy opens, I'll grab your pain meds and antibiotics, but the doctor said you should be good until then."

"Mmmhmmm."

Dustin's hand brushed over the tear stains on her cheek and he was so glad she hadn't cried for long.

"Hey," Charlie called from the doorway. "How's the patient?"

Dustin stood up and faced his brother. "She's a little loopy right now, but no surgery was needed. Just pain meds, antibiotics, and lots of rest."

"I can sing though, right?" she mumbled.

"All you want." Dustin snorted. "Apparently, they gave her the good stuff."

"Lucky girl." Charlie shot Dustin a meaningful look. "We'll talk in the morning."

Dustin nodded, and when Charlie disappeared down the hallway, Dustin closed and locked the door. He'd considered sleeping in one of the guest rooms, but he didn't want to be that far away from her.

He got undressed, leaving on his boxers, and crawled under the covers next to her. He pulled her against him and she snuggled close, sighing against his chest.

"I am really sorry I'm so much trouble."

Dustin kissed her forehead softly. "Didn't you know? I love trouble."

"I did hear that somewhere."

His fingers stroked down her back as he waited for her to fall asleep, his mind racing as he thought about what could have happened if Asher had wanted to do more than scare her. What if he'd broken the window, gone inside, and hurt her? There was no guarantee he would have heard her if she'd screamed, and if anything more had happened to her, he didn't think he could live with himself. Imagining a world without Rylie in it was impossible. Her smile. Her voice. Her laugh.

It was as though he couldn't remember what life was like before he really knew her and he never wanted to go back there.

"Talk to me," she whispered.

He rubbed a hand across his face, banishing his dark thoughts. "What do you want me to talk about?"

"Anything." Her soft voice was slurring slightly and he wondered how much longer she was going to stay awake.

"I loved the doughnuts."

"I knew you would."

He chuckled, then sobered. "The cheesecake was supposed to be a thank-you, but I guess I kind of ruined it, huh?"

"You were a dick."

"Yes, I was."

"Why?"

What exactly did he tell her? That he liked her? That he was starting to think she wasn't just another one of his hookups?

She'd never believe it, even hopped up on painkillers. She'd think he was feeding her a line.

"I guess I was just surprised," he said, honestly. "I was getting used to having you around."

"Just because I don't live here doesn't mean we won't still see each other. We still work together." She yawned against the front of his chest. "We're friends."

Dustin knew all that, but there was something different about having Rylie so close. Knowing that he could just walk down the steps to get a glimpse of her. That she'd pop through the door in the morning to say hi to Victoria and he'd sometimes stand on the stairs and listen to them gossip at the table.

Well, Victoria would gossip and Rylie would listen, which was just another thing to like about her. She didn't spread stuff around like the rest of town.

"I know we're friends, but it won't be the same with you living across town." His arm squeezed her affectionately as he added, "I'll miss your little noises when something tastes good. The way you roll your eyes when I annoy you. But I think I'm going to miss your zombie walk when you first wake up most of all."

Her hand half-heartedly smacked his chest. "Be nice."

"I thought I was being nice."

"You called me a zombie."

"I also said I would miss you."

She grew so quiet he thought she might have fallen asleep. Only a few moments later, she mumbled, "I'll miss you too."

Dustin traced his fingers from her temple to her cheek, until the soft rustle of her deep breathing fell from her lips. It was another thing he'd learned about Rylie; she had this funny little snore that almost had a wheeze on the end. On any other woman, he'd have found it annoying, but on Rylie it was…cute.

Yep, it was official. Four weeks of living next door to this woman and he'd lost his damn mind.

Chapter 20

On Saturday, Rylie sat in the front seat of Dustin's car, grumbling as she stared out the window and trees whizzed past.

"I was okay to drive, you know. I can totally work the pedals with my left foot."

Dustin shot her an annoyed glance, which she'd gotten used to the last six days. "And I said that I did not want you pulling out your stitches again. Do not aggravate me, woman."

Rylie huffed, her own irritation hitting Defcon Five. The day after she'd sliced her foot, she'd tried to walk down the steps of his house and pulled out a couple of stitches. Dustin had rushed her to Dr. Turner's office in town. He'd been quick about sewing her back up, and told her to keep off it for a day or two. After that, she was good to use her crutches.

When they got back from the doctor's office, though, Dustin had brought her a laptop and a stack of magazines and told her to stay in bed. That she could just holler if she needed something. She'd argued that she'd needed to pack up her stuff, but he'd simply shot her one of those dark scowls and left the room. He'd been hovering ever since.

"You're being ridiculous," she said for the hundredth time that week.

He pulled down the driveway of her new house and parked next to Luke Jessup's truck. Marley and Luke had helped Dustin and her pack up her stuff yesterday, but it had gotten too dark to drive the boxes over.

If she was being honest, having Dustin's undivided attention hadn't been so bad, and Rylie had been happy to share a bed with him for one more night. They didn't do more than talk and sleep, but she'd enjoyed the sensation of waking up in his arms and was going to miss it tonight.

Once the car was in gear, he turned in the seat and leveled her with a stern expression. "Now, I am going to carry you inside and you will sit where I put you. You will not try to get up and help; just pretend you're the overlord and we are your serfs."

"God, do you ever get tired of being bossy? Why did we bring my crutches if you were going to carry me around everywhere?"

"Because tomorrow you are on your own, but today, I will brook no disobedience," he said in a very bad Sean Connery voice.

"Maybe you're the overlord," she grumbled.

Dustin made a sound as though he was cracking a whip before he got out of the car and came around. He knew she was perfectly capable of using her crutches, but for some reason, he seemed to like taking care of her.

Which was okay with her. For one more day, at least.

Dustin lifted her out of the car and she wrapped her arms around his neck, her fingers traveling across the warm skin. A dull ache settled in her chest. They had one more week of wedding preparations and then that was it. They wouldn't be neighbors, partners, or lovers... Would they still be friends without the close proximity?

She had her doubts and it made her grip on him tighten.

"You afraid I'm going to drop you?" he asked.

"No, I trust you."

Dustin's blue eyes narrowed as they reached the front door, and she wondered what he was thinking. Before she could ask, someone opened the door for them. Marley stood in the opening wearing a dirty pair of jeans, a *Supernatural* T-shirt, and her blond hair thrown up in a haphazard bun.

"Ready to see your new home?" Marley asked.

Dustin stepped past Marley, and Rylie's jaw dropped.

"Surprise!"

Rylie's gaze swung around the fully furnished living room, and into the smiling faces of all her friends. Marley and Luke. Kelly and the bridesmaids from Something Borrowed, including Wendy. Tayler and the staff at the shelter. Dustin's brother, Charlie, stood off to the side with Kenzie.

"What... What is going on?"

"This is your housewarming party!" Marley said.

Rylie looked up at Dustin, completely overwhelmed. "Did you do this?"

He shrugged as he set her down on a soft gray couch. It was almost exactly like the one she'd picked out from the *Better Homes and Gardens* magazine he'd given her. Her eyes narrowed on the coffee table, and scanned the rest of the room, noting all the items that were all too familiar.

She should have been suspicious when he'd brought that stack of magazines to his room and set them on the bed. He'd told her, if she was bored, to circle what she'd put in her dream home and like an idiot, she'd gone along with it.

The only things that weren't new were her father's old recliner, the antique coffee table that had been her grandmother's, and the wall of photos that her friends must have pulled out of storage.

Tears blurred her vision. "I can't accept any of this."

Dustin squatted down and lowered his voice so only she could hear. "I'd told Kelly to give my bonus and commission to you because you've done most of the work and you deserve it."

Rylie's eyes widened. "But that's not true!"

He covered her fluttering hands with his. "I don't need the money, Rylie, but you do. So, technically, *you* bought all the furniture. Since she'd already cut me the check, instead of handing the money over, I furnished your house."

"I... I don't know what to say."

"How about...*thank you, Dustin.*"

What she wanted to do was throw her arms around him and kiss him with everything she'd been holding in her heart, but she couldn't. Especially not in front of a room full of people.

"Thank you, Dustin," she whispered. Clearing her throat past the lump of emotion, she added loudly, "This is amazing. Thank you. This is the best surprise I've ever had."

"A bonus surprise is Raider is in your bedroom, taking a nap in his crate. He was a little overwhelmed by all the strangers, so I gave him a calming tablet," Tayler said.

Rylie's eyes filled with tears and she sniffled. "This is so *nice!*"

"You deserve better than nice, Rylie," Dustin said softly.

Her hands gripped Dustin's and she didn't want to let go. "Thank you."

"What are friends for?"

She stared into his deep blue eyes, searching for something more. This week, she'd thought maybe there'd been a growing intimacy and closeness, but he hadn't tried anything. Even his pervy comments had been at a minimum.

But if there was really nothing between them, then why was he being so generous to her? He didn't even offer breakfast to his sex partners... Victoria hadn't been shy about sharing that.

"Come on, I want to show you the rest," Marley said, holding out her hand.

Dustin frowned. "I don't think she should be walking."

Marley huffed at him. "The stitches have had four days and she was hobbling around yesterday. Don't be such a mother hen."

Dustin got up from the couch with a sigh. "I'll get her crutches from the car."

"I think I'll be okay. I can limp," Rylie said.

Rylie let Marley help her to her feet despite Dustin's protests, and leaned on her friend as they explored the kitchen. She couldn't wait to see the rest of it.

The kitchen was big enough to cook comfortably without banging her elbow on something and the stainless-steel appliances were new, except for the mixer that sat on the counter next to the fridge. Rylie calculated the expense in her head and knew that Dustin's bonus in no way covered all the furniture plus appliances. She was going to have to pay him back; there was just no other way.

The light-colored cupboards and daisy wallpaper were new and complemented the oak table with four chairs that sat in the breakfast nook. The little dining area sat before three large windows with gauzy yellow curtains drawn over them.

"It's perfect."

Marley squeezed her arm, and whispered, "Dustin planned everything and we all got together this week when we could. All the Something Borrowed girls put up the wallpaper and Dustin, Charlie, and Luke updated the cabinet doors. I have to admit, there might be more to him than just a manwhoring asshat."

Rylie giggled. "That's a big concession coming from you."

"I was just happy he was there for you." Marley's expression darkened as she added, "And I'm glad you finally got that restraining order on Asher."

Rylie nodded. The police hadn't been able to prove he was the one who'd thrown the brick, but Dustin and Luke had convinced her that at least the RO would give them more to work with.

"Me too. I just hope it doesn't make things worse."

"It won't, I'm sure." Marley squeezed her side and steered her around a corner. "Come check out the laundry room. Someone has a new washer and dryer!"

"Seriously?" Rylie hobbled along with Marley into the little room off the kitchen and wished she could dance. The silver set was exactly what she would have purchased, down to the brand. It was the first time she'd ever had her own stuff and for some reason, it made her want to break down and cry again.

"Are you okay?" Marley asked.

"Yeah, I just… I've never been on my own before and it's big."

"There's more. Do you think you can handle it?"

Rylie couldn't wait.

"Has that guy you went out with called?" Marley asked as they headed down the hallway toward the bedrooms a few minutes later.

Rylie glanced back toward the living room where Dustin was, but couldn't see him. "Yeah, he asked me out again, but I told him I hurt my foot so it would be a while. He wanted to come over and cook for me and I said I'd let him know."

When they reached what would be her bedroom, she barely looked at the comforter set as she hobbled toward Raider's cage. He started barking excitedly as soon as he saw her and she sat down to open the door. He burst forward, licking her as he whined excitedly.

"Aw, hey my baby. Are you so glad to be home? I know I am."

Marley clicked her tongue. "Poor dude. I can't believe someone did that to him."

Rylie kissed his nose and crooned, "Some people are just assholes. Yes they are."

"Let's get back to you. Why don't you want to set up another date with Will? I thought you liked him."

Rylie made a face. Having friends was a blessing and a curse sometimes. "I do. I just don't think I *like* like him."

Marley sat on the bed and harrumphed. "This wouldn't have to do with someone we both know, would it?"

Rylie shook her head, although she couldn't really meet Marley's eye. "Like I said before, Dustin and I are just friends and I want it to stay that way."

* * * *

Dustin was in the kitchen, putting away the food that was left over from the party, when Marley came into the room. Luke and Marley were the only ones left, and Dustin was surprised that Marley was seeking him out. Although their relationship was less hostile than it used to be, they still weren't exactly pals.

"I want to thank you for everything you've done for Rylie."

Dustin leaned back against the kitchen counter and folded his arms over his chest. "You don't have to. She's thanked me enough."

Marley gave him a curt nod. "I just want to make sure you know how wonderful she is. And that if you do anything to hurt her, I will chop off your penis and pickle it."

Dustin choked on a laugh, realizing that if she thought he was mocking her, she might just follow through. "As much as I admire the imagery, you don't have anything to worry about. Rylie and I are just friends."

"Yeah, she fed me that BS too, but I've seen the way you watch her when she's not looking. You feel *something* for her. I'm just not sure what, and I don't want you leading her on and breaking what's left of her heart. Rylie is one of those bright, bubbly people who sees the good in everyone and if you squash that in her, I will come after you with a fury that you've only imagined."

Dustin didn't get angry or tell her to mind her own business, which he considered progress. She was just looking out for her friend, something Dustin could fully understand. Rylie brought out that kind of protective instinct in him too.

"I know the kind of guy I am and so does Rylie. Trust me, she doesn't want to get involved with me."

Marley opened her mouth to say more, but Luke came into the room. "Hey, I just wanted to say that Rylie looks pretty wiped, so maybe it's about time we take off?"

"Yeah, it's getting late," Marley said. "I'll go say good-bye to Rylie."

Marley shot him a warning look from behind Luke's back before she disappeared into the living room.

"You need a ride, Dustin?" Luke asked.

Dustin held his hand out to Luke to shake. "I appreciate it, but I'm okay. I'm just going to make sure she's all settled in and then call my brother."

"Well, good job. I don't know Rylie well, but she seemed really happy with everything."

"Thanks for helping out, Luke."

"Anytime. And hey, if you play poker, some of us get together every week. If you're interested, I'll text you the details."

Dustin was more than a little stunned that Luke would invite him into his boys' club. He'd figured the guy had only agreed to help out Marley.

But he'd learned that he genuinely liked Luke. He was a decent guy. "Let me know when and where and I'll try to make it."

"Will do."

They walked into the living room, where Rylie was curled up on the couch with a blanket, her new dog lying on his back behind her legs.

"You're letting him up on your new couch?" Dustin asked. His parents had never let him have a pet growing up, because they carried parasites. He'd traveled so much up until moving back to Sweetheart that it hadn't seemed fair to have one.

He still wasn't sure if he had one, though, he'd let it up on the furniture.
Rylie scratched Raider's chest. "It's his house too, and he likes to snuggle."
So do I.

Dustin almost laughed aloud as the thought crossed him mind. He couldn't believe he was jealous of a dog.

"Well, y'all have a good night," Luke said, a bit of his Texas twang coming through.

Marley waved at them as Luke led her out the front door. "Call me tomorrow."

Once the door was closed, Dustin sat down on her other side and put his arm around her shoulder. She leaned into him, placing her face against his chest, and he pulled her a little closer.

"How are you feeling?"

In response, she yawned loudly. "Tired, and my foot is a little sore."

He didn't tell her she overdid it, although it was touch and go for a minute there. "Want me to get you something for the pain?"

"Nah, I already took one a few minutes ago."

His hands brushed over her shoulder, loving how good she fit against him. He'd gotten used to touching her whenever he wanted this week. Taking her hand, slipping his arms around her. He wasn't ready to give that up.

A low woof drew his attention to her new pet, who had lifted his head. The dog's gaze was focused on his hand on Rylie's shoulder.

"Is Fido going to take off a limb if I move?"

"No, he just wants you to pet him and not me," she teased.

Dustin couldn't miss her eager expression and knew she wanted him to make friends with the dog.

"Hey, dude," Dustin said, leaning across Rylie's lap. "Don't eat me."

He held his hand out, fingers curled under in case he decided he was hungry. Instead of teeth, his hand was bathed in a long pink tongue until he started rubbing Raider's cheek. He leaned into the scratches and something warm spread through Dustin's body. "You like that, huh?"

Raider tried climbing over Rylie's legs to get closer to him, and she laughed. "Do I need to move and give you two a moment alone?"

"Nah, I should probably let you get some rest." Dustin gave Raider one last pet, and sat back, preparing to stand.

When Rylie's arms went around his waist, he jumped in surprise. As he looked down into her eyes, he noticed she seemed almost embarrassed at practically tackling him.

"I've kind of gotten used to sleeping with you this week. I don't know how I'll do it alone tonight."

Dustin's whole body came alive at her admission and he scrambled for a response that didn't have a sexual innuendo attached to it. What he wanted to say was he felt the same way, except he wanted more than just sleep, more than one night. He didn't know what it meant but he wanted…more.

He must have taken too long to respond, because Rylie pulled away, her cheeks red. "I'm sorry. I guess if Raider sleeps on the bed, I won't be able to tell the difference."

"Are you saying I'm easily replaced by a dog?" Dustin asked, offended.

"No, but it isn't fair to ask you to babysit me anymore. And if you have to get home, he's the next best thing."

Dustin glanced at Raider. "I always figured you for more of a toy breed type of girl."

"Nope, I'm all about what's under the surface, and Raider is the best dude in the world." The dog's thin tail started smacking the couch at her high-pitched croon.

"So, be straight with me. Do you want me to stay?" He hated that he almost held his breath as he waited for her to respond. Something had happened between them this week that had nothing to do with sex or friendship. Dustin had enjoyed being with Rylie, the intimacy of sleeping with her and waking up next to her. Of talking to her and making her laugh. He didn't just like Rylie; it seemed as though he needed her.

Which was a crazy, emotional trap he'd vowed to never step in. Words like *need* set you up for vulnerability and he wasn't looking for that. He wanted the spontaneous, freewheeling life he'd always lived.

Yet when Rylie turned those chocolate brown eyes up to meet his, he forgot all about what he wanted.

"Yes. Please stay."

He knew that it wasn't sexual, that there was no way he was getting laid tonight. Two months ago, that would have been the deal breaker but tonight, he didn't care.

There was no one and nowhere he'd rather be than with this woman in his arms.

"Sure. Sure I'll stay."

Chapter 21

On Tuesday morning, Rylie was a nervous wreck. Tonya and her fiancé were scheduled to arrive today, four days before their wedding, and Rylie was hoping that the two of them would mesh as well in person as they did over the phone and via e-mail.

Someone rapped on her door, and she got up from her chair with a grimace. Her foot was still sore and she prayed that it would be completely healed by the time Saturday came around. She didn't want to be limping down the aisle.

Not to mention she was hoping to dance with Dustin at the reception.

She knew it was crazy to think about that. She'd woken up on Saturday to find him gone, and she'd driven herself into work to meet with Kelly and a new bride. Besides a few text messages, she hadn't heard anything from Dustin until he'd come into work yesterday, acting as if everything was same old same old between them.

The man was driving her crazy and it was her own damn fault for seeing things that weren't there.

When the person knocked again, Rylie realized she'd gotten lost in thought and called, "Come in."

The door opened and Dustin stepped inside, dressed in a green dress shirt and khakis, the most casual she'd ever seen him in the office.

Also, the sexiest, in her opinion.

I need to stop. I slept in the same bed with the man for almost a week and he didn't even try to cop a feel. Obviously, he's over whatever was between us.

"I figured you were probably nervous and thought you could use something to calm your nerves. And since you don't like wine, I figured this would be way better," Dustin said.

He held up a bottle of whisky and two glasses, and she gasped. "Are you crazy? I'm not drinking before meeting our client for the first time!"

Dustin set the stuff down on her desk and took her shoulders in his hands. "You need to calm down. Everything is going to be fine."

"What if she gets here and hates everything?"

"She okayed it via e-mail, so why would she do that?"

"I don't know. Because she might be one of those crazy celebrity kids?"

He pulled her against him, rubbing his big hands down her back. "Breathe."

She let out a shaky breath and relaxed against him, her body suddenly tingling with every stroke. "That's really nice."

Rylie waited for his dirty comment but it never came. Her eyes flew open and she pulled away, staring up at him in bewilderment. "Are you feeling okay?"

"Yeah, why?"

She frowned. Since she'd gotten hurt, Dustin had been her rock, and it was wonderful, but he'd stopped treating her like a woman he desired and it bothered her.

Why? I wanted him to stop coming on to me and after our fabulous night together, things were supposed to cool off. This was a good thing.

But if she truly believed that, then why was she so frustrated with their current relationship?

Rylie's cell rang before she could ponder her flip-floppiness further, and when she saw the caller ID, she grimaced. It was the second time Will had called her, and she needed to talk to him, to let him know that she just wasn't interested, but with Dustin standing there she didn't want him to get the wrong idea. Like she was turning down the date for him.

"Is that your boyfriend?" Dustin asked.

Rylie's startled gaze jerked up to meet his. "Yes. I mean no. He's not my boyfriend."

Was it just her imagination, or did he look a little put out?

"Go ahead and answer it. I've got plans tonight, so can we make our dinner with Tonya and Blake at six instead of seven?"

"Um, sure."

"Great."

He walked out of her office as if he hadn't just dropped a giant bomb on her, and her chest tightened. What were his *plans*? Now that she wasn't living next door was he having overnight guests again?

She answered Will's call, swallowing past the lump in her throat. "Hey, Will."

"Hey, Rylie. I know you're at work, but I was thinking about dinner. Do you prefer chicken or beef?"

Rylie had no idea what he was talking about at first and then it struck her. He'd called her on Sunday when she was still half asleep and asked if he could come over and cook her dinner on Tuesday.

Which was tonight.

God, she was a complete jerk. "Oh, Will, my client is flying in today and we're supposed to go to dinner. I am so sorry I forgot."

Silence stretched across the line and she checked to make sure he hadn't hung up. "Will?"

"Yeah, I'm here. You got a work thing. I understand. But just so we're clear, are you asking me for a raincheck? Or is this your nice way of blowing me off?"

She hesitated, but she needed to be honest with him. "No, I don't think so. I mean, I'm not blowing you off or asking for a raincheck. I like you—"

"There's really no need to give me the *it's not you it's me* speech. I get it. Some things just aren't meant to be."

The bitter, almost angry tone was out of character, but then again, she'd probably hurt his feelings.

"I'm so sorry," she said.

"Yeah, me too. Bye, Rylie."

He ended the call and she stared down at her phone. It was the right thing to do, for both of them, but she still felt queasy. She didn't like causing anyone pain.

Another knock on her door and she turned, jumping when she recognized Tonya.

"You're here!"

"Rylie." The gorgeous young African American woman had long, wavy hair and smooth, beautiful skin. She crossed the room in no time, and wrapped Rylie up in a tight hug. Rylie had studied everything about Tonya, but had forgotten that she was six foot one without her heels. When she pulled away, Rylie had to look up at her. "I am so happy to finally meet you."

"Likewise. How was your flight?"

Tonya released a tired breath. "Long, but worth it. I was so excited to get here and see in person everything you and Dustin have planned."

"Where is your fiancé?" Rylie asked.

"He went on ahead to say hello to Dustin. I only caught a glimpse of him, but whoa. That is one good looking man." Tonya tapped her finger to her red lips. "That's just between us though."

Rylie smiled, although the mention of Dustin brought back the sick feeling again. "Do you want to go and rest? Dustin arranged for you and Blake to stay at Castle Vineyards, in the honeymoon suite. Or we could walk the grounds and show you where everything is."

Tonya smiled sheepishly. "To be honest, I'd love to grab a drink and get to know you. I love Blake, but talking wedding stuff with him is like him trying to talk sports with my mother. Nothing but blank stares. Unless you've already gotten started without me?"

Rylie cocked her head at Tonya's grin and followed her gaze….

To the whisky bottle on Rylie's desk.

Rylie's cheeks flamed and she stammered, "That's…um… It's not mine. Dustin thought I was too nervous about meeting you and tried to give me something to relax."

"Oh, honey, I'm just playing. I prefer margaritas anyway." Tonya looped her arm through Rylie's and led her out of her office.

"What is this hitch in your giddy-up?"

Rylie realized Tonya had noticed her limp. "I cut the bottom of my foot last week, but it should be fine by Saturday."

"Ouch! What a terrible place to get sliced."

"Yeah, it's definitely been a hindrance."

They bumped into Blake and Dustin in the hall, and although Rylie had only seen pictures, the six foot seven basketball player for the Los Angeles Lakers was seriously smoking hot. He'd retired at the end of last season at thirty-five, nine years older than his fiancée, but Rylie thought he looked the same age.

"Tonya, this is Dustin," Blake said, holding his hand out to Rylie. "And you're Rylie?"

"Yes. Good to meet you, Blake." Giggling as his hand engulfed hers, she added, "I gotta say, you are so much bigger than you look on television."

The wide smile revealed even white teeth. "I get that a lot."

Tonya squeezed her arm and waved her free hand in a shooing motion. "Well, we're going to have some girl time, and will meet you two for dinner later."

Blake threw up his hands, addressing Dustin. "See, didn't I tell you? She's sick of me shrugging when she asks if I like ivory or white better."

"No, I just know in four days I'm going to have you all to myself for two whole weeks." Tonya leaned up and gave her fiancé a long, lingering kiss. Rylie looked away, only to catch Dustin's gaze. He smiled at her and there was something warm in his blue eyes, something she'd never seen before.

"Have fun, baby," Blake murmured.

"We will." Tonya took her by the arm and led her out the door.

* * * *

Hours later, Dustin sat next to Rylie at Bow Ties Italian Restaurant. It was torture to be so close to her and not touch her.

Across from them, Blake and Tonya held hands, kissed, and practiced being as nauseating as possible. He liked them, especially Blake, who he'd always admired... But it just reminded him that he couldn't have what he wanted.

The past week he'd been her friend, her support system, and her champion, three things he'd never been for any other woman. He had no idea why or how it had happened, but for the first time in his life, he wanted to be a boyfriend. It was weird to even think about that; he'd never experienced envy when he was around couples, but today, as Rylie was leaving with Tonya, he'd wished he had the right to kiss Rylie good-bye.

He knew that Rylie didn't feel the same way and it completely stumped him. Every woman he'd ever met had wanted more from him, yet the only woman he'd ever thought twice about was perfectly content to just stay friends.

It was maddening.

Their food arrived, and Rylie took a bite of her gnocchi alla vodka and made that little moan he loved. "God, if I could eat anything forever, it would be this."

"What is that?" Tonya asked.

Rylie waved her fork. "Try it."

Dustin chuckled as Tonya hesitated. He'd been the same way when Rylie had offered to share food with him.

After a few seconds, Tonya stabbed one of the potato nuggets and popped it into her mouth. Her eyes went wide, and she pointed her fork at Rylie's plate. "I should have gotten that."

"Want a bite?" Rylie asked Blake.

"Nah, I'm good."

Rylie got a generous bite on her fork and turned toward Dustin. "Have you tried it?"

He shook his head and when Rylie held the fork out to him, he closed his lips around the utensil, staring into her eyes as he chewed. The spicy sauce set his mouth on fire and he reached for his wineglass before taking a healthy swallow.

Rylie giggled. "You're not a fan of spicy?"

"Not in my food."

Rylie's cheeks turned red and his lips curved into a smile as he chewed. Did she wonder what kind of spicy he did enjoy?

He sure hoped so.

He caught the look Blake and Tonya shared, and froze. *Crap.*

The last thing Rylie needed was their clients mentioning to Kelly that they thought there was something going on with Rylie and Dustin. Dating within the company was frowned upon.

"So, Rylie, are you seeing anyone?" Tonya asked.

"Not at the moment."

"That is crazy. You are so gorgeous." Tonya focused on Dustin. "Don't you think?"

"Without a doubt."

Rylie slyly poked him in the side and he grabbed her wrist, running the pad of his thumb over the inside. She pulled away, but not before he'd felt her tremble.

Tonya took a sip of her water, seemingly oblivious to what had just transpired. "So, why are you single, Rylie?"

"Babe," Blake said warningly.

"What?" she asked.

Rylie waved her fork at Blake. "No, it's okay. I broke up with someone a little over a month ago."

Tonya looked contrite. "Oh, I'm sorry."

"It's okay. It was a good thing. I do have a new man in my life though."

"Oh?"

"Yep. His name is Raider and he loves belly rubs," she joked.

"Okay then," Tonya said with an awkward laugh.

"She's talking about her rescue dog," Dustin said.

"I figured it was a pet," Tonya said. Rylie pulled out her phone and turned it so Tonya could see the picture. "Oh, what happened to him?"

"Some mean people set him on fire. I still think he's handsome though."

"He's definitely got character. Love his smile."

"Thank you," Rylie said, putting her phone away.

Then Tonya addressed him. "How about you, Dustin? Anyone special?"

He debated how to answer and ended up going for honesty. "There is."

Rylie stiffened next to him and Tonya leaned forward, completely ignoring her dinner. "Really? What's she like?"

"Special."

"That's it?" Tonya asked.

"Tonya…" Blake growled.

She held her hands up in surrender. "Okay, okay. You don't want to talk about her with a total stranger. I get it."

He could feel Rylie shooting him glances, but he didn't meet her gaze. It was one thing to want her, but it was another thing to tell her that. Especially when she was still making plans with that Will guy.

They finished the rest of their meal, and by the time the check came, the happy couple was yawning. Dustin grabbed the bill before anyone else could and when they all protested, he waved them off.

"Please, this is a small thing. You two just go back to your suite and relax. We'll meet you at the winery for breakfast, and take a tour of the grounds."

"You're right, he is bossy," Tonya said to Rylie.

Rylie laughed at his incredulous look.

"You told her that?" he said.

Tonya winked at him. "Oh, she wrote about you a lot in her e-mails."

Rylie's whole face turned red and Dustin was suddenly dying to know what was in those emails.

They all walked outside, and said their good nights. Before Rylie could escape, Dustin called out to her. "Can I get a ride back to my car? I came with Blake."

She nodded as she unlocked her doors. "Of course."

Dustin got in and when she'd put the key in the ignition, he teased, "You know, I find it a little sexist that you didn't open my door for me, and yet, I always get it for you."

"It's a sexist world, my friend. You could always stop getting my door."

He put his hands over his heart, as though she'd offended him just by suggesting it. "But I'm a gentleman. It's engrained."

"Harrumph."

The rest of the ride was silent, until Rylie parked next to his car.

"Have fun with your *plans*."

Dustin rotated in his seat and watched her expectantly. "Why do you say it like that?"

"Like what?"

"As if I'm not actually doing something now."

"Oh, I believe you're *doing someone*."

Dustin stared at her for several ticks and then threw back his head, laughing with masculine pride. Rylie was jealous. She thought he was going out with someone else and was pissed about it.

Maybe she wasn't as okay just being friends as he'd thought.

"Actually, dirty girl, my brother and I are meeting Luke Jessup and some of his friends for a poker night."

He couldn't tell if she was blushing, but she looked apologetic. "Oh."

Dustin reached up to turn on the dome light, and caught the tail end of her embarrassment. "I gotta ask though… Why were you so upset when you thought I was hooking up?"

"I wasn't."

He clucked his tongue. "Good little girls shouldn't tell lies."

"I've got to get home. Raider is waiting for me."

Dustin took her hand off the keys and brought her fingers to his lips, kissing them. "I think you miss me."

"What? I've seen you almost every day for three months. How could I miss you?"

"Fine, I think you miss *this*."

Dustin caught her by the back of the neck with his other hand and brought her mouth to his. He traced his tongue along the seam of her lips and when they parted with a sweet little sigh, he slid his tongue inside. She tasted of the peppermint candies they'd grabbed as they left the restaurant and he was tempted to press deeper, to completely lose control.

Give her a taste and make her want more.

He pulled away and watched her dazed expression with satisfaction.

"If you get lonely, all you gotta do is text me."

Without giving her a chance to recover, he got out of the car and shut the door with a thud.

Chapter 22

Rylie stepped out of her car the next day and stared out across Castle Vineyards. The main house sat on top of a hill, and below it were acres of grapevines, stretching across the rolling hills. In front of her were the guest quarters, the main event hall, and the honeymoon suite—big cedar buildings with green roofs. It was beautiful, the perfect rustic setting for an outdoor wedding ceremony.

The sun sparkled across the surface of a large pond, and Rylie tried to imagine growing up in a place like this, surrounded by beauty. With room to run and play. Her dad had let her go to the Sweetheart community park sometimes with friends, but that was nothing compared to this place. Dustin had been so lucky.

Then she remembered the crisscross scars across his back, and took back her opinion. Nothing was ever perfect.

Rylie heard gravel crunching behind her and the sound of an approaching vehicle. She turned to find Dustin pulling up alongside her car in a yellow Jeep. Her whole body hummed thinking about the kiss from last night, and then she remembered she was mad at him. That kiss was unexpected and inappropriate and disturbing....

And God, she wanted more of it.

When he climbed out, she shifted her glance between them and the shiny new car, then laughed.

"When did you get that?"

"I own it. I usually only drive it in the winter, but it felt like a Jeep kind of day."

Rylie scoffed. "Must be nice."

"It is." He stepped up to her and tapped the end of her nose with his finger. "If you ask me really sweetly, I might let you take it for a spin."

"I'm always sweet," she said.

"I remember."

Rylie's heart slammed at his deep murmur, and every rational reason for why she was angry with him flew right out of her head as his head dipped. His mouth drew closer and her eyes fluttered closed, waiting...

"There you two are!" Tonya called.

Rylie's eyes flew open and she jumped away from Dustin. Tonya stood just a few feet away with Moira Kent.

Dustin's mother.

Oh, God, what if she saw that and got the wrong idea?

What, like maybe I've fallen in love with her son?

That thought scared the hell out of her. Falling for him was just asking to have her heart broken. He was so far out of her league in means and experience... There was no way he'd be happy with her long-term, even if by some insane chance the feeling was mutual.

And there was no way Kelly would be happy about two of her employees dating.

"Hey, Tonya. Hello, Mrs. Kent," Rylie said, praying her voice sounded steady.

Moira was beautiful, with golden blond hair and the same gorgeous blue eyes her son had. Dressed in a powder blue dress and cream pumps, she wore a rope of pearls around her neck that looked very real. She screamed money and sophistication, two things Rylie lacked.

"Good morning," Moira said, her warm voice at odds with her cool appearance.

"Hey, Mom. Tonya. Have you eaten yet?"

"No, we were waiting for you two. Hello, Rylie. It's been a long time since I've seen you." Moira stepped forward and pressed her lips against Rylie's cheek, surprising her. "You look lovely."

Rylie ducked her head, intimidated by this incredibly classy woman. She'd put on a simple floral blouse and black pencil skirt. She'd forgone her usual heels in lieu of a pair of comfortable Toms, and standing next to Moira and Tonya, who looked like a million bucks in a yellow maxi dress and strappy white sandals, she was regretting the decision.

"Thank you, ma'am."

"Is Blake inside?" Dustin asked.

"Yeah, he couldn't wait. He was pretty hungry this morning."

There was something about Tonya's smile that told Rylie *she* was the reason for her soon to be husband's voracious appetite, and Rylie almost tittered. She liked the fact that Tonya wasn't stiff and fake like some of the celebrities they handled. She was genuine and nice.

"Well, let's go join him." To Rylie's surprise, Moira linked her arm through hers and walked alongside her up to the lodge. "I must say, I am so excited to see what you and my son have been doing for Tonya's wedding. She has told me about everything."

"I really hope she's as thrilled with the finished products as she is the mock-ups," Rylie said.

Tonya bumped Rylie's shoulder. "I'm right here and I know I will be."

Rylie looked over her shoulder at Dustin, who was walking slowly behind them. He shrugged. "Oh, don't mind me. I'm just here to smile and look pretty."

"That's right, dear," his mother said, winking at Rylie.

This was not what she'd expected. She'd hardly spoken to Dustin's mother, besides a passing hello, but she'd always imagined she'd be stuck-up and cold.

How wrong she had been.

They walked into the dining area, and Rylie greeted Blake, who was shoveling a forkful of eggs into his mouth.

"Baby, I swear, sometimes I think you were raised in a barn," Tonya said, sitting next to him.

Blake oinked at her, and everyone laughed. Moira sat at the head of the table and Dustin pulled out the chair next to her for Rylie.

"Thank you."

"One thing I can say for my son is I did raise him with halfway decent manners," Moira said.

"Thanks, Mom."

Dustin picked up the dishes and served Moira, Tonya, and Rylie. Blake pointed his fork at Dustin. "You're making me look bad, man."

"Why don't you pour the orange juice then?" Dustin said.

Tonya held up her glass. "I'm waiting."

More laughter before eating became their top priority. Rylie snagged one of the raspberry scones, and took a bite, humming in approval.

"Who made these?"

"I did," Moira said.

"They are delicious! I'd love to get the recipe. My scones aren't bad, but these are so much better. They are almost creamy."

Moira's smile widened. "Well thank you. It's a family recipe though. I'm afraid you'd have to become my daughter-in-law in order for me to share my secret."

Rylie choked on the piece of scone in her mouth. Dustin thumped her on the back and the hunk flew out onto her plate. It was completely mortifying and she refused to look at Dustin.

"Subtle, Mom."

Moira turned innocent blue eyes past Rylie, and she suddenly knew where Dustin got that *I-wasn't-implying-anything* look.

"What? I have four sons and not one of them has gotten married. It's bad enough that two of them moved away from me, but they don't even give me the consolation of daughters-in-law and grandchildren." She shifted her gaze between Tonya and Rylie. "Now, I ask you, girls... Is that fair?"

"Okay—new topic," Dustin said.

Rylie finally met his gaze and realized that he was blushing. She'd never seen him do that, and it made her smile.

Sorry, she mouthed.

Dustin shrugged.

"When is the rest of your wedding party showing up?" Rylie asked.

Blake took a long drink of orange juice before answering. "My boys are driving up from L.A. and should be here Friday."

"And I'm picking up my two cousins and best friend Thursday night from the airport," Tonya said.

Rylie nodded. "Well, we did what you asked. Tuxes will be ready to be picked up, and the bridesmaids' dresses are going to be perfect."

"I'm sure they will be," Tonya said.

"How do you like working at Something Borrowed, Rylie? I will admit, my son doesn't talk about it much," Moira said.

"I love it, Mrs. Kent. I love the details and the dresses. And someday I want to open my own bakery and hopefully bake all the cakes for Something Borrowed's weddings. I'm basically banking my entire future on the success of it, and I would do anything to help it continue."

Abruptly, Dustin stood, looking a little pale. "Would you all excuse me a moment?"

He left the dining hall at a rapid pace, and Rylie watched him with her mouth hanging open.

What did I say?

* * * *

"Yeah, I know what I said, but you're just going to have to tell them I backed out."

Dustin had walked out below one of his favorite oak trees to make the call to his literary agent in New York. David Brown was a bulldog, and Dustin had liked that about him when they'd first met.

Now? Not so much.

"You want me to pull a book that we've been offered seven figures for? Are you crazy?"

Dustin scrubbed his hand over his face. He could understand David's frustration. When he'd first pitched him the book about a bridal party for hire business that catered to the stars, he'd been intrigued, but when Dustin had pitched it as an exposé, David couldn't send off the proposal fast enough. That had been fine when he hadn't really known Kelly, or Marley....

Then Rylie had happened.

And even though he wasn't taking any money for being a professional groomsman, violating the confidentiality clause would ruin Something Borrowed. Rylie deserved to have her bakery, Marley deserved to have her wedding venue and Kelly, well, she had gone from being a shop girl in a bridal boutique to having her own company. It had hit him like a ton of bricks that if he did this, he would be ruining their lives, and Rylie would never forgive him.

"Yes, I want you to pull the book. Say that I made the whole thing up."

"And what if they want it as a work of fiction?"

"Tell them I'm not writing it, and if I don't, no one is."

David was breathing hard on the other end, and Dustin hoped he wasn't having an anxiety attack.

"Look, Dustin, I don't know what's going on, but I think you need to take some time to think this through."

"Pull the book, David, and I'll make sure you are compensated."

Dustin clicked off the phone call and let out a shaky breath. God, he really was an asshole. Every time someone had asked him why he was working at Something Borrowed, he'd just smirked. All of this had come about because he was bored and miserable, and liked making other people around him just as unhappy.

He was like the Grinch or Ebenezer, only this wasn't a Christmas redemption tale. It was real life and he'd almost screwed up and hurt the woman he...

Loved?

"There you are! Is everything okay?"

Just the sound of her voice rose goosebumps across his skin. Was this what love was? Finding joy in just the other person's presence? Putting their happiness before your own?

No wonder he'd avoided this for so long.

"Yeah, everything is good."

She cocked her head to the side and her gaze clearly said she wasn't convinced. "You sure? Because you looked a little pale when you ran out here and I heard you using your bossy voice."

"What else did you hear?" he asked hoarsely.

"I couldn't hear what you said, just how you were speaking." She took several limping steps closer to him and touched his cheek. "Are you feeling okay? You seem tense."

Dustin's heart slowed as he forced himself to relax. Rylie didn't know what he'd almost done and she was out here, worried about him.

That was a win in his book. He didn't need to focus on his feelings for her right now. Besides, it seemed as though they should try their hand at a date first before they started dropping the L bomb.

"I'm fine, really." He wrapped his arms around her waist and her eyes lifted to meet his. "I have been thinking though. About you and me."

"You and me?" she squeaked.

"Yeah. We've worked together several months and were neighbors for five weeks. I feel like we're friends. Am I wrong?"

"No, I mean, yes. Of course we are friends."

"Who on occasion have kissed," he said.

"What are you getting at, Dustin?"

"I propose that Monday morning I walk into your office and I ask you out. And when I do, you're going to say yes."

Rylie's hands came up to rest on his shoulders. "What if I say no?"

He pretended to consider this outcome. "Ehh, I think I'm still going to give it a shot. I'm like ninety-nine percent certain you're going to say yes."

"And until then?" she asked.

"I'm going to be a professional and keep my hands to myself."

"You mean the hands that are currently resting on my lower back? Those hands?"

He dropped his arms from around her and grinned sheepishly. "Starting now."

Rylie gave him a gentle push. "I guess we'll see on Monday then, huh?"

"I guess we will."

Chapter 23

Dustin waited inside Kelly's office later that afternoon, his leg wiggling impatiently. He'd already decided to give Kelly the heads up about what he'd planned to do and tender his resignation. He was hoping that coming clean would score him some brownie points and maybe she wouldn't share his nefarious plot with Rylie and the rest of the company.

Did he need to tell her? No, she'd probably never find out that he'd almost ruined her. But just in case, he'd rather have everything out in the open than hide it and have it come back to bite him in the ass.

"Dustin," Kelly said, as she came in the room behind him and he stood up. "I wasn't expecting you in here. Should I close the door?"

"Please."

The door clicked shut, and she shot him a curious glance as she came around her desk. "Is there something wrong?"

"You could say that." He cleared his throat, calling for the nerve. "I'd like to tender my resignation."

She stilled for several seconds, half sitting, half standing, and finally sunk into the chair. "All right. May I ask why?"

"I was hired under false pretenses."

Kelly's eyebrows arched. "Oh?"

"I applied here because I thought I could write a tell-all about celebrity bridezillas."

She leaned forward on her elbows, resting her chin on her folded hands. "Uh huh. And you no longer think you can write the book?"

"No, I know I could," he said. "I just don't want to."

"I see. Well, why tell me this at all then? If you no longer wish to pursue the book."

"I'm one of those people who believes when you keep secrets, they eventually rise to the surface and destroy you. So, I'd rather be honest and forthcoming now than suffer the consequences later."

"I appreciate the honesty. Can I ask what changed your mind?"

He shifted in his chair uncomfortably. "I didn't want to hurt you or the business."

"Anyone else?"

He grimaced. "Yeah. But she doesn't know anything about this."

"Oh, I know. There is no way Rylie would have kept something like this from me."

"How are you not pissed right now, threatening to sue me for all I'm worth?"

She scoffed. "Please, did you think I didn't know you were up to something? A millionaire playboy wants to be a hired groomsman?"

"Then why did you take me on?"

"For all the reasons I told everyone else. You run in the right circles and you look good in a tux."

Dustin shook his head, laughing. "I guess those are valid. I could have ruined you, though."

"Maybe. Or I may have ruined you. You can't bullshit a bullshitter. We always have one more ace up our sleeve."

She reached into the cabinet below her desk and brought out a large file. "When you gave all your commission to Rylie, I took the liberty of having you investigated. I figured you were trying to slip out of the non-disclosure agreement by not accepting payment. Let's just say if you ever are tempted to expose my clients' secrets, I'll expose yours. Because as honest as you may be, we all have things we'd rather stay hidden."

Dustin took in her deadly expression and gulped. "You know... I am really glad I didn't cross you. You're terrifying."

She stuck the file in the drawer and closed it. "Thank you."

"About Rylie..."

"If you're worried I'm going to fire her over your office romance, you can rest easy. Since you're tendering your resignation, it's not an issue anymore."

Dustin stood up. "Then I guess that is it. I'll have my office cleaned out on Friday, and after the wedding on Saturday, we'll be square?"

"Not quite yet," she said, leaning her elbows on her desk. "I want one more thing."

"What's that?"

"I want a wedding deposit. In the event that you get engaged before turning forty-five, Something Borrowed is commissioned to help you plan your wedding."

He almost laughed until he realized she was dead serious. "What if you go out of business?"

"Your money will be returned in full, same as if you never get married."

"But if I do, you plan everything."

"Every...last...detail."

"This feels a lot like blackmail," he said.

"Let's call it insurance. It has a sweeter ring to it."

Considering she could have rained a whole lot more hell down on him, this didn't seem like a bad deal.

"I'll cut you a check now."

* * * *

After work, Rylie grabbed a cart from the front of the supermarket and headed for the pet aisle. She wanted to get another Kong toy for Raider and she was going to bake a special cake for Tonya's last night of freedom. She'd asked Rylie earlier if they could do a sleepover at her house, and she'd been unable to come up with a reason why they couldn't.

Well, she'd had a ton of reasons, but Tonya's pleading look had demolished every single one of them.

She threw a couple of new toys into her basket and turned the corner, only to slam her cart into someone.

"Oh, I am so sorry! I wasn't paying attention."

Her gaze traveled over the big hands wrapped around the end of her cart all the way up to the familiar bloodshot brown eyes of Asher Reid. Besides the eyes, she barely recognized him. In the last month, he'd lost weight and his cheeks were hollow. He seemed almost dazed as he stared back at her.

"Sorry," he mumbled. "It's a small town and there's only one grocery store. If I knew you were going to be here, I would have waited to shop."

Rylie bit her lip, that sick feeling of guilt twisting up her gut.

He threw a brick through Dustin's pool house window. What do I have to feel guilty about?

She didn't respond, surprised when he asked, "How's your foot?"

Rylie stared up at him. "How did you know I hurt my foot?"

"Everyone has told me. When they're not calling me an asshole and crazy." What was she supposed to say?

"You wouldn't leave me alone and after...that night, I had to do something."

"I didn't throw that brick. I wanted you back. I didn't want to hurt you." He moved as though he was going to come around the cart and she took a step back, keeping it between them. "Are you really scared of me?"

Taking in his disheveled appearance, his wild eyes, and the bitter twist of his mouth, she nodded.

His face flushed nearly purple with rage. "All I did was try to show you I cared, that I was willing to work on things and what did you do? You shacked up with that rich son of a bitch, Dustin Kent." He came all the way around the cart and she moved, keeping the metal basket between them. "Does he take care of you and buy you pretty things? Is that how he got you?"

"You... You need to go, Asher. You're violating the restraining order."

"You've already destroyed my life! Did you know I was fired from the garage? Once they heard that you'd accused me of throwing a brick through that prick's window, Paulson let me go."

Rylie backed down the aisle. "Just leave me alone."

"Why?"

The way he said it, so cold and empty, caused sweat to break out across her body. She glanced over her shoulder, calculating if she could make it to the end of the aisle before he caught her.

"Because you'll be violating the RO if you touch me."

He sneered at her. "It's just a piece of paper. You really think that or your new boyfriend can protect you?"

"Is there a problem here?"

Rylie had never been so happy to hear Luke Jessup's Texas drawl behind her.

"Asher. If memory serves, you're supposed to be five hundred feet away from Rylie."

"How the fuck was I supposed to know she was going to be here?"

Luke took her arm and stepped between her and Asher. "I heard the lady ask you to leave from the next aisle over. So, you had a chance to walk away, and now I'm going to have to arrest you."

Asher shoved her cart at Luke and took off out of sight. Luke chased after him and as she followed behind, it was as though she was floating, watching all of this take place in someone else's world.

Another deputy had Asher pinned to the floor and pulled something from his pocket. Rylie couldn't hear what they were saying over the blood pounding in her ears, but knew this couldn't be happening. This wasn't her life. She wasn't the girl who dated abusive assholes and watched them get arrested in the middle of a supermarket.

Her gaze lifted and she realized there were a lot of people standing around watching and she couldn't breathe. Couldn't think.

Rylie turned and ran, losing her heels as she pumped her arms. She didn't slow at the pain in her foot or when her bare skin hit asphalt. She unlocked her car with shaky hands, tears rolling down her cheeks as she climbed inside.

She peeled out of the parking lot, ignoring angry glares from several older women from church. She didn't care what anyone thought of her, not right now. All she knew was she was scared and wanted to feel safe, to forget about what had just happened. There was only one place that offered her that.

She took the main road out of town to Dustin's house.

The road blurred and she dashed at her eyes, trying to clear her vision, but it was like trying to use wipers in the pouring rain. It just wouldn't stop.

When she pulled up in front of his house, she stumbled out of her car and raced to his front door. She didn't see his car and prayed he'd just pulled it into the garage.

She banged on the door, and after several moments, the door was pulled open.

Only it wasn't Dustin but Victoria.

"Rylie? What's happened?"

"I...I need... I need Dustin."

"Oh, baby, he's not here right now, but I'll call him. Come inside and I'll make you some tea."

"I ca-can't. I have to get home and let Ra-Raider out. I just... I just needed to see him."

Victoria took her hand and dragged her inside. "You're going to come into the kitchen and let me make you a cup of tea. Then I'm going to call Mr. Kent."

Rylie let Victoria pull her into the kitchen and push her toward a chair. "I want you to sit there while I make you some tea."

Rylie sat and waited, while Victoria picked up the phone and dialed. Rylie stared out the window as she listened to Victoria leave Dustin a message.

She didn't want to be here without Dustin. As much as she loved Victoria, she didn't feel comfortable talking to her.

When Victoria went into the other room, Rylie stood up and left. If she couldn't be with Dustin, she'd rather be alone.

Chapter 24

Dustin got Victoria's message while he was having dinner at his mother's house with Charlie. He rushed back inside and told them both good-bye, ignoring their questions.

As soon as he made his escape to his car, he called Victoria.

"Is she still there?"

"No, she took off when I had my back turned. She was so upset, I really don't think she should be driving."

"I'm going by her place."

"Please let me know she's safe," Victoria said.

Dustin hung up and stepped on the gas, heading to Rylie's little house. He didn't know what was going on, but Rylie wouldn't have showed up asking for him if it wasn't important.

By the time he stood on her porch, knocking on the front door, he was sweating and ready to tear the slab of wood off the hinges to get to her.

She pulled the door open, her face puffy and red, and the heart he never knew he had fell apart.

"Aw, baby. What happened?" He stepped inside and closed the door behind him, waiting for her to say something.

Rylie walked straight into his arms and he caught a glimpse of her face crumbling just before it buried into his chest.

"Rys, you're scaring me."

"I just…don't know…what I did," she wailed.

Dustin wrapped his arms around her, trying not to step on Raider who was circling them. When he managed to angle them toward the couch, he sat down, and pulled her across his lap.

"Now, what the heck are you talking about?"

"I… I bumped into Asher at the grocery store."

Dustin stiffened. "That son of a bitch."

"It was an accident, but then he got hostile. Blamed me for getting him fired and he… Luke was in the next aisle and heard everything, and they arrested him, right there in the middle of the store. He looked so awful. He's thin and I think he might be sick. The way he looked at me… I've never had anyone hate me so much."

He smoothed her hair back from her face and cupped her cheeks, tilting her face until she met his gaze. "Baby, it has nothing to do with you. You did nothing wrong."

"Are you sure? Because it doesn't feel that way. I keep thinking if I'd done something different, helped him in some way, this wouldn't be happening."

"Some people are just miserable and there is no saving them. And even if you could, it is not your responsibility. You owe it to yourself to be happy, and you were not happy with him. You owed him nothing."

She sniffled, laying her cheek against his chest. "My mother thought that way too. She got diagnosed with cancer and took off to find herself. Left my dad and me for a tennis instructor in Palm Beach, because she wanted to live her life before she died. We didn't make her happy."

"That's not the same thing," he said.

"Isn't it? She found out she was dying and realized she wasn't happy, so she went off to find it."

"Did your dad beat your mother?" he asked harshly.

She jerked back, scowling at him. "Of course not. He was wonderful. Kind and supportive—"

"That is one major difference. Your dad was a good man. Asher is an abusive asshole and you can't tell me he isn't. I didn't see much, but I know what it looks like when a man is hurting his woman."

To his surprise, Rylie cupped his cheek, her brown eyes filled with sympathy. "Or their kids."

His throat closed and every instinct told him to run, to keep his family's darkness locked away.

But she was pouring her heart out to him; it only seemed fair to share.

"Yeah, that happens too." He took a deep shaky breath before he laid it all out for her. "When I was really little, he didn't. He hardly spoke to me until I was eleven or so. I knew he hit my mother though. She was good at hiding the bruises and he became more careful about where he left them, but I saw them. I felt her wince when I'd hug her."

She made a sympathetic sound and it should have irritated him, made him pull away and shut up, but it was comforting.

"The first time he took his belt to me, my mom was gone at some charity thing. He always made sure she was out of the house. I never told her about it, but I found out recently that she knew. It was why she'd always tried to find places for me to go when she had to leave the house. She couldn't leave him, but she tried to protect me."

Rylie's arms wrapped around his shoulders and she squeezed him tight. "He must have hit you pretty hard to leave those marks."

"That and he used the end with the buckle."

"Oh my God. Why didn't you tell your mother?"

"I don't know. We never talked about it. But when I was fifteen, I almost beat him to death. I told him that if he ever touched my mother again, I would finish the job."

Her lips pressed against the side of his neck and he closed his eyes, leaning into the caress. "He never touched me again after that. Or her, at least, as long as I was there."

"I am so sorry."

"It happened. He's gone now, and there's nothing much I can do about the past."

"Why didn't your mother ever tell anyone?" Rylie asked.

"He had her sign a prenup that pretty much screwed her over no matter what she did. I believe she tried to protect us. At least she's free now and the happiest I've ever seen her." His lips found her temple, and against her skin he whispered, "But this was supposed to be about you, not me."

"I'm glad you feel like you can tell me things. When it happened, all I could think about was getting to you. That you'd make everything better."

Dustin's chest swelled at her admission. "I feel the same way when I'm with you. The first time I saw you, swishing past my office in a pair of those killer heels, I knew I had to meet you. And when I did, none of my usual game worked."

"Only because I thought you were a dog. It was really hard not to like you."

"Back at you. In fact, I told myself I was going to stop flirting with you when you moved into the pool house."

She snorted. "That lasted what, two seconds?"

"What can I say? I find you irresistible."

"I might believe you if I didn't know firsthand how hideous I am right now."

He slid his hand under her chin and tilted her face up to his. "It's not about how you look. It's about the way you make me feel when I'm near you."

He couldn't believe he was saying all this to her, but when she brushed her thumb over his mouth, he didn't think she hated it.

"How do I make you feel?"

"Like I can be the kind of man you deserve."

She brushed her lips across his and that contact was more than a sizzle or a shock. It was like standing in a field during a lightning storm. Thrilling and hot.

"You're not perfect, but I don't care. I don't want anyone else to have me. I'm all yours."

* * * *

Rylie had no idea if what she was saying made any sense, but when Dustin cradled her face and took her mouth with his, she figured she must have said something right.

His hand grabbed the bottom of her T-shirt, and she held her arms over her head so he could easily remove it. She wasn't wearing a bra, but she didn't have time to be shy or embarrassed because Dustin's lips were wrapped around her nipple and she closed her eyes, moaning at every tug and every suck.

Canine whimpering broke the mood when Raider started licking her cheek. She busted up, shaking her head. "He thinks you're killing me."

Dustin gripped her thighs and stood. She automatically locked her legs around his waist as he spoke to her dog.

"Look, Raider. Your mom and I are going to go have some grown-up time while you hang out here, because honestly, I don't trust you not to bite my butt while I'm making her happy."

Rylie was wheezing with laughter as he carried her down the hallway to her room, kicking the door shut before Raider could join them.

"Hang on, let me give him a treat."

Dustin let her down, his mouth moving over her neck. "Do I get a treat?"

"Yes, you pervert."

Once she'd handed the dog biscuit to Raider and closed the door again, she turned around to find Dustin stripping. He unbuttoned his dress shirt, revealing tight, tan muscles, and she didn't think she would ever get tired of watching him. He dropped his shirt on the floor and she leaned against the door as her legs went a little weak.

He crooked his finger at her as he kicked off his dress shoes. "Come a little closer, baby."

Rylie took one step and then another until she threw herself against him, knocking him back onto the bed. She giggled as she lifted up over him, sitting back on his thighs as her hands went to the belt in his slacks.

"You know, I've fantasized about this a few times," she said.

"What? Having sex with me? May I remind you that we've already done that, multiple times in one night if memory serves."

"But I never got to unwrap you like a Christmas present."

Dustin grinned, putting his hands behind his head. "By all means. Unwrap me."

Rylie tried to pull his belt out with a flourish, but it turned out, that didn't work when the guy was lying down. When she finally had it free and on the floor, she slipped the button on his pants out of the loop and slowly lowered the zipper.

"Can't you go any faster?" he groaned.

"I'm savoring it."

"Baby, there are better things to savor than me dropping my drawers."

She stood up with a laugh and pulled his slacks down his thighs until he was lying on her bed in just blue boxer briefs and black socks.

"I'm feeling kind of exposed here," he said.

"Hmmm, want me to even the score?"

His gaze dropped to where her hands were playing with the sides of her yoga pants, slipping them down an inch.

"Seems only fair."

She pushed them to the floor and stepped out of them, wearing nothing but a smile as she climbed back onto the bed. Rylie pressed her lips against his stomach, loving the way the muscles jumped under her mouth, and trailed kisses down to the edge of his briefs. She could see the outline of his cock through the thin cotton and couldn't wait to push the barrier out of the way.

As she peeled back his boxer briefs until they were halfway down his thighs, she dropped light little nips along his tip and shaft. It jerked away at the contact and she laughed again.

"Can you not giggle that close to my dick?"

In response, she wrapped her hand and mouth around it, sucking his head hard. The air whooshed out between his teeth and she let him go with a little pop.

"I'm so sorry I made you uncomfortable. All better?"

His deep chuckle turned into a groan when her lips covered him again, bringing her hand up to meet her mouth on him, listening to the noises he made. It had been a long while since she'd gone down on a guy, but it was really like riding a bike. Especially if she enjoyed the ride.

"Okay, okay, okay, you gotta stop," Dustin said.

She released him and crawled up his form, her whole body throbbing with need. She placed her hands on his chest and rubbed her wet center over his stiff cock. When the motion hit her clit, she whimpered with need.

"Do you have a condom?"

"Not on me."

"I thought men were always supposed to be prepared?"

"I was never a Boy Scout." He lifted his hips. "Are you on the pill?"

"Yes."

"Then I think we're good. I know I'm clean and I trust you."

Rylie shifted her hips until the tip of him slid inside her, smiling. "I trust you, too."

The moment he was all the way in, she leaned back on her hands and rocked her hips, closing her eyes as the steady drumming built at her center. Dustin's hands came up to cup her breasts, playing with her nipples until her motions were no longer smooth and controlled, but jerky, fast, and sloppy.

Her orgasm hit and she cried out as she kept moving, prolonging the pleasure. When Dustin's hands gripped her hips and took control, she couldn't keep quiet as she climbed that mountain again and fell over with him, his deep, growling shout the hottest sound she'd ever heard.

It wasn't until she came down that she realized Raider was howling outside the door.

"Oh, God, is he howling because we were loud or because he's locked out?"

"Probably both," Dustin teased, earning a light slap on his chest.

She climbed off him slowly and stumbled to the door, her legs like rubber as she walked. When she opened the door, Raider bounded in, jumping around and barking at both of them, as if scolding them for excluding him.

"I'll be back," Rylie said.

Dustin lay sprawled across her bed with his underwear around his knees and his socks still on. "I'll be here."

Rylie escaped to the bathroom and closed the door before she started laughing. She was still fighting the giggles after she'd finished cleaning up and came back into the bedroom.

His socks and boxer briefs were now on the floor, and he was under her covers.

"So, what now? Snuggle? Snack? Or sleep?"

Rylie climbed into the bed with him and cuddled up against his side. "All of the above."

Chapter 25

Rylie stood by the mirror, watching as Tonya's mother slid the veil into her daughter's intricate up-do. It was a bittersweet moment for her, as she knew that when her time to get married came around, she wouldn't have a mother to help her get ready or her dad to walk her down the aisle.

She shook herself out of her doldrums, refusing to shroud one second of Tonya's big day with sadness. Of all the weddings she'd ever been a part of at Something Borrowed, she had a good feeling that this couple had a real chance at the rest of their lives.

"You look gorgeous," Tonya's cousin, Glenda, said. Glenda was kind of a ball buster and had given Rylie a ration of shit for not having alcohol at the slumber party last night. When she'd explained that there would be plenty of drinking going on at the reception and they didn't need to be hung over for the ceremony, she'd just huffed and pouted until Rylie had brought out the "Man-Candy" movies and "Last Night of Freedom" snack mix. After that, they bonded over abs and sweet and salty popcorn.

But in this instance, she was right. Tonya was beautiful in her strapless ivory dress that glided down to the floor. Her hair was smoothed back from her face in a thick bun, threaded with silver thread and pearls under her veil.

"Thank you. You all look wonderful too," Tonya said.

Rylie agreed. Tonya's best friend was short and curvy, while both of her cousins were five foot ten and stacked up top. The off-the-shoulder dresses were flattering and the wine color looked amazing on all of them.

"What about your mother?"

Tonya stood up and went over to her mom, kissing her on the cheek. Her mother was an older version of Tonya, only her hair was straightened and hit just below her chin. Her dress was a formal silver dress made out of chiffon with capped sleeves.

"You're beautiful, Mama."

Rylie's eyes stung and she desperately tried to blink back the emotion.

Someone knocked on the door and when they all said come in, Tonya's father, Governor Richard Rolland, popped his head in. His graying hair did nothing to detract from the imposing figure he cut in his black tux.

"Are we ready to get this show on the road?" When his gaze landed on his daughter, he stepped all the way into the room and held his hand over his chest. "This can't be my baby girl."

Oh, God, I'm going to lose it. Rylie's eyes filled with tears as she watched them embrace, so much love in the room it was overwhelming.

"I'm ready, Daddy."

Her father led Tonya and her mother from the room, followed by the maid of honor, her two cousins, and Rylie pulling up the rear. When they stood just outside the double doors of the chapel, Rylie's heart flipped in her chest as Dustin came through and held his arm out to Tonya's mother. He looked amazing in his tux, and she didn't blame Tonya's mom one bit for giggling.

"My, you are a handsome devil."

"Mom," Tonya scolded.

"What, he is. I'm married, not dead. Right, honey?" she teased her husband.

Her husband shot Dustin a stern look. "You just be sure to keep your hands to yourself, young man."

"Of course, sir. Besides, my girl would skin me alive if I didn't."

Rylie's jaw slid open as he winked right at her and then disappeared behind the doors.

All eyes swung her way and Tonya tsked. "Someone's been keeping secrets."

Rylie hid her face behind her bouquet, praying they wouldn't have time to ask her any questions.

Luckily Blake's college friends joined them, holding out their arms to Tonya's cousins and her relationship was forgotten for the moment. Rylie waited impatiently for Dustin to return, her emotions warring between excitement and horror. She hoped that Tonya didn't tell Kelly they were dating before she got the chance. Technically, there was nothing in the employee contract about dating coworkers, just groomsman, but she still didn't think Kelly would be thrilled.

When Dustin came back through whistling his way to her side, she shook her head. "I can't believe you said that. What if Kelly fires us?"

The bridal procession lined up and since they were up first, they walked to the front.

"Kelly won't fire you because I already quit."

Rylie stumbled and was grateful that they hadn't opened the doors yet for everyone to see her klutzy move. "Why would you do that?"

"Well, as you pointed out, I don't need the money. And there was the whole tell-all book I was planning to write."

"What?" Rylie cried, earning a roomful of sour looks.

"Maybe we should talk about this later," Dustin said. "We're almost there."

"Then you better slow your pace, 'cause I want you to explain that last part to me."

But there wasn't time and as they stood across from each other, Rylie worried her lower lip. Dustin had joined Something Borrowed in order to write a tell-all? Was that why he'd let her stay at his place? Because he wanted more dirt on other clients? Is that why he'd given her the commission? So he wouldn't be held to their non-disclosure agreement?

Okay, I need to calm down. He never once asked me any questions about my clients.

Still, the other questions nagged at her, but after the ceremony and pictures, she lost him. She was searching for him when she bumped into Kelly coming out of the restroom.

"Hey, where are you going? I wanted to congratulate you. You and Dustin did a phenomenal job."

"Thank you. Have you seen Dustin? I need to speak with him."

"I haven't, but is everything okay?"

Rylie's loyalties fought against each other before she finally blurted, "Did you know he was writing a book about Something Borrowed?"

To her surprise, Kelly wrapped her arm around her shoulders and squeezed her. "Why don't we pop into this room over here and talk?"

Rylie allowed Kelly to guide her, and when Kelly closed the door, it hit her like a ton of bricks. "You knew?"

"Not specifics, but I knew he was up to something."

"When did you find out for sure?"

"When he came to my office on Wednesday and told me. Then he quit."

Rylie was still trying to wrap her head around the fact that Dustin had planned to betray Kelly and yet, Kelly didn't seem pissed at all. She seemed absolutely fine.

"Why did he tell you?"

"I guess because he decided not to go through with it."

"But why not?"

"I think you already know the answer," Kelly said gently.

Rylie stood there, remembering every time she'd told him she needed her job, how important it was to her.

"I am sorry. I didn't mean for this to happen and I swear, it never affected my job."

"Rylie," Kelly said, taking her hands. "You're fine. We're fine. Sometimes, you can't help who you fall in love with. You still have a job at Something Borrowed for as long as you want."

"Thanks, Kelly. But I want to discuss moving into a different capacity. Maybe baking the wedding cakes, like we talked about?"

Kelly hugged her hard. "Yes. We'll get the details straightened out on Monday. Although I will hate to lose you as a bridesmaid, I know this is your true calling."

"Thanks. By the way, what did you get out of him?" Rylie asked.

Kelly grinned devilishly. "What do you mean?"

"Come on, I've known you well enough to know that no one gets away scot-free."

"Do you really want to know?" Kelly asked.

"I wouldn't have asked if I didn't."

"When the time comes, Something Borrowed is going to plan Dustin Kent's wedding—and it is going to be fabulous."

* * * *

Dustin stood on the edge of the dance floor, scanning the room for Rylie. He was pretty sure she wouldn't leave the festivities no matter how mad she might be at him.

"And who are you looking for?" his mother asked.

He hadn't even noticed her move up next to him and he gave her a hug. "Just Rylie. You know, my partner in wedding planning."

"Oh, I just saw her talking to your employer, Kelly. I have to say, at first, I couldn't understand you wanting to do this, but after seeing everything you and Rylie put together, I get it."

"Sorry to disappoint you then, but I quit three days ago."

His mom stared at him. "Why?"

"Because it wasn't my thing."

"Ah. So what are you going to do now?"

"Real estate investments and restoration," he said.

"Really?"

"Yep. We'll see how this first project goes, but I'm hoping to bring Charlie in as my partner. Won't you be happy having two of your boys here?"

His mother's eyes filled with tears. "I would love it."

Dustin caught sight of Rylie across the room and kissed his mom's cheek. "We'll talk later, okay? I've got to run."

"Give Rylie my best."

Dustin didn't have time to respond before he was standing in front of Rylie, holding his hand out to her.

"May I have this dance?"

She slipped her hand into his with a smile. "It's not time for dancing yet."

"Well, I have a playlist on my phone, and it's a beautiful night outside. I think that's as good a reason as any to dance."

"I'm only going with you because I want to talk, not dance."

"You haven't heard my playlist though…or seen my best moves."

"Oh, I've seen *all* of your moves and there will be no move making until we have a very frank conversation."

Dustin led the way, ready to get this over with. Once they'd put the appropriate distance between the reception and them, Dustin dropped Rylie's hand. He faced her with his arms over his chest, ready for the explosion. "So, I'm waiting for you to blast me. Go ahead."

To his shock, she stepped into him and wrapped her arms around his waist. "I already talked to Kelly and know that you pulled the book deal. And I also have a pretty good guess that it was because you didn't want me to lose my job. How am I doing?"

"Spot on, baby."

"But see, I have a confession too. Kelly actually asked me to keep an eye on you and report any suspicious behavior."

Dustin quirked an eyebrow. "And did you?"

"No. There was nothing to report, and besides, I couldn't very well admit that I had slept with the enemy."

He unfolded his arms with a grin and wrapped them around her. "What a couple of star-crossed lovers we are."

"Not anymore. Since you no longer work for Something Borrowed, there's nothing standing in our way… Unless you've changed your mind."

"Nope. In fact, I was wondering if I didn't have to wait until Monday to ask you out."

"Oh yeah? What did you have in mind?"

Dustin gave her a deep, fast kiss. "Meet me right here at ten and I'll show you."

Chapter 26

Rylie held the bottle of champagne in one hand and the skirt of her dress in the other. She stood beside D'agostini Pond, a large reed and tree-filled swamp that was just outside of Somerset. The D'agostini family owned a lot of the area.

When they'd left the wedding, and headed out of Sweetheart, she hadn't minded when Dustin had taken a left down the private dirt road that led to the pond. She'd even been cool when he'd parked the Jeep and announced they were going to play sexy truth or dare. It had sounded exciting.

Until she'd picked dare for the second time. "Let me be clear, you inferred that this was to be a date and that it would be *fun*."

Dustin laughed from his position beside the Jeep. "Sexy truth or dare is fun!"

"No, there is nothing sexy about swimming in a swamp. Why did I let you talk me into this? This is something small town high school kids do when they lie to their parents about going to the movies!"

"Are you punking out?" he challenged.

Rylie glared at him.

"I do not want to swim in this. It is slimy and there are probably snakes!"

"Nah, the snakes are all sleeping."

She started to inch her toe near the water and could have sworn she saw something move beneath the surface. She stumbled back with a squeal. "I hate you."

He sighed as though he was a benevolent king granting her greatest wish. "All right, you want to use your pass on this one?"

Rylie nodded enthusiastically. "Yes, yes!"

"Fine, my turn."

Rylie pulled out her phone and scrolled through her music. "I dare you to strip while doing the Macarena."

"Yeah, I'm not doing that."

"Oh come on! That's easy compared to what you wanted me to do."

"Okay, but if I see your camera come out, you're taking a swim." He hopped down from the hood of his Jeep and Rylie climbed in to flip on his headlights.

"What are you doing, trying to bring the cops down on us?"

"You need a spotlight if you're going to perform." She pressed play on her phone and giggled. "You're up, Chippendale!"

She took a swig of champagne from the bottle as she watched Dustin do a very clumsy version of the Macarena. When he crossed his arms, he pulled his bow tie loose and by the time he put his hands on his hips, he pushed his pants down to around his ankles.

A flash of blue and red from the main road caught the corner of Rylie's eye, and she turned off the music and lights. "Shit, it's the fuzz."

"Did you just say the fuzz?"

She ran over to him and grabbed his hand. "Come on, we've got to hide."

"Or we can just get in the car and if they happen to meet us on the road, we can just tell them we came down here to make out."

"Again, not in high school. We are adults. And I am too tipsy to deal with this situation."

Dustin bent over and pulled his pants back up. "Get in the Jeep, Tipsy, and let's get out of here."

By the time they started backing up, a patrol car had blocked them in.

"Ah, crap! They're going to think we were going at it."

"Do you want me to tell them the truth?" Dustin asked.

"Oh, God, where do I put the champagne bottle?"

Dustin took it from her and stuffed it under the backseat.

A lit flashlight tapped on his window, and when he rolled it down, Rylie recognized Luke right away.

"Hi, Luke," she said.

"Rylie. Dustin. You two know you're on private property, right?"

Dustin slid his arm behind her seat and squeezed her shoulder. "Yeah, sorry, Luke. We were coming back from the wedding at my mom's winery, and Rylie said I had to pull off so she could kiss me and—ow!"

Rylie pinched him on the arm and shouted, "He's lying, Luke! He tried to get me to go skinny dipping in the pond."

Luke shook his head and rubbed a hand over his face. "Guys, I am way too tired for this. I'm going to write you a ticket for trespassing on private property and then I want you to take your extracurricular activities home. Capisce?"

"You got it, bud. Still invited to poker this week?" Dustin asked.

"Only if you bring two hundred bucks and promise to be on a losing streak."

"I will do my best."

When Luke walked away, Rylie shoved his shoulder gently. "I cannot believe you did that."

"Well, since we've been ordered home…your place or mine?"

"Hey, buddy, I don't know who you think I am, but I don't put out on the first date."

Dustin tangled his fingers in the curls falling from her up-do and kissed her so thoroughly that her toes were practically double-jointed by the time he'd pulled away.

"You were saying?"

She licked her lips. "My place, but you have to give me five minutes to pick up."

"Come on, I don't care what your house looks like."

"Easy for you to say, Victoria always has your home looking like a magazine and I had four women over last night. I still think there are little dick straws all over the place and I need to do some damage control."

Dustin laughed and kissed the side of her neck. "Fine, I'll go home and grab a bag while you clean up. Think a half an hour will give you enough time?"

"That's perfect." She kissed him sweetly, which turned into a full-on make-out.

A tap on the car door broke it up and Luke cleared his throat. "If you two don't separate immediately, this ticket is going to double."

Dustin took it from Luke and his jaw went slack. "A thousand dollars?"

Luke grinned. "Next time you want to get it on, take her back to your castle, rich boy."

Once Luke was backing away, Dustin turned to her, flashing her an evil smile.

"I am going to destroy him on poker night."

Fifteen minutes later, Rylie hopped out of the Jeep with her tote from the day in hand and blew him a kiss. "See you in a half an hour."

"Not a minute more," he said.

She closed the door, floating all the way to her house. She put the key in the knob and then turned it. As she was coming through, she realized she hadn't heard the click that usually happened when she unlocked the door. Had she forgotten to turn the deadbolt when she left this morning? She shut it behind her and heard Raider's frantic barking from his crate. Still buzzed from the champagne, she fumbled in the dark toward her bedroom.

"Hey, baby, do you need to go potty?"

As she passed by the bedroom, it registered two seconds too late that there had been a large shadow on the wall.

Suddenly, she was slammed against the wall in the hallway, a sweaty hand covering her mouth.

Raider's barking became high and hysterical and the clink of metal told her he was throwing his body against the cage. She tried to scream, to tell him to stop, but she couldn't make a sound. She stared up at the ski-masked face, his eyes glittering in the dark.

"If you make one sound, you're dead. You understand?"

Oh, God. She knew that voice, and it wasn't Asher.

It was Will.

Chapter 27

Dustin whistled as he pulled out onto Highway 16, pressing a little harder on the gas. He was eager to go home, pack, and get back to Rylie. He'd had Victoria pick up a bunch of ingredients he needed to bake his mother's scones, and he was hoping that he didn't screw them up. He wasn't exactly a culinary master.

Something silver flashed between the trees on the right and for some reason, Dustin slowed down to a crawl to see what it was. He flipped around half a mile up the road and came back, pulling off across from the place. He got out of the Jeep and jogged across the road, listening for oncoming cars, since the curve was blind.

Using the flashlight app on his phone, he pushed through the trees and shone the light around.

It was a silver Chevelle in mint condition. He stood there for a minute, trying to figure out why someone would leave such a nice car behind the trees and where he'd seen it before....

He looked in the window, and when he saw that the door was unlocked, he opened her up. The car was immaculate, and there wasn't even a receipt lying around.

He opened the glove box and found a black leather wallet and a metal box. He peeked inside to find a driver's license and froze.

It was Will. Rylie's date.

Parked less than a mile from her house.

Dustin dropped the wallet and ran through the trees before taking off across the street. The flash of high beams and blare of a horn scared him shitless, but he kept going. He frantically turned the key and shoved the Jeep into drive, peeling out onto the road.

I'm coming, baby. Just hang on.

* * * *

Rylie fought back tears as Will kneeled in front of her, waving the long, serrated knife just under her nose. He'd strapped her hands together behind her back with zip ties, and set her down in one of the kitchen chairs. She hadn't called him by name, or given any hint that she knew who he was, hoping it would keep her alive. So far he'd only spoken to issue orders, but hadn't told her what he wanted.

Finally, tired of his silence, she asked, "What do you want? If it's money, I can give you my card and pin and you can just go—"

"Shut up. I don't want your money, whore."

Whore?

Panic settled into her gut. God, if Will had been the one to throw a brick through the window, then she really *had* ruined Asher's life.

But she didn't want to accuse him of anything, so instead, she tried to remind him who she was. That she was a person.

"I'm not a whore. My name is Rylie Templeton. I've lived in Sweetheart all my life. Both of my parents are dead—"

"I said shut up," he shouted.

Pain exploded across her cheek as he backhanded her, knocking her off the chair. She hit the floor hard, crying out as her shoulder popped.

Losing her calm, she screamed, "I don't understand! If you want to kill me, then just get it over with!"

He lifted her off the ground and back into the chair.

"It's not always about what *you* want. I know *you* think that we should worship the ground *you* walk on, but *whores* are only good for one thing."

Rylie watched in horror as he adjusted himself through his pants, and did what she did best.

She pulled her legs up and kicked him so hard in the jewels that he flew back, smacking into her kitchen cabinet.

And the chair fell back, her head cracking against the wall.

Then she felt nothing at all.

* * * *

Dustin came in through the laundry room just as he heard two crashes. With the hammer he'd found out back in his hand, he came around the corner, ready to bash the bastard's head in.

He lowered the hammer as he looked down at Will in a ski mask, crying and moaning on the floor.

Then he spotted Rylie.

Every instinct told him to rush for her, to make sure she was all right, but he needed to take care of Will first. He'd already called the cavalry, which should have been pulling in any second.

He hauled Will to his feet and planted a hard-right hook in the middle of his face. The guy slumped to the ground, and Dustin dragged him into the living room, where he found a gym bag full of twist ties, knives...

Condoms.

Dustin resisted the urge to pound the guy into meat. He bound his legs and hands with zip ties behind his back and added a bit of duct tape for good measure. Once he was sure he wasn't going anywhere, Dustin raced back to the kitchen.

"Rylie, sweetheart, talk to me." He kneeled next to her and cupped her cheek. "Please, be okay. Help is on the way."

Sirens wailed down the driveway as the kitchen lit up blue and red.

"Do you hear that? They're already here."

Then he heard her voice, hoarse and soft.

"About time."

His laughter broke as he lifted her into his arms and held her tight, rocking with her as uniforms burst through the door.

"He's in there," Dustin said, waving toward the living room.

When Luke came through and joined them, he smiled grimly. "Long time no see."

"Yeah, I know. She needs to go to a hospital," Dustin said.

Rylie shook her head, then moaned. "No, I'm fine."

Dustin scoffed. "She always says that. Don't listen to her."

"And he's always bossy, so don't mind him."

Luke's gaze shifted between them and then he burst out laughing.

"What's so funny? She's hurt, man," Dustin said, anger leaking into his voice.

"Sorry, it's just...never mind."

He got up and walked into the other room. When the paramedics came in and got her onto the gurney, he kept a hold of her hand.

"You're going to stay with me, right?"

He squeezed it. "Sure, I'll stay.

Chapter 28

On Monday morning, Rylie woke up with her face buried in the back of Raider's fur, the smell of baked goods wafting into the room. She started to sit up and winced as her hand grazed the bump on the back of her head.

Raider flipped over onto his back, giving her a goofy grin. The poor guy had several cuts and abrasions on his muzzle and body from trying to break out of his cage during her attack. She'd made Dustin take him to the vet to make sure he was all right, and found out that afterward they'd gone through the McDonald's drive through for burgers. The last thing she needed was her already spoiled dog thinking he'd get cheeseburgers during every car ride.

"Who is mama's brave boy?" She kissed his nose and climbed out of the bed, padding down the hallway to the living room. Dustin had wanted her to come back to his home after she'd been discharged, but she refused to let Will ruin her first chance to be on her own. She had been grateful that Dustin had hired someone to clean it before she'd come home. She didn't want to see blood on the ground where Will's nose had gushed after Dustin had broken it.

She shivered as she thought about what had almost happened in such a small, idyllic town. And from what they found in Will's car, it turned out she wasn't the first woman he'd stalked and...

Well, he hadn't had the chance to do worse, but as of yesterday, they had connected Will to five unsolved rapes in El Dorado County. There was a good chance she'd have to testify when it came time for his trial, but she wasn't scared of facing him.

In fact, the last few months had shown her that she didn't need to be afraid of anything. She was strong. She was smart.

And she was in love.

She rounded the corner with Raider tripping her up and found Dustin in a pair of sweats, shirtless and dancing as he mixed up something in one of her good Pyrex bowls.

"Whatcha you got there, Chef Boyardee?" she said.

He jumped, and spun around, never slowing his mixing. "I'm making you something special."

"Oh yeah? I want to taste."

"Nuh uh!" He held the bowl away from her. "You will wait for the finished product." In a terrible French accent, he said, "Now, geet out of my keetchen."

Rylie leaned against the doorjamb and smiled. "I love you."

Dustin froze, staring at her like a deer caught in a set of headlights. "What did you say?"

Okay, so maybe she wasn't as brave as she thought. Suddenly, her palms were sweating bullets and her heart wouldn't stop racing.

"I said that I'm in love with you. And it's okay if you don't feel the same way, but I wanted to tell you because life is too short not to say it. You know? Dustin?" He was like the Tin Man without his oil. "Blink once if you're okay, twice if I need to call for help."

"I…damn it." He set the bowl on the counter and crossed his arms over his chest. "Why do you always surprise me?"

"I'm sorry?"

"I had a plan. I was going to make you my mother's raspberry scones, and then after breakfast, slip you the recipe."

"But she said she'd only give it to family."

He took several steps until he'd eaten up the distance between them and took her hands in his. "*You're* my family. Rylie, I've shared more with you than with people who share my blood. You've seen me be a complete and utter dickhead, and you didn't write me off. I want to be with you and only you."

Rylie couldn't believe that Dustin, who had only two months ago sworn to avoid relationships at all costs, was declaring himself.

And it scared her just a bit. "I want you to be sure about this, because if you're not, if this is just some kind of experiment, I'm out."

He smiled softly, his gaze full of such tenderness that a ball of emotion clogged her throat. "I wouldn't be offering you my mother's secret recipe, which will definitely incur her wrath, if I wasn't sure."

That was good enough for her. Rylie dropped his hands and wrapped her arms around his waist, leaning her cheek against his chest. She could hear the rapid thump of his heart and smiled, knowing he was scared shitless. It was kind of nice having the always cocky Dustin Kent off his game.

"If you don't believe me, Rys, I'll prove it to you. Just give me time."

"How much time do you need?"

"As much as you're willing to give me."

She looked up at him, her chin resting on his chest.

"How about forever? Does that work for you?"

He dipped his head to kiss her, his lips warm and gentle. When he finally pulled away, he traced his finger down her cheek with a smile that still wrecked her every time.

"Forever sounds perfect."

Epilogue

Four Years Later

Dustin was a nervous wreck as he paced the "Groom's Saloon," one of the restored buildings in Buzzard Gulch that was made for the groom and his party to get ready for the big day. Charlie, his best man, sat on one of the barstools, nursing a beer while Luke and his other two brothers sat around a card table playing poker.

Dustin checked the clock again as he passed by. "This is ridiculous."

"Are you really that nervous, little brother?" Charlie teased.

Dustin didn't want to admit that he was terrified. From the moment that Rylie had finally agreed to marry him, he'd known what was coming. Kelly and her minions had complete control over his wedding and unless his bride had interceded, Kelly would finally have her revenge.

"Hello, boys," Kelly said, pushing through the swinging saloon doors. She was wearing a red and white floral dress and bright red cowboy boots. In her arms were five shoe boxes and behind her were two of her newer bridesmaids for hire, holding garment bags.

Kelly set the boxes down on the nearest table and clapped her hands. "I've got everything you need to get ready right here. Ceremony starts in twenty minutes, so you better get going."

Dustin flipped the lid on one of the boxes, his mouth falling open. "Cowboy boots."

"Yep. It's a themed wedding. Welcome to the Old West."

"She's kidding, right?" Charlie asked.

"Hey, what's wrong with cowboy boots?" Luke asked.

Dustin held up one of the boots…in bright red leather.

* * * *

Twenty minutes later, Dustin stood under the floral-covered arbor in his black suit with red tie. On his head sat a black cowboy hat and he had squeezed his feet into those fire engine red boots. If Kelly thought she could break him, she was wrong. He'd waited too long for this to let a few practical jokes scare him off.

Rylie had been the one who wanted to wait at least three years before she'd consider living together, let alone marriage. In that time, they'd completely restored Buzzard Gulch and Rylie had saved the money she'd earned working at Something Borrowed and baking the wedding cakes for the company to open her own little gourmet bakery. Seize the Cake had filled a void when the other bakery in town had been shut down due to health code violations. Plus everyone loved Rylie's treats.

A haunting country love song played over the speakers, and everyone in the chairs stood.

Dustin's twin nephews, his older brother Paul's boys, came up the aisle in little black suits, making every woman sigh and coo. The boys each had their own pillow with no actual rings on it. They were only two, after all. His mother had been pleased to finally get a daughter-in-law and grandchildren, but as his brother and his family lived in Seattle, the pressure was still on him and Charlie.

He hadn't told his mom yet that Rylie was already eight weeks pregnant. They hadn't planned it, but they hadn't been preventing it either.

Next was Marley and Luke's daughter, Chloe, holding on to her mother's hand the whole way down the aisle. The little girl's brown eyes took up half her face as she stared around nervously. Her white tutu dress with red sash was perfect with her bouncing blond curls.

If they had a little girl first, Dustin hoped she had Rylie's smile.

Marley let Chloe run to her grandmother, Rose, and then took her place. She winked to him when he caught her eye and he smiled back. Marley had warmed to him over the years after a lot of groveling on his part, but Luke and she were counted among his growing group of friends.

Marley was wearing a red off-the-shoulder dress with black cowboy boots. She was soon joined by Tonya, who Rylie had become good friends with after her wedding, and two of Rylie's friends from Something Borrowed, Emmy and Darcy.

And then Rylie was standing at the end of the aisle, her arm looped through Charlie's. Raider sat at her side, wearing a red bow tie.

Dustin would have laughed if he wasn't completely captivated by his bride to be.

She was wearing an ivory halter dress, the skirt gathered in waves. Her hair was swept up with curls rioting down her neck and red baby roses pinned in the brown strands.

When Charlie finally passed her hand to his, he brought it to his lips and she grinned at him.

He blinked. Rylie's front tooth was missing.

"What happened?"

"What's wrong?" she asked innocently.

"Where's your tooth?" he practically shouted.

The whole crowd bust out laughing, including the pastor, and Rylie.

"Relax, honey, it will come off before pictures," Rylie said.

He was stupefied. "You helped Kelly punk me?"

"You know what they say. Revenge is a dish best served cold," Kelly hollered from the front row.

Dustin tipped his hat to her. "Well played."

"So, think you can marry a woman with a blackened tooth and a heart of gold?" Rylie asked, wrapping her arms around his waist.

Dustin pretended to consider, then hugged her back.

"Hell yeah. What are we waiting for?"

Acknowledgements

I would first like to thank my husband and children because after four and a half years, they know how to work the mommy-is-on-deadline system and leave me alone (for the most part). I love you, honey and babies. I am grateful to my fantastic agent, Sarah, and my uber awesome editor, Norma, for being there for me and making this book great. To the rest of #TeamKensington who made my beautiful cover, copy edited, formatted, and organized my publicity, I appreciate all that you do. I need to thank my extended family and wonderful friends for reading and sharing my books. To my Rockers, who amaze me and always brighten my day with their warm hearts and sexy man pics. I love your guts. To my amazing friends Darcy Burke, Rachel Lacey, T.J. Kline, and the ladies in our Contemporary Crushes group, I adore you! And to all the readers who took a chance on this series... I hope I made you smile.

Be Mine, Sweetheart

Turn the page for a sneak peek at
the next book in Codi Gary's Something Borrowed series!

Available in August 2018 from Lyrical Shine.

Chapter 1

Kelly Barrow stared down at the court papers, completely flabbergasted. Her company, Something Borrowed Wedding Solutions, and personal attorney, Christian Ryan, sat across from her, and she could tell he was fighting a grin.

"This is a joke, right?" she asked.

Chris shook his head. "No joke. I received them this morning."

"Who in the hell sues someone for"—she read the amount again and scoffed—"thirty-two dollars and seventeen cents?"

"Apparently, someone who doesn't appreciate you walking out on a date with them."

"I didn't walk out! I told him that I had a work emergency and had to go."

Chris shrugged his broad shoulders. "Guess he didn't believe you because he is suing you for the cost of your dinner and your ticket to… *Pirates of the Caribbean.*"

This is why she hadn't dated in almost ten years. Men were absolute idiots.

"Can you just take care of this? Send him a check or whatever so he will go away."

"Not that simple, Kel," Chris said. "The man wants a formal apology and for you to be his date for his sister's wedding."

Kelly looked down at the papers again and sure enough, it was in bold print. "Why would he want me to be his date if I pissed him off so bad he had to file a lawsuit against me?"

"The guy must be hard-up. I can't think of a single reason he'd want to take you…oh wait. There's the fact that you're beautiful, intelligent, and will no doubt make whatever ex-girlfriend he's afraid of bumping into jealous."

Kelly stuck her tongue out at him, but he just laughed at her childishness. She'd known Chris since eighth grade, when he'd walked up to her for his friend, Ray Jackson, and told her Ray liked her. Since that moment, it had been the three of them together; Ray and her as sweethearts and Chris as their dear friend.

Then high school had ended, and Chris had gone away to college while Ray had joined the military. And Kelly, well, she'd gotten a job at the local bridal boutique and stayed right here in Sweetheart, California. She'd missed them dreadfully, and when Ray came home on his first leave and asked her to marry him, she'd said yes. They started making plans for when his four years were up. She was already taking courses at Consumes River College, and when Ray got out, he would get his degree too. They'd get jobs, then get married and eventually, have four kids. The plan was to be happy and in love forever.

Only Ray had never come home. He'd been killed in action just before his twentieth birthday, and Kelly had been a mess. Her parents. Her friends. No one could bring her out of her misery.

Until Chris had come home and sat on the bed next to her prone form. At first he'd been patient and understanding. When she still wouldn't acknowledge him, he lost his temper. He'd grabbed her by the shoulders and turned her around to face him.

"You aren't the only one who loved Ray, and he wouldn't want you behaving like this. So wrapped up in your own grief that you don't give a shit about anyone else who may be hurting."

She'd come out of her depression enough to slap him, and the rush of emotions that followed had her pummeling his chest, screaming at him. Chris had just wrapped his arms around her until she stopped fighting and just wailed. Screaming and sobbing her heartbreak all while he cried into the crook of her neck. It had been Chris's tears that had been the key to fully waking her up.

After Ray's funeral, Chris had gone back to Stanford, but they'd stayed close. And when he'd finished law school, she'd begged him to come back and set up shop in Sweetheart.

And now, here they were. Poring over a frivolous lawsuit.

Kelly shot Chris a pleading look. "I don't really have to go out with him again, do I?"

Chris laughed, throwing his head back, and Kelly studied him. At thirteen, Chris had been a towheaded kid, bean pole thin with glasses. As a man, his white blond hair had darkened to a mix of mahogany and rich gold, and he wore contacts over his light blue eyes. Kelly wasn't oblivious to the fact that Chris had become a handsome guy; it just didn't matter. He would always be Chris. Ray's best friend, and then hers.

"No, Kelly. I'll handle it."

"Thanks, C. What would I do without you?"

"Continue to date losers?"

"Ha ha," she said. "So funny."

"What did prompt you to go out with this guy?" Chris asked.

Kelly shifted in her chair awkwardly, embarrassed to tell him that she had joined an online dating site, but she didn't lie to Chris.

"I signed up on LastFirstKiss.com, and that guy was one of the top matches the website spit out."

"Seriously?"

"Yes. When he contacted me and I looked at his profile, it all looked good."

"So what happened?"

She grimaced. "He lied on his profile."

"Shocker. What did he say? That he was six two instead of five two?"

"Well, he lied about his job, what he likes to do for fun, and he was a complete douche nozzle to the waiter at the restaurant. Frankly, I was glad that Veronica called me and pulled me out of the movie because the way he chewed popcorn was just…disgusting."

Chris chuckled. "Ah, Kel, I love you."

"I know."

They shared a smile over the desk. Since the first time they went to a *Star Wars* marathon in high school, Chris and she had done the Han Solo and Princess Leia bit. It used to drive Ray crazy, but that had never stopped them.

Kelly leaned her head back in the chair and groaned. "Ugh, I don't know what to do. I haven't been dating since LFO was cool and it was only ever with one guy. I don't know how to do this."

"So don't. No one says you have to date."

She met his gaze sadly. "It's time. I used to think that my future died with Ray, but the truth is, watching all my friends find love and get married, start families… It made me realize I still want those things. I'm thirty-two years old; I need to move on."

Chris didn't say anything for several moments, and she sat forward. "Don't you think?"

She couldn't tell what he was really thinking, but when he nodded, she almost sighed aloud in relief. She couldn't have Chris mad at her. He was the most important person in her life.

Chris reached across the desk, taking her hand in his.

"You deserve to be happy, Kel. I'll support you in whatever you do. You know that."

Meet the Author

An obsessive bookworm, **Codi Gary** likes to write sexy, small-town contemporary romances with humor, grand gestures, and blush-worthy moments. When she's not writing, she can be found reading her favorite authors, squealing over her must-watch shows, and playing with her children. She lives in Idaho with her family.

Visit her on the web at www.codigarysbooks.com.

CPSIA information can be obtained
at www.ICGtesting.com
Printed in the USA
LVHW02s1440300118
564591LV00002B/231/P